THE TUNNEL

Neil Page

Book Guild Publishing
Sussex, England

First published in Great Britain in 2007 by
The Book Guild Ltd
Pavilion View
19 New Road
Brighton
BN1 1UF

Typesetting in Baskerville by
IML Typographers, Birkenhead, Merseyside

Printed in Great Britain by
CPI Antony Rowe

A catalogue record for this book is available from
The British Library.

ISBN 978 1 84624 117 8

THE TUNNEL

*This novel is dedicated to my parents,
David and Stephanie Page.*

Contents

It was watching him – yes it was inside there all right, keeping quiet, distant, yet close enough to entice him inside. He could feel its pull, like he was made of metal and a powerful magnet was forcing him forward against his will. And quietly it watched him from the opening, waiting.

Billy entered.

Prologue

They both felt it. It was undeniable ...

And with only a week before the summer holiday began it was now time to do something about it. Their skins were itching, deep beneath the surface, reminding them that their time was now. They would only be young once and that itching, that felt like a thousand insects tinkering over their skins, was unforgiving.

The Tunnel was calling out to him. He did not know why or how, but it was. It was mostly in his dreams. It was damp and cold, and there was something waiting inside. Every dream was the same. He was standing in front of the opening wearing his pyjama bottoms and white T-shirt. The air was still, eerily quiet and hiding something. Yes, something all right. There was something watching him from inside the darkness, calling out to him. He walked forwards, had no other choice. He was cold and scared. The entrance to The Tunnel looked like a huge endless mouth wanting to swallow him whole.

There were sounds of dripping water, the air cool. The Tunnel was more like a cave now. The roof and walls were damp and musty, forgotten in time. It was hard to believe that trains used to run through it, trees and tall grass now surrounded it, encompassing a route that used to be so active. The stone was crumbling away. No-one cared for it any more. So why was he here?

His bare feet felt cold and hurt as he walked along the dirt-ridden track that was really only used now by the odd hiker or person walking their dog, or perhaps junkie seeking a fix. But to come this far out to The Tunnel was rare. He knew it. It was a ten mile walk and the path was anything but inviting. Then there were the stories, stories that were legend, that made his skin crawl. The Tunnel was haunted. The dead walked in that place. It was a place that one would not venture alone, especially at night.

He stopped in front of the entrance and looked into the darkness. There was nothing but an echo, carried along in the wind, seductively calling out his name.

Billy … the voice only echoed, lonely, there was nobody there.

He went inside.

The journey continues … And never ends.
It's not about the ending; it's the journey that matters …

J C

Boys don't cry …

B C

1

Home Life

1

So much had happened to his family over the past year. A shy retiring boy by nature, twelve-year-old Billy Cooper did not know what to do any more. School was lousy and his home life wasn't a whole lot better either. His parents were distant, and barely spoke to him, and recently it had become even worse, if that was possible. They used to speak. They used to be a proper family. However, that was a long time ago now, another lifetime. The year had brought with it the foul stench of misfortune to the Cooper household. And it wasn't through yet.

It was the morning of Monday 7th July 2003 and time for school again. Billy entered the kitchen with his white school shirt all creased and hanging out over his black trousers. His straight brown hair was all ruffled and his blue eyes showed signs of too little sleep again. He didn't sleep at all well any more. Guilt and dreams of Justin plagued him like a disease. Sometimes the dreams made him cry out, just like the guilt always did. He had cried again last night. But the dream had not been just about Justin. No! There was something else as well, that made him feel like there was an anvil hanging over his head about to drop any second now. In short Billy was afraid of something, but what?

He was greeted by the usual heavy silence as he entered the kitchen. His mother, Kate, was waiting for the toaster to spit out her breakfast, and his father, Alex, was reading the morning paper, occasionally taking a sip from his coffee cup. He never once looked up to acknowledge his son. Billy avoided his mother and went over to the fridge. The only thing he fancied this morning was a glass of pure orange juice. The toaster popped and made Alex look up from his paper. He looked older than his forty-one years. His black hair was receding, showing the early signs of greying, and heavy marks lay underneath his eyes. Kate buttered her toast and sat down next to her husband. She was pretty, with long brown hair, but never wore any make up these days. She never really took pride in herself any more and no longer cared for life, not since Justin anyway.

Billy sipped his juice, keeping an eye on both parents. They didn't speak. The room was heavy and the atmosphere could have been cut with a knife. Billy smiled secretly, imagining himself jumping through the air with his mother's butter knife.

His father carried on flicking through the newspaper whilst his mother ate her toast looking down at the crumbs on her plate. Anything was better than having to look at her husband. Neither of them made any eye contact. Billy suddenly felt like he was part of some sort of science experiment here, the nuclear family and all the shit that comes along with it.

Billy finished his juice and put the empty glass in the sink. His mother used to pack him up for school, but there were no sandwiches today, nor would there be tomorrow or the day after or the day after that. He would get something at school, maybe. And come to think of it he was looking a bit underweight these days.

School wasn't so bad, he guessed, not compared to home anyhow. It saddened Billy, made his stomach turn, to realise that he actually preferred being at school to home. He went to his bedroom and grabbed his bag and put some change in his pocket that he found lying around in the front room, most probably belonging to his father.

He heard his father's car reversing down the driveway and watched out of his bedroom window. He watched the car being driven away by a man he barely knew any more. It might as well have been driven by a total stranger. He suddenly felt very upset, his throat was lumpy and his chest all heavy. Billy sat down on the end of his bed and cried.

Come on, Billy, boys don't cry, remember? What are you going to say to Amy if she sees that your eyes are all red? Come on pull yourself together. Boys don't cry. Now repeat after me: Boys don't cry...

'Amy!'

He wiped his eyes then looked into his bedroom mirror. His eyes were red, but not as red as they had been after Justin died.

2

Kate was washing up when Billy re-entered the kitchen, his young face was awash with hurt and sorrow but she did not notice, Kate hardly noticed anything any more. She gave him a quick glance but did not smile. Billy had his bag over his right shoulder and simply looked at her. She had been scrubbing the same plate for almost a minute now, seemingly uncomfortable with the notion that her only son may want to confide in her.

'I think it's clean Mum,' Billy noted, leaning against the table.

She stopped scrubbing the plate and turned to him, blowing a little piece of her hair away from her face. She looked down at the plate and placed it onto the draining board rack. She took a deep breath then removed her yellow rubber gloves, then just stared out of the window. The wind was blowing the trees, and a light drizzle had started. Any distraction would suffice it seemed.

'Mum ... I ...'

'Time for school now, Billy,' Kate said harshly, looking at the clock on the wall. 'I don't want you being late again.'

She threw her gloves into the hot soapy water and went into the living room, walking straight past Billy, like he was a ghost and not something tangible. Billy was left standing alone with only the ticking sound of the clock for company. He looked around the kitchen, his young face once again displaying far too much dismay for one so young.

'I'm a ghost,' he muttered underneath his breath.

He then left the house and started walking to school.

The rain had stopped. Billy waited at the bottom of his driveway and looked back towards his house, a house that he no longer cared for much. He felt lost, like a piece of driftwood floating down a river, not going anywhere in particular, just seemingly guided along by an unseen force. And as the cool morning breeze swept through his untidy brown hair and made his bright blue eyes water he thought about Amy. Thank God, he had Amy. He crossed the road and started running. He didn't want to miss her this morning for Amy was the only reason he had for living these days.

3

Billy had been waiting almost ten minutes when he saw her. He was sitting on a wooden bench in a park not far from his house. There were a row of shops on the opposite side of the road and a chip shop too. Billy sniffled and wiped his eyes. The cold biting air was making everything run this morning. Even though it was the final week of school, and early July, the morning was still very cool and fresh.

He was thinking about the dream again when he saw Amy walking towards him. She was wearing a black cardigan with a white shirt on underneath and a black knee-length skirt. Her long brown hair was combed back, still looking a little damp, and her hazelnut eyes seemed to be dazzling him. She smiled when she saw Billy waiting for her. Billy picked up his bag and stood up. He put the dream to the back of his head for the time being and smiled. After all, this was Amy Johnston, the love of his life.

Billy and Amy were best friends, and had been now for almost a year. Their meeting had been as weird as most other things in Billy's life. They simply connected and she was the only real friend Billy actually had. He really liked Amy, more so than ever lately. She was blossoming and Billy took notice. In short, Billy was in love with her.

Billy placed both hands inside his pockets. He wanted to look cool. Yes, let Amy know he was a right cool geezer.

'Thanks for waiting for me.'

'No problem,' Billy said, beaming. He noticed Amy did not have her school bag with her today.

'I don't need it today,' Amy said smiling.

'What?'

'My bag ... You were wondering why I didn't have my bag.'

Billy frowned and removed his hands from his pockets quickly as if they had suddenly been burned by something in there.

'How do you do that?' Billy asked.

'I'm a mind reader.'

'Yes you are.'

Amy giggled and placed her arm around Billy's.

'You're very easy to read, Billy Cooper.' Amy paused and smiled at him. 'Come on then, we don't want to be late again.'

Amy did have some other-worldly knack of reading Billy's mind. He often put it down to her knowing him so well, but still … Lately she seemed to be doing it more and more frequently. She freaked him out sometimes. He felt like his mind was a book and she was reading it. Since Justin, he had poured his heart out to her on more than one occasion. She always listened and found the right words to say. Incredible, he thought.

The walk to school lasted a little longer than usual. Billy deliberately dawdled with a purpose. He talked to Amy about his home life, and about how his mother and father couldn't look him in the eye any more. He told her about how they still screamed at one another, more often than ever lately, especially at night time. Billy's father had recently started drinking too, and was an awful drunk. Billy stayed out of the way. Then there was the dream. He had spoken of it before to Amy, but this time she seemed particularly interested.

'Perhaps we should go then.'

'What?' Billy said, suddenly stopping.

'That place in your dream, The Tunnel!'

Billy frowned, almost terrified by the very thought of it. The stories, he remembered the stories, and Amy must have heard them too. God, was this girl insane? The very thought of going to The Tunnel made Billy want to cower and shit his pants.

He suddenly remembered the rules and smiled.

Boys show no fear, remember? Especially in front of girls they have a little crush on.

'Over the summer holidays,' Amy added. 'We should go … See what we find there. It could be fun.'

Fun! God, she is insane.

Yes, of course she is. Remember the dead walk in that place, Billy.

'Holy shit!' Billy muttered underneath his breath.

'Pardon?'

'Nothing.'

Billy paused for a few seconds then said, 'All right then, we'll go.'

They smiled at one another then carried on walking to school, Amy once again with her arm around Billy's.

They were both late again.

4

10 am, Mr Harris's maths lesson, good to get the lousiest lesson of the day out of the way as soon as possible.

But the second hand was slowing down. Had it actually stopped? Billy felt like time had temporarily stood still. Mr Harris wasn't the greatest at keeping someone awake. His voice was slow and exaggerated. He spoke like a robot. His voice was flat, boring. But it wasn't just that. Billy's mind was elsewhere, it had been for the past couple of weeks now. Or had it been for the past couple of months? He didn't know for sure. Mr Harris could have been giving a lecture on the female reproductive system for all Billy knew. He was just staring at the clock, rolling his yellow pencil back and forth along the desk.

The dreams? If only he knew what they meant. Always the same they were. They started the same and ended the same. Billy saw The Tunnel again last night in his dream. Justin had been there and so too had Amy. But why? Billy hated Justin not being around. Things wouldn't be so shit if he was still here, of that much he was certain. His parents would still be talking and not treating him like he was an invisible outsider.

Click.

The second hand stopped. Billy suddenly shuddered, like cold feet were walking down his back. The room was suddenly still, heavy and damp with moisture. He could now see his breath firing out in front of his mouth like on a cold November morning. There was a dripping sound, like someone had not turned a tap off properly. Billy looked up. The room suddenly started going dark, like a huge plane had flown overhead. The metal legs of his plastic chair screeched against the cold floor as he pushed it backwards. He stood up and stared at the wall. Something was appearing on it.

A black dot appeared, drawn by an invisible hand. Billy watched. He had no other choice. The black dot gradually grew bigger on the wall, engulfing it. He could no longer hear Mr Harris's ramblings on about equilateral triangles. He could hear nothing any more, except for the beating of his own heart.

What had started out as a small dot was now a huge black mouth filling up the entire wall. Billy stared into it, endless darkness. The air was freezing, and there was still the noise of water dripping and something else. It was a steady regular sound, getting louder, or nearer, coming towards him with a purpose.

Billy looked transfixed, like one who had been hypnotised. His small frame started leaning forwards as the noise grew louder and louder. An archway had opened up in the wall, looking like an entrance belonging to a cave. It was The Tunnel.

Billy blinked, flinched, shook his head, and did all the things that he could think of to try to convince himself that what he was seeing was not really there. The air was suddenly fresh and clean and through the murky darkness Billy saw something.

A man stood in the entrance of the cave, looking at Billy. Billy wanted to run, but couldn't. The man's complexion looked very pale, his face stern, showing no emotion, and his clothes looked like they hadn't been washed in ages. He was young, thirties maybe, but his clothes were old, very old. His face scared Billy – there was something sinister looking about it. But standing in the archway of The Tunnel the man looked at home.

'Billy,' the man hissed.

His voice floated like the wind. It was quiet but direct, almost a whisper. Billy felt afraid. The man scared him, terrified him. This was like his dream from last night, except ...

Billy blinked and swallowed hard. His young innocent face suddenly looked red and flustered like he had been running. He wanted to run.

'*Billlyyy ...*'

The man started walking towards him.

Holy shit ...

Billy's mouth opened wider as the man stepped out of the wall and into the classroom. He pointed at Billy with a long right index finger then motioned with it as if to get him to follow. Billy cried out and looked away, but The Tunnel was still calling out his name.

5

Tick ... Tick ... Tick ...

Billy was back. He was standing in front of his desk with the entire classroom giving him the evil eye.

'Are you all right, Billy?' Mr Harris asked, looking over the tops of his spectacles.

Billy looked around, felt confused. What the hell had just happened? His heart was racing and a light layer of sweat had appeared on his brow.

'Billy,' Mr Harris said again. He walked to Billy's desk. 'Billy, look at me.'

Billy did so.

'You were daydreaming, Billy ... Now are you all right?' Mr Harris placed one of his chunky hands onto Billy's right shoulder. 'You called out, Billy.'

Billy had no words to say. He looked confused, lost again. He could still see the man standing behind Mr Harris, watching him, waiting for something. He slowly disappeared, fading away into the daylight.

'Come on son,' Mr Harris said.

He lcd Billy out of the classroom.

When the door closed the entire classroom erupted into a roar of laughter, everyone except for Amy that is. She sat there silent, just looking down at her text book.

Billy Cooper now had a mission and the force driving him was not going to let him fail. Something was happening to him, had happened, and he could no longer ignore it or pretend it wasn't there any more, because it wasn't going to go away.

6

He knew he wasn't alone in the sick room. Someone was holding his hand. The good thing about being in the sick room was that you got to skive off from lessons like maths. Billy just wished he had been taken here under different circumstances. A headache, sore throat, hell, even the shits would have been better than day-dreaming and calling out in class, that was not good. Seeing cave entrances appearing in the middle of classroom walls, followed by a thin strange man with pale, dead skin, emerging from it was not good either. The black cloud was getting thicker. But at least he had Amy.

He opened his eyes and quickly sat up.

'Are you OK now?'

Billy turned his head and saw Amy sitting next to him. She was no longer holding his hand.

'How long was I out for?'

'Quite some time.' She smiled. 'What's the matter, Billy Cooper, did you know we were going to have that test today or something?'

'Very funny,' Billy said with a smile, he then felt a yawn coming on.

'I saw what happened,' Amy said, 'so I wanted to sit with you. I hope you don't mind.'

'No,' Billy said stretching out his arms, feeling slightly embarrassed, but glad Amy was here with him just the same. He then paused, remembering how the friendship he had felt for her now suddenly felt so much more.

'I'm glad you're here, Amy.'

She smiled, her pretty face lighting up like a candle.

Billy got up from the bed and stretched his back. He felt like he had just awoken from the best sleep of his life.

'They laughed at me, didn't they?' Billy said, turning to Amy.

'Yes they did,' Amy said. She noticed Billy frowning. 'But who cares what that lot think, Billy? You should only care about what I think.'

Billy stopped frowning, and then smiled. He did care about what Amy thought; she was the only person whose opinion actually mattered to him these days. But he didn't say so.

'What time is it?' Billy asked.

'Four.'

'What?'

God, I've been out for hours!

'Reception tried calling your home but no-one was answering. So I said I would wait and take you home.'

Billy's heart fluttered. God, he loved her.

'Thanks, I mean cool, no big deal.'

Amy got up from the bed and walked over to Billy. 'Come on,' she said, taking his arm again. 'You can tell me all about what happened on the walk home.'

Billy grabbed his bag and followed her out of the room. The black cloud had lifted a little but the problem was it was not going to stay away, and Billy didn't really know what was happening himself any more.

7

Billy savoured his time spent with Amy like a connoisseur would a glass of fine wine. When he was with her he forgot about Justin and about how his parents both appeared to loathe him with a passion. He once told her, only inside his head, that he loved her. That she made him feel better than he was.

'That is weird,' Amy agreed after Billy had explained his vision.

'I know,' Billy said, looking at her. 'Especially since I dreamt about it again last night. Well, except for that strange man being there.'

'Well that settles it then.'

'What does?' Billy asked frowning.

'The Tunnel. We're definitely going now.'

'We are?'

They both stopped again.

Amy smiled, seeing Billy's face suddenly awash with terror.

'Not a big old scaredy cat are you, Billy Cooper?'

She then let out a small giggle.

'Of course not,' Billy said firmly. 'I don't get scared.'

That's right partner…

'Good. That settles it then. This will be our summer adventure. What do you say, Billy Cooper?'

Billy smiled. He had nothing to say.

They then carried on walking up the road to Billy's house.

Of course he wasn't scared of going to the old tunnel with Amy. He was only afraid of what he might find there, waiting for him in the darkness. Yes, he could only wonder at that.

Billy's house was on a small quiet road, shared with ten others. Five Maple Green Road was a comfortable house, with a small garden and wall at the front and a long block-paved driveway. Billy's father was an insurance adviser so they were reasonably well off. But the pleasant exterior of the house hid a foul stench inside. His family was falling apart around him, like a house of cards, and there was nothing he could do about it except watch and dodge the occasional falling debris. And the worse aspect of it was that Billy reckoned he was the only one that noticed, or perhaps even cared.

Amy stopped at the top of the driveway, her black shoes glued to the Tarmac. Billy turned and looked at her. Her face looked sheepish, all of a sudden uncomfortable.

'Not coming in?'

'No. I think I'd better get going. My mum and dad want me home on time tonight, Billy Cooper!'

Billy didn't believe her, but didn't blame her either. He didn't really want to go inside himself. The uncomfortable atmosphere and heavy silence were not very good incentives for him either.

'Are you going to be all right?' Amy asked, shuffling her feet.

Billy nodded his head. 'I guess so.'

He then quickly remembered the rules once again. 'Don't worry about me, Amy. I'll be fine.'

He looked at her, and she at him. There was silence for almost a minute. It was a comfortable one, one that could only be shared by friends, with neither one of them feeling like they had to say something ridiculous to break it.

'The Tunnel then,' Amy said finally. 'We go next week.'

'OK,' Billy said, half-heartedly. 'Next week it is then.'

Amy suddenly thought that Billy looked really sad. His bottom lip trembled and his eyes looked lost in a sea of heartache.

'It's going to be all right, Billy,' Amy said, gently rubbing his left arm. 'I promise.'

Billy wanted to believe her, more than anything he did. But nothing felt all right any more, nothing … It was hard to believe that anything good could come out of any of this.

Amy walked forwards and then hugged Billy. He slowly hugged her back and wanted to cry right there and then on her shoulder, but didn't. Boys can't show emotion, not in front of girls – Billy knew this better than most.

'All right then, Billy Cooper?'

'Yes.'

Billy's heart fluttered again as they released one another. Amy was the one person that seemed to understand him and he was glad he had her in his life.

'Bye, Billy.'

He watched her walking away from him. The further she got away the more lost and empty inside he felt. It was like little pieces of his essence were falling out of him the further she went away, and being replaced with with hurt and sorrow.

'Bye, Amy,' Billy muttered.

He went inside his house. The atmosphere was horrid. Something nasty had just happened.

8

Amy felt Billy's pain. She knew he was brave and reluctant to break down. She knew of Justin, and of the dreams about The Tunnel. She had luckily entered Billy's life when he had been at his most lost and lonesome. They had become close friends really quickly, like brother and sister. A connection had been made. She loved Billy. But she was also afraid for him and for his family. There was just far too much hurt going on in his life at the moment. The Tunnel held the answers, she was sure about this, especially from what Billy had told her, and even though she masked it with jokes she was sure The Tunnel was the key. But to what, she didn't know. There was something drawing Billy to that place. And whatever that was it was not going away.

The Tunnel was ten miles away, an old disused railway line.

The path was going to be a long and arduous one. Amy knew this. She also knew that not many people would wander that far out, not after hearing all of the stories anyway. The Tunnel was calling to Billy, its voice undeniable. A supernatural force had entered Billy's life, and Amy was going to try to help him discover what it wanted. They would go to The Tunnel and find out together.

Amy crossed the road into the fading light and headed home, still thinking about Billy and The Tunnel.

2

Home Life Part II

1

Billy stayed in his room for most of the night, only coming out twice, once to eat his dinner and the other time to use the toilet. There's only so long your body can put off the need to take a dump. Yes, he wanted to hide tonight. He felt safe inside his bedroom. He knew his parents were both sitting in the front room and the television was on, providing them both with adequate distraction from one another.

They had once been so close as a family. Billy never envisaged this day in his worst dreams. Nobody talked any more and nobody seemed to care, or even noticed. Nobody cared to care. Billy hated it. He wanted to scream at the both of them, slap some sense back into his parents. He wanted to apologise for Justin. But would that really help? Would that make any difference? Billy didn't think so. It wouldn't bring Justin back would it?

He got up from his bed and looked out of the window. It was dark outside. He wondered what Amy was doing right now. She was probably not hiding in her bedroom like he was. Was she thinking about him the same way he was thinking about her? Yes she was.

He thought about The Tunnel and the young man he had seen, looking like he'd belonged in a 1930s fashion parade.

He tried forgetting him. He didn't want to see that face again, especially not this close to bed time. He was just so tired, everything was a struggle for him, and the last thing he wanted was another sleepless night. He lay down on his bed and looked up at the ceiling. He could hear the television coming from the front room. He closed his eyes and rested his young body. He would wake again soon.

2

He dreamt of Justin again.

He called out and opened his eyes. He found himself sitting upright in his bed looking into the darkness. His breathing was rapid and a thin layer of sweat had appeared on his brow, looking like tiny diamonds stuck to his skin.

Billy wiped his face and leaned back against the headboard. Except for the occasional creaking from his bed the room was silent. Cloudy visions from the dream remained inside his head, like mist on a cold morning. They floated, filled with images of Justin and The Tunnel. Billy closed his eyes. The images did not fade away. Not this time.

Billy suddenly felt sick. He threw his duvet over to one side then made haste to the bathroom.

The bathroom felt cold. Billy shuddered as he leaned in over the toilet. His stomach jolted and cramped tightly. Billy retched. Two minutes later Billy was sitting down on the bath tub staring at the red carpet. He could always see faces in the carpet when he looked at it for long enough. Billy hadn't been sick because he was unwell. He had been sick because of the way his life was affecting him emotionally. Hurt and sorrow were building up inside of him, making him feel like a coiled spring at maximum tension. He did now feel a little better. He wiped his brow and sighed.

He left the bathroom and headed back to his bedroom. He

stopped in front of his bedroom door. He became aware of a faint noise. He turned slowly, looking into the dark hallway. He then walked to where the sound was coming from.

3

In his haste to get to the bathroom so he didn't chuck up all over the carpet, Billy hadn't noticed the light coming from the living room.

He arrived at the living room door and stopped. The door was ajar and a beam of light, looking like a laser beam, stretched out, highlighting the grey patterned kitchen carpet. Billy felt his heart racing, but didn't know why. Should he be afraid? The sound was louder now and unmistakable. He closed his left eye and peered through the spacing between the door and the frame with his right.

The small lamp in the corner of the room was on, blowing up someone's shadow against the far wall. Billy never entered the room. He just watched silently with his right eye.

Kate Cooper was sitting in one of the beige armchairs, her long brown hair looking all messy and partially covering her face. She was sitting with her feet underneath her bum and holding an object in both hands. When Billy first looked into the room she was holding, no, grasping, it against her cleavage. After almost a minute she held the object up and looked at it. Kate Cooper was crying and occasionally wiping her eyes with a tissue taken from her sleeve. She looked like a child, Billy thought. Lost and desperate. He had never seen his mother looking so distraught. She had cried over Justin, sure, but this was different. Kate wasn't just crying now, she was looking hysterical, broken.

Billy wanted to enter the room. He wanted to tell his mother that he understood the pain and loss she was feeling. He wanted to tell her that ever since Justin had died he too had lost his way in life a little. Every day seemed to get a little darker as opposed to lighter, and Billy didn't know why that was. Isn't time supposedly a great healer? But maybe the answers needed could not be sought from a twelve year old boy.

Billy watched her for two, maybe three more minutes before going back to bed. She never put the photograph of Justin down in that time. She flicked her hair away from her face and when the light from the small lamp highlighted her distraught features, Billy could see her eyes were blood red, awash with anguish and hurt that only a mother's pining love could bring about. Billy wanted to hold her hand, and tell her that he loved her. And to tell her that everything was going to be all right. He wanted to tell her that he knew too that the wrong son had been killed on that tragic day. He wanted to apologise for being such a bitter disappointment. He wanted to apologise for taking away their proudest achievement. He wanted to apologise for being the one that lived. Billy hated himself in that moment. He was a twelve year old child with the weight of the world on his shoulders, and he hated himself. But all he really wanted was for both his mum and dad to love him, like he thought they once had. Just for once he wanted them both to look at him the way they used to look at Justin. He wanted them to be proud of him. He wanted them to notice that he was growing up into a handsome young lad that they could both love.

Billy quietly moved away from the door and made his way back through the darkness and into his bedroom. He closed his eyes to sleep, still hearing his mother's distant sobs, and he was gently taken away into a world where sometimes he was happy again.

Kate stayed up for most of the night. Her red eyes had hidden something that Billy had not seen. Alex had hit her before Billy had come home tonight. In a drunken onslaught of stupidity and cowardice he had finally hit rock bottom and raised his hand to the woman he had sworn above all else to love and protect. Alex hadn't even realised what he had done, and come tomorrow morning would even ask his wife what she had done to her face. That would be the only question he would ask her all day.

4

In his dream he was always eleven years old, feeling lost like a child all alone in the woods, with something dark and sinister chasing him.

He wasn't sure why but there was a significance to that. Justin was eighteen, the same age he'd been before he died. They were both walking down a long stretch of desolate road. The road never bent or changed gradient. The scenery around them flickered by fast, in a brilliant white light. Everything was unrecognisable. Billy was holding Justin's hand and feeling afraid. He knew something was going to happen, it always did. Eventually the scenery slowed down. It was no longer fast moving white rays of light. Billy was trying to pull Justin along the road. He wanted to get his brother away to safety. The slower the images moved, the more danger Billy sensed. Something was coming, being formed within the images around them. Billy tugged and pulled at his brother's right hand, desperately trying to get him away.

The images all around them, that at first appeared like speeded up cars at night with lights on now revealed a canvas. The images were still moving, but only very slowly now.

'We have to run,' Billy said, sounding distressed. 'If we don't look at the picture then it will never happen.'

There were sounds coming from the moving canvas all around, so Billy pressed both hands up against his ears to shut them out. He never wanted to hear them. He closed his eyes as well. He never wanted to see.

'It's OK, Billy,' Justin said. He was a good looking boy with short blond hair. He kneeled down in front of his younger brother. 'Billy ... Look at me,' he said, trying to move Billy's hands away from his face.

Billy didn't want to look. He knew what would happen if he did, what always did.

'We have to go,' Billy said. His hands were still hiding his face.

'There's nothing to be afraid of, Billy.'

'If I open my eyes and look you will go away again.'

The moving scenery had almost stopped. Billy and Justin were standing on the road but also in the pictures all around them. The scenery was now just one massive picture canvas telling a story, moving with the memories that Billy had of it.

'Billy ... Open your eyes.'

Billy slowly moved his hands away from his face and looked up. Justin was gone. The scenery was moving again and he was now only a part of that, standing all alone. Billy watched as he always did. Clouds floated by quickly, like time was speeding up again. The heavens looked grey, like it was going to rain.

He watched in horror as the images of Justin high in the sky began shaking violently, with small cracks appearing in them. The entire sky looked like it was made of glass. The clouds were no longer moving and neither was Justin. Billy wanted to close his eyes but had to watch. The image of Justin suddenly smashed into a thousand pieces and fell to the ground like droplets of rain. Billy cried out as little pieces of his brother poured down over him. The glass cut deep into his skin and the memories of Justin cut deep into his heart. They always did.

Every moment that ever mattered which he had shared with Justin had been shown to him in the heavens. They were a collage of memories and moments that Billy had dreamt of, each one forming in the scenery around him, even up in the heavens. But there was always one memory that he tried to keep the door shut on, the one that never did as it was told. And all those memories he had formed, like a collage, were falling down around him. Billy recognised all of them. Every magical moment shared with his brother had been shown to him, and then just like in real life taken away again. Like Justin had.

Old memories, new memories, Billy watched them cascade into a million pieces now all lying on the road in ruins, impossible to fit back together again. His brother was gone again, extinguished like a candle blown out by the wind. Billy was once again left alone to pick up the pieces, his shattered dreams lying all around him.

Billy turned uncomfortably in his bed, his face distraught. He muttered something barely audible then cried out in his sleep. He was now coming to the end of the dream, and the worst part.

When he looked up again he was facing the opening of a cave. It was dark and cold and Billy could barely see his own hands in front of him. The sky was clear and the moon full. He had a soft breeze for company and that was all.

Billy's shoes crunched on loose stones and threw up little pockets of dust as he walked along the road. Perhaps road was not the best description. It was more like a dirt track. Trees on his right rustled as the wind swept through them, blades of grass danced underneath the pale moonlight, shadows scurrying for Billy under the moonlit sky. The entrance was getting closer and Billy had no choice except to carry on walking. The gentle wind he felt against his face was now pushing him forwards, and the huge black mouth was waiting.

Billy tried stopping, his shoes scuffing against the track, but the invisible force pushing him forwards was relentless. His shoes carried on sliding across the dirt track, making a rough grinding sound. He couldn't stop. The opening was getting wider and wider. Then he heard something. He cried out.

'Billy,' the voice echoed out of the opening. 'You must come to me, Billy. I have something for you.'

Billy stopped, his body was shaking like he had been suddenly doused in ice cold water. He looked on, his face full of terror.

What was in there waiting for him? What was in there that knew his name? It was watching him right now, willing him to come forward.

'Come to this place, Billy. You must come to this place. You must come to me. I have something for you, Billy.'

'No!'

Billy looked around. The bricks above the entrance gleamed underneath the moonlight. The trees rustled unnervingly, and then the light wind blew him forwards into the darkness again. And then Billy woke up.

5

He always woke up at that point. He never actually got to go inside The Tunnel to find out what was in there. Did he really want to? A little part of him did. However, another part, a much bigger part, was just thankful that the dream always ended before he had the chance of finding out what was waiting for him inside.

Billy had become certain of two things in his short life; number one was that he would most probably dream about Justin and The Tunnel every night for the rest of his life, and number two was that he would be greeted by the same uncomfortable silence by his parents every morning. It was getting a little ridiculous. Every morning was the same. His father would be ignoring him, sitting at the table munching on his toast, reading the morning paper, whilst his mother would be standing at the sink looking out of the window, most probably thinking about Justin or some other far off place that was just as unreachable as the sun.

Kate looked tired and her eyes were all red. Billy knew why and suspected that his father did not. He didn't know how long his mother had stayed up after he had returned to bed last night. Judging by how tired she looked it had probably been for most of the night.

Kate turned and acknowledged Billy with a nod of her head, her shiner discreetly hidden away underneath layers of make-up. Billy smiled. She then went over to the bread bin. Billy watched his father biting down into his toast, making little crunching sounds which he found extremely irritating. He looked up and noticed Billy staring. 'Don't dither about, Billy,' Alex spoke in a firm voice. 'I don't want another phone call from that school of yours telling me that my son has been late, yet again.'

'Yes sir,' Billy said.

Kate was now standing still, watching the both of them. She didn't know how things had become so bad either. It was just the way it was. And it just seemed too hard to fix now.

'Get your juice, Billy,' she said.

Billy nodded then went over to the fridge. Kate went over to the toaster and put her bread into it. Billy downed his juice in one go and then returned to his room. He didn't want to look at his father any more.

6

Billy watched his father driving off like he always did every morning. He still loved him and his mother, but the problem was he didn't think that they loved him any more. He wanted to cry again but didn't. The lump inside his throat would go, eventually, like it always did. He walked over to his bedroom mirror and stared into it. He didn't recognise the person looking back at him any more and that scared him. He was only twelve years old but looked and felt a lot older. The bags underneath his eyes were darker today, but still told the same story. He wanted his parents to love and hold him. He wanted them both to say that they were glad he had survived and that it hadn't been his fault. Billy needed them more now than ever, but all they seemed to do was leave him outside standing in the cold. He thought about Amy and then his pain went away again just like it always did.

Billy got dressed and when he arrived back in the kitchen his mother was washing up. She was still looking out of the window, miles away. She probably didn't even realise he was standing there. Billy almost wanted to look out of the window also, to see what was so fascinating to her. He suddenly felt the need to make conversation with her. Maybe tell her that Amy was coming around for tea again, anything to break the horrid silence that had cocooned the room.

'Mum,' Billy said tentatively. 'I heard you crying last night.'

She turned away from the window and looked at him; her eyes flickered, almost looking scared because he had seen her showing emotion.

Billy maintained eye contact with her.

'I just wanted to say sorry and that if you want to talk –'

'Please go to school, Billy,' Kate said, her voice trembling a little. 'I don't want you being late … You know your father doesn't like it when you are late.'

Perhaps Billy facing up to the problems their family was obviously going through had caught her off guard a little. Kate preferred silence to talking. Maybe admitting that there was a problem was harder for her than actually trying to find a solution to it. Yes, if you don't admit the problem exists then it is easier to ignore, isn't it?

Billy carried on looking at her, his innocent stare holding her, making her feel even more uncomfortable.

'I think we should talk about last night, Mum. I reckon that...'

'BILLY!' Kate shouted smashing a glass against the sink.

Billy flinched and stepped back. He was now scared, scared of his own mother, his throat all of a sudden going all dry.

Kate looked at the broken glass in the sink then pressed her left hand up against her forehead. She hadn't meant to break the glass or to scare Billy. She had failed miserably on both accounts.

It hurt Billy to see her reacting in such a way. He swallowed hard and wiped his teary eyes. He now felt empty inside. To think that his own mother could act in such a way towards him when all he was trying to do was help her both confused and saddened him. As much as he wanted to cry he was not going to, not in front of her, not today.

Billy quickly grabbed his school bag and left the house. Kate watched as he closed the door then looked back down at the broken glass again. She then collapsed onto the floor and sobbed into her hands like a child, doing what Billy had wanted to do for a year now.

7

The morning dragged on, like only a morning at school can. It was now finally lunch time and Billy and Amy were sitting on the field behind the science buildings. It was warm and Billy could feel the sun on the back of his neck. A soft breeze occasionally blew across his young face.

Billy had just finished off one of the sandwiches which Amy had given to him when she looked at him.

'You're awfully quiet today, Billy,' Amy said. She noticed the hand he was holding the sandwich in was shaking. 'Do you want to talk about it?'

'I didn't see you this morning before school,' Billy said, deliberately changing the subject.

'I know,' Amy said, squinting because of the sun. 'I had things to do earlier on. But don't change the subject with me, Billy Cooper. Now what is it?'

Billy didn't mean to shut Amy out. He just didn't want to talk about what had happened with his mother earlier on. The pain was still too fresh. Amy was totally aware of Billy's situation at home but still … To speak the words out loud made it even more real. To admit that to himself felt like giving up. Billy wasn't ready to give up on his family … yet.

He just craved a normal conversation for once, not about The Tunnel, not about his parents or Justin, or about how shitty he was feeling again this morning.

'I'll tell you when I'm ready.'

'I know,' Amy said tenderly, brushing his right arm with her hand. 'But we're still going to The Tunnel, right?'

Billy was still going. He had to. There was something there that was reaching out to him through a haze of elaborate dreams. A force which needed him there for a reason, but why? Billy didn't know. In the back of his mind he thought it had something to do with Justin, why now and how, he didn't know that either. He was positive about one detail though and the very thought of it dried his throat and made his heart thump fast. It was going to be dangerous. He had absolutely no idea of what he was going to find at the end of his journey. And there was something else. He didn't want Amy to come with him. He loved her too much to place her in a dangerous situation. Even though they had talked about going together he would go alone. Bright and early Saturday morning he would leave and find the answers to his nightmares.

Dreams, Billy thought with a smile, remembering Justin.

'What?' Amy asked.

'Nothing,' Billy said, shaking his head.

But the dreams, no, nightmares...

They had been far too scary and real to be just dreams. Billy was convinced there was a hidden message within them and that The Tunnel was the key. And Billy was right, The Tunnel was harbouring something, and he was going to have to face it if he ever wanted to be free and happy again.

'Billy,' Amy said, almost hearing his mind turning with thought. 'What are you up to? Please tell me what is wrong.' Billy forced a smile again. It's nothing,' he said.

'Promise,' Amy said, putting her lunch-box back inside her bag.

The bell rang and children all over the school began heading back inside the school.

Saved by the bell, Billy thought.

Billy and Amy said bye to one another then went in separate directions. They had different classes this afternoon. Billy hated lying to her, even though technically speaking he hadn't. But still, she was his best friend. But he wasn't going to place Amy in danger, and The Tunnel was going to be dangerous, of that much he was certain of. Hell would freeze over before Billy Cooper placed Amy in harm's way.

Billy walked to the entrance to the science block then turned to see if he could still see Amy. She was gone again, lost in a crowd of children who were all talking and laughing with one another.

Billy never went to class that afternoon. He knew he wouldn't have been able to concentrate even if he had. All he could think about was The Tunnel and Justin. He went to the park and started planning his trip. He would leave in three days so had a lot of planning to do. Billy was ready to take on his journey, his adventure. The way he saw it was that he had no other choice. And sitting on the wooden bench watching the world going by, Billy thought about Amy again.

Whichever way he looked at it he always came back to the same conclusion. It was just too dangerous to take her with him.

3

The First Step

1

He was standing at the threshold ... He felt the pull; an almost yearning sensation had overcome him.

Billy skipped school again the next day. Instead of going he ventured down to the track that would eventually lead to The Tunnel. Ten miles as the crow flies, so he reckoned. It was now Wednesday morning and a thin layer of mist hovered above the moist ground. It made Billy think of candy floss. He stopped by a wooden gate at the beginning of the track and rested his right foot on it. He looked at the dirt track and started thinking. This was the beginning all right. A ten mile walk and he would then eventually reach the place in his dreams. Why did he feel like he had to go? Why did he feel like if he didn't then he would never sleep again? What did The Tunnel have to do with ...? Suddenly feeling frustrated he stopped digressing.

I don't really know ... I don't feel like I know anything any more...

He looked up and saw an old man walking his dog. The animal started taking a dump and the old man stood by watching, plastic bag at the ready.

Billy smiled ...

Billy's mind started wandering again. He knew the stories about The Tunnel. Most people in the small town of Market

Harborough had heard about them at some point or another. When Justin had told Billy about them they had scared him shitless. A week's worth of sleep had been lost at the very least. No child likes ghost stories, so why did The Tunnel have such a strong hold on Billy now?

There were so many voices inside Billy's head telling him not to go, but the voice that was the loudest was the one telling him that he had to. That was the voice that would always win out in the end. His fear wanted him to stay put, but his desire to go, to realise the truth, was just too overpowering. He was torn between what he wanted to do and what he knew he really should do. Either way, he couldn't win.

The track leading to The Tunnel was surrounded by trees, high grass and bushes. It didn't look particularly inviting. The track was beaten up badly, uneven, cracked, neglected over time. There were small puddles formed on the track left over from when it had rained two days earlier. Even though the track was still used by dog walkers and the occasional keen runner or cyclist, rarely anybody ventured up as far as Billy was going. Billy never knew of anyone who had before.

Billy wanted answers, needed them, and knew the only way he was going to get them was to go, and he was not going to take Amy with him. This was one venture that he was going to do solo. Perhaps he would go down in history as the first person brave enough to venture the ten miles to The Tunnel since the line had been abandoned. If he made it back alive that is.

The dirt track Billy was going to follow was the bed of a disused railway line. The line, which was closed down in the 1980s, used to link Market Harborough to Northampton, some sixteen miles away. There was certainly a history to the line. Billy started wondering why the line had been closed down in the first place. Was it really haunted? Had that been the reason why? Billy started remembering the stories he had been told long ago ...

35

One of the stories was about a boy who had hung himself. Apparently Kyle Jacob had tied a rope around a tree atop of The Tunnel then placed the noose around his neck. Nobody had ever really known how long he had been hanging in space before being hit by an oncoming train because there hadn't been enough of his body left to salvage to determine anything. Supposedly, the ghost of Kyle Jacob walked the disused line at night time, haunting it and The Tunnel, with the noose still around his neck. Billy, suddenly feeling goose pimples rising up on his cool flesh, shuddered. He had pictured a boy hanging over the entrance of The Tunnel, blowing in the wind, rope creaking against the tree. He had only been eighteen at the time and the reason why Kyle had killed himself was never determined. One of life's mysteries Billy thought. And now he had one of his own to unravel. The dreams had been plenty, but the vision, or hallucination he had seen whilst sitting in the classroom was new to him. Had the figure he'd seen been Kyle Jacob?

Holy shit, Billy thought shuddering again. *What if…?*

No, stop it – you have to stop it, Billy. It was not Kyle Jacob, it was…

A cool hand touched his shoulder.

Billy spun around, almost slipping.

The cool July morning made her cheeks look rosy. She smiled.

Billy was surprised to see her and couldn't hide the fact. It now looked like they were both going to skip school today.

'I'd thought you'd be here, Billy,' Amy said resting her left elbow down onto the fencing.

'I had to come,' Billy said.

'I know.'

They both shared a moment's silence. Only leaves rustling in the wind and the distant sound of traffic could be heard.

'I waited for you this morning,' Amy eventually said. She shuffled her feet. 'I wanted to make sure you were OK. You bailed on me again, Billy Cooper.'

Billy started feeling a little guilty. He had known at the time that he shouldn't have just left her waiting for him in the park. But it wasn't just that. He felt guilty about not wanting her to come with him to The Tunnel. It was just something he knew he had to do alone. And besides he had no idea what was going to be waiting for him when he finally reached … it.

Kyle Jacob, Billy, that's who …

'We can still make school,' Amy noted, looking at her watch.

'I'm not going,' Billy said, turning to her. 'I have to be here today.'

And he did. Even though he was still miles away, standing here made it seem far less. His mind didn't feel so heavy for some reason. It was almost like he needed to be here. The Tunnel was calling out to him, and just standing here, on the threshold, was enough to quieten that voice for the time being.

'Please don't get into trouble, Billy,' Amy said looking worried. Her long brown hair was blowing in the wind. 'Whatever is going on, we will work it out. We are going on Saturday anyway. It will be all right …'

Billy knew Amy wasn't just referring to The Tunnel here. Besides risking getting into trouble herself, Amy had come to find him. She had once again said the right thing to him. Amy always did. Billy believed her in that moment. He started thinking that perhaps things would be all right and believing his parents would one day love him again. And that they needed him just as much as he needed them, but they just didn't know it yet.

'Thanks,' Billy said, smiling. 'But you go, Amy. I don't want you getting into trouble because of me. I will be OK. I just want to stay here for a little while longer.'

'What about you?'

'What about me?'

'The school, Billy,' Amy said looking worried. 'They will phone your house to see where you are again.'

37

'I'll be all right,' Billy said casually. 'My parents won't give a shit anyway.'

'Billy!'

'Amy, please. Just go to school. I can handle my parents. I just want to be alone.'

Amy knew Billy was shutting her out. She didn't feel upset because he was, rather because she knew the trouble he was going to get into.

'Talk to me when you are ready then, Billy,' Amy said, putting her hand onto his arm. 'I'll be waiting for you.'

She started walking away and Billy watched her. She then stopped and turned around. Billy knew what she was going to say.

'Don't you dare go without me, Billy Cooper,' Amy shouted, almost pleading, her young face uncertain.

'I won't, Amy,' Billy said shaking his head. 'I promise.'

Amy smiled, put her bag over her right shoulder then carried on walking back towards the main road. Billy watched until she had disappeared out of sight.

Billy could not keep the promise he had made to Amy. It was as false as the blame his parents had laid onto him over Justin's death. He looked back down at the dirt track and stayed where he was for a long time with only his thoughts for a companion.

2

When Amy passed the house she stopped and turned. It felt and looked like a house she had seen before in a dream. She knew it, yet strangely she didn't. The weird thing was that she and Billy had walked past the house every day on the way to school and this was the first time she had paid any attention to it. She dropped her bag down and stared at the house. The grass looked like it hadn't been cut for some time and the upstairs and downstairs windows were all boarded up. The property looked like it was in serious need of renovating, and was perhaps even too dangerous to enter. She looked further up the house, even a section of the roof had fallen away.

Amy had lived there before, that was how it felt to her. Or had it been Billy? But that wasn't possible. She had lived with her parents in the same bungalow in town since she had been born. She suddenly felt afraid and wanted to run. She couldn't understand why she was feeling the way she was. It just didn't make any sense. Why such a run-down house would intrigue her so much. The boards creaked and the blades of grass blew in the wind, yet no memory of the house would release itself to her. She suddenly wanted to go inside. And go inside she did.

She forced herself to look away from the house, like it was holding her in some type of hypnotic trance, then picked her bag up. Something was wrong here, just like with Billy and The Tunnel. Was the house connected somehow?

The house intrigued, yet scared her at the same time. A tall weeping willow alongside the house seemed to be inviting her to come inside, twigs and branches blew in the wind. Amy shuddered. The house was black and nothing about it was inviting. Yet to her it was. Like Billy and The Tunnel, she too had something from her past that was important to her. Something from both their pasts was reaching out to them, and the only way they could face it would be together.

Amy didn't think getting inside was going to be too much of a problem. Those old boards didn't look particularly rigid. She would come back with Billy and together they would go inside, maybe tomorrow, because right now she no longer wanted to look at the house.

It feels like ... She thought turning away. *But it can't be. The Tunnel, this has something to do with The Tunnel.*

And walking to school that morning the images of the house never left her.

3

The desire for food was the reason for him leaving, that and the sudden urge to speak to Amy, and something else too. One thing Billy had learnt during his twelve years was that his bowels always had the uncanny desire to empty at the most inconvenient of times.

He had lost track of the time. He had even forgotten what day it was. It was Wednesday, wasn't it? Monday he'd had the day-dream in class, yesterday he had bunked off school in the afternoon. Yes, it was Wednesday all right. Billy had forgotten his watch, he didn't like wearing it all of the time just in case he damaged it, so had no idea what the time was. But it was dusk and cars were driving with their lights on. He could see the headlamps seeping in through the trees and bushes, yet the sounds of the engines were still so distant.

Billy had been waiting by the fencing for the best part of the day. He wanted answers and knew where they lay. Billy reluctantly left, looking over his shoulder three or four times until the threshold was no longer visible.

Billy waited by the main road not far from where he had been standing. Cars whooshed by, their lights making them look like huge insects all heading in the same direction. Billy suddenly felt light-headed. He was going to faint. The road was not two feet in front of him. He hadn't eaten all day. He had the weight of the world on his shoulders. Were all of his inner demons suddenly catching up with him? Billy suddenly felt like the world was spinning and he was now looking at it through a thick fog. He was going to fall down into the road, probably to get crushed like a grape by the next oncoming car, when something on the opposite side of the road caught his attention. It was hazy but it was there. Billy felt its pull like a magnetic charge. It was relentless.

Billy had seen him before. The pale faced man standing on the opposite side of the road was a haunting figure who seemed to encapsulate all of Billy's fears.

The classroom, Billy thought. *You were from the classroom.*

The man's stare pierced straight through Billy. He couldn't look away, didn't want to. The pasty-faced man was saying something but Billy couldn't hear him over all the traffic. The fading light surrounded him, and the hollow words of a man he strangely recognised blew over him, his mouth opening and closing yet no sound coming out. Then Billy did hear something. It was unmistakable. A horn and screeching of tyres. He turned and saw two huge eyes coming towards him. He had wandered onto the road. He flinched then went into darkness. There was no pain any more.

The pale looking figure standing on the opposite side of the road watched on. Billy couldn't see any more.

The figure didn't move for a few minutes then disappeared into the fading light, leaving Billy all alone with only his dreams.

4

Amy had lied to her mother. She had phoned her from school with some cock and bull story about working late in the library on an assignment with, yes, you guessed it, Billy. She had also mentioned that she was getting a lift back home with him so her mother needn't worry. Oh what webs we weave? But this girl was on a mission. She had two things on her mind at the moment. Billy and the boarded-up house she had passed on the way to school which filled up her mind like the remnants of a bad dream that would not disperse. Billy was in more pain than usual at this present time. Amy felt it. She wished she had not left him alone now. She knew she shouldn't have. Would he really go to The Tunnel without her? She didn't think so, yet her pace quickened just the same.

At one moment walking back towards the house Amy thought that she had seen Billy. He was standing by the side of a busy road, his face all pale and blank, seemingly looking off into nothingness.

'Billy?' she suddenly muttered.

Amy then shuddered as ice-like fingers crawled down her spine. Amy stopped by the side of the road. She then looked at what was in front of her. A huge looming shadow reached out to her. The sky was now looking grey. No birds were flying today.

'Willow Crest Avenue,' she muttered reading the sign. 'Billy!'

Amy knew something was wrong. She and Billy were such close friends they could sometimes read each other like a book, and feel each other's pain, like twins sometimes can. But the house was too inviting for her to turn away. She had followed the path back and her curiosity was what had guided her. She felt strangely drawn to the house. She wanted to, had to go inside.

The upstairs and downstairs windows were still boarded up. They still creaked in the wind, moaned with voices long forgotten. Amy walked down the long forgotten driveway towards the rear of the house. The ground felt sandy underfoot and made her teeth screech inside her head. Weeds had started protruding between the spacing around the slabs. No-one cared any more. But Amy still wanted to get inside. The house looked uninviting, something out of a horror movie, but Amy still wanted to get inside. A black cloud hovered over above; it was going to start raining soon.

The rear of the house was a spectacle of neglect. High grass and weeds surrounded by a wooden fence that leaned like a drunken sailor. It would fall before too long. In the top right corner was a shed. The wood had rotted away. The house stood alone and the black cloud still hovered. Yes, no-one cared any more.

Billy! The Tunnel...

But the house, she had to go inside and quickly look around. If she was right, then this would help Billy with his quest.

Amy only weighed about six stones, and was not five feet yet, but the boards came away easily enough. She thought she might have needed Billy; he was taller by a couple of inches and was over seven stones, she thought. Her strength sufficed though. Behind the boards there was no glass. Amy climbed into the house.

She was now standing inside the kitchen. She could hear the faint sound of water dripping. It was dark and cold, murky in appearance. The worktops were covered with a thick layer of dust. Huge cobwebs hung from the corners of rooms and between hanging wall lights. Amy prayed she would not meet the spinner.

Her steady steps against the wooden flooring echoed along the empty rooms. The house was damp and unclean. The walls were all stained. Dry rot was setting in. Amy couldn't understand how a house could have become so neglected. She coughed and wiped her hand across her face. Something brushed passed her hair. A cobweb maybe. She shuddered then frantically started rubbing her long brown hair with both hands.

Amy left the kitchen and was now standing in a much larger room. It was the living room of the house. The wooden boards creaked underfoot and the dust floated in the air making her want to sneeze again. What furniture remained was covered with white sheets. Amy stopped in the centre of the room below a hanging light that didn't look secure. A large boarded-up window on the far wall allowed a little light in, Amy could see dust falling over the rays then disappearing forever.

A ray of light highlighted something which immediately grabbed her attention. Was this deliberate? She wiped her face again then walked over to a large mantelpiece standing over a forgotten black fireplace. Amy looked down. It appeared to her in that moment as if deliberately pointed out to her by the weak rays of light fighting through the cracks around the wooden boards. She shuddered again, felt afraid. She also felt surprised, confusion all rolled up into one.

'How can this be?' she said in a barely audible voice, trembling. 'I don't understand. Billy!'

She could not look away from the mantelpiece. It held her. She only wished now that she had not entered the house. She wished the truth about Billy had not shown itself to her in such a horribly cruel way. She didn't want to know any more so fell to the dusty floor and started crying. She now wanted to go home more than ever, but the house had her now. There was no escape.

5

Kate Cooper looked at the clock. Billy was late. She then glanced over at her husband, Alex. He hadn't remembered hitting her, and with the cover Kate had applied over the bruise now revealing part of it, he hadn't even bothered asking her how she had done it.

The television was on but neither of them was paying much attention to it. It's only purpose was to provide a low rumble in the background to mask the deathly silence the two of them had become so accustomed to these days. Any sound was good, less pressure on each of them to make small talk.

Kate flicked a piece of hair behind her left ear then curled her feet underneath her bum like a cat. She hated the silence. She hated what their family had become. It wasn't anyone's fault really. Just a series of unfortunate events had led them all up to this point, a harsh point that was awash with misery.

Alex was staring at the shelf on the wall just above a bookcase. His black hair was all ruffled and he was badly in need of a shave. He always used to be clean shaven. But at least he wasn't drinking tonight. A small light above the shelf highlighted what he was looking at, a picture of Justin.

'Billy's a little late.'

Kate's eyes moved from the clock on the wall. The atmosphere was thick. You could cut it with a knife.

Alex's eyes cast a quick look her way. He didn't say anything though. Did he hate and loathe Billy? No he didn't. But there were deeper more hurtful sensations he had acquired since the death of his first born. Those being blame and guilt. The guilt belonged wholly to him. The blame was all Billy's.

Alex remembered that day like it had been yesterday. Every sound, every smell was there. His mind often travelled back. The 'What ifs' plagued him like a swarm of hungry locusts. Alex was a good man deep down. He just couldn't let go of his dead son. And somewhere along the way the man had been consumed by his own blame and regret.

Kate looked back at the clock again. It was getting late. She fidgeted then got up from her chair and went into the kitchen. She could always phone Billy's friend's house to see if he was there.

Alex meanwhile carried on looking into the picture, and as tears slipped out of his eyes, looking like pearls on his cheeks, his mind once again went back to the most painful day of his life.

4

Justin Part I

1

The day had finally arrived with the familiar scent of freshly mown lawns hovering in the air, blossoming trees, and long evenings that felt like they would never end, were like magic at Billy's age. Billy could feel it. The last week had been one of the longest of his short life, God how it had been.

It was July 2002 and Billy's wait was finally over. The last few days had dragged along in an almost deliberate fashion. Something strange had not long ago happened to him, and he was now desperately in need of some answers. More so now than ever he needed them. He knew where they lay.

Two days earlier Billy had had a dream. It was the type that did not go away. He wanted to tell Justin all about it but so far had not been given the opportunity. Billy had experienced nightmares before, but this one had been different, this one had been something else. And to make matters worse the humidity and pollen levels on this particular warm Saturday afternoon were playing havoc with his asthma. He had used his inhaler plenty, but his chest still felt like it had a clamp around it that was forever tightening.

It was the first Saturday of his summer holiday. No school for seven weeks, sheer bliss, right? Billy didn't think so. Every time he closed his eyes fragments of his nightmare remained, torturing him in an unforgiving way. It was pretty obvious that this dream was not going to go away and Billy was afraid. It had felt real, so much so that he had thought it was really going to happen. He didn't want to talk to his parents about it. Alex and Kate were great with him but they had enough on their plates at present. Justin was going travelling in less than a week's time, with his girlfriend, Lisa. They had been planning this trip for some time now. Justin was also going away to university at the end of the holidays so Alex and Kate were cherishing every bit of time spent with their first born before he flew the nest.

Justin was great and Billy loved him more than anyone. He was eighteen years old, and seven years older than Billy. Billy idolised him. Justin was a popular guy. He played football for the town's team and had a zest for life that was sometimes a little intoxicating. In short he was Billy's hero. They always talked, guy's stuff you understand, Justin was Billy's confidant, the guy that he would speak to when it seemed like the whole world was crashing down around him. They shared some good times too, like when they had both gone camping last summer on some fields that Justin used to run past on the outskirts of town. That was when Justin had told Billy the stories about The Tunnel, and Billy hadn't slept properly since.

Billy's parents were currently sitting down in a couple of chairs beside the barbecue. The strong smell of onions and burgers should have tantalised his taste buds but all they did was make Billy want to be sick. He didn't want to eat at the moment. All he wanted was to sit in his little bit of shade offered by the side wall of the house and rip up blades of grass whilst staring at Justin, occasionally making eye contact with him. Jesus Christ! Aunt Mary did go on sometimes, and it was always when you wanted to get away from her. There would be a slight pause, making you think that she had finished and you could finally escape from her clutches, when she would start off again with another ridiculous anecdote. Billy knew it was probably going to be some time before Justin escaped her evil clutches. She was like this huge spider, so that when caught in her web escape was impossible. Billy didn't like the way she always pinched his cheeks and almost asphyxiated him with layers of flab that would have made a walrus envious whenever she greeted him. She always had terrible body odour as well and Billy thought her breath smelt like turds. But hey, he was only eleven and what eleven year old does like being smothered and kissed by a woman that looks big enough to pick him out of her teeth?

Billy hadn't really felt that way about her though. He was a good kid, quiet and inoffensive. He liked her really. It was just at this present time she happened to be keeping the one person he really wanted to talk to away from him.

Aunt Mary lived across town. Her house was spacious with a huge garden that backed on to a small river. The property was out in the country and was very picturesque. She was twenty years older than Billy's mother and had been a widow for seven years. Uncle Bob had collapsed one day at work from a massive heart attack. Billy didn't really remember him.

Billy hardly recognised any of the twenty or so other party goers Aunt Mary had invited. He wasn't in the party mood anyway. His chest was beginning to feel tight again and Justin was looking in no danger of escaping the spider's web. There weren't even any children of Billy's own age here to play with.

A soft breeze blew through the air. Billy threw the blades of grass he had pulled up into the air and watched then getting swept away by the wind, all going off in different directions. He watched them disappearing, carried off by the wind. He only wished that his nightmare could be carried away so easily.

Billy made a deep breath and felt the clamp tighten around his chest again. He got his blue inhaler out from his pocket and took another puff from it. It didn't help much. It seemed on these hot days his inhaler was becoming less and less effective. He wiped his brow, he was sweating now, and then leaned back against the cool wall.

It was going to be a long day.

He heard laughter so looked up. It was Justin. Aunt Mary was laughing also and had one of her podgy hands on one of his broad shoulders. Billy watched for a few moments then looked back down at the lawn again. He had never felt so lost and afraid in his life.

2

The shadow had consumed him like a black hole.

His parents were eating burgers and wiping ketchup away from their mouths. There was also some music coming from inside the house. Billy turned around and looked through the window. People he didn't recognise with names he probably wouldn't remember danced to the music. Most were drunk. Christ, it wasn't even 3 pm yet. Someone broke a glass. Billy didn't care though. He just wanted to go home now. He hadn't felt like coming here in the first place. His parents had insisted. And the truth was he wouldn't have minded if he had got to spend more time with Justin. Where was he now anyway? Billy suddenly panicked, thinking that Justin had bailed on him, perhaps secretly sneaked out to go and meet Lisa. Billy knew about that kind of stuff, he had seen his brother and Lisa together plenty of times to know what they got up to, and why she had such a hold over him, but in a good way.

'Aunt Mary hasn't seen you in such a long time, Billy,' Kate had said.

'It will only be for a few hours son,' Alex had added. 'Besides you are too young to be left alone in the house.'

Billy had looked around frantically at the dinner table, feeling hard done by, looking for any help here, no matter how little, and then noticed Justin looking at him. He smiled cutely, and so too had Billy. They both remembered at the same time, when Justin had supposedly been baby-sitting his younger brother and sneaked out to be with Lisa instead, that was playing through both their minds in that sneaky exchange.

Back to the garden of delights then, and the sky was not as blue as it had been earlier. The wind was up and Billy's asthma was steadily growing worse. He coughed then had another deep breath from his inhaler. He was starting to panic a little. He hadn't had an attack for some time now, and his inhaler was no longer helping. Just keep calm though, that was the secret, right? Panicking only makes matters worse. It was too late for that though. He was feeling weak and tired, and dared not even attempt to stand up through fear of collapsing.

Even while it was still warm Billy felt cold. A fine layer of sweat appeared on his brow again. He wiped it away with the back of his hand. He started frantically looking around. He needed help. It was in that moment that Justin came over to him.

He stood over Billy, looking like a giant. The sun was beaming down over his shoulders causing Billy to squint when he looked up at him.

'Billy,' Justin said going down to his knees. 'Are you OK, buddy?'

Billy took a shallow breath and shook his head. 'I ... I need to talk ...' He took another shallow breath and realised he wasn't going to be able to complete his sentence.

'Have you used your puffer?'

Billy nodded. 'It ... ra ... ou ... noww,' he gasped then

dropped the empty inhaler onto the lawn next to his badly stained white trainers. He coughed again; a horrible wheezing noise – sounding like something had become loosened inside his chest and was now rattling around inside there.

'Shit,' Justin said. He ran his fingers through his fair hair then looked around. 'Where are mum and dad?' A short pause followed. 'No time.'

Billy gasped again. His blue eyes widened, his little frame jolting uncomfortably as he fought to oxygenate his lungs.

'Come on, buddy,' Justin said helping him up. 'I won't let anything happen to you, I promise. You're coming with me.'

Justin picked Billy up, and carried him off, looking more like his father now than older brother. Billy placed both his arms around Justin's neck and held him tightly. He was less scared now, because he was with his hero, and he always knew what to do.

Most people were now inside. Justin and Billy had now left Aunt Mary's superficial get-together. They were in a race against the clock. It was Billy's clock, and time was now running out.

It was ten minutes after Justin and Billy had left before anyone even noticed.

'*Where are the boys?*'

'*Probably skimming stones by the lake…*'

3

I won't let anything happen to you buddy … I promise.

Those words were still as distant now as they had been when Justin had spoken them, almost a year ago to the day.

Billy's mind had temporarily returned to a time in his life that he wished to God he could have back again. It had been one fateful day when everything around him had changed for the worse, and he had been forced to grow up and to stop being the kid he still was. It saddened him to think about it, but there was no use in dwelling on the past. He couldn't change it, could he?

Friday 18th July 2003 and the last day of school had finally arrived, and not soon enough as far as Billy Cooper was concerned. Since he had skipped school for the best part of the week and fortunately got away with it, he thought that he'd better come in for the last day. It wasn't as if there was going to be much work to do anyway. Billy was a bright boy, used to belong to the chess club, used to get all As, but since Justin had died his grades and overall interest in school had slumped like a drunk at a bar. Everything had slumped. What had once seemed important to him now felt inferior, like losing someone you love can often do to you.

Billy had waited for Amy in their usual meeting place this morning but she had failed to show. He had looked for her at school but hadn't been able to find her there either. He was ready to talk to her now but it seemed she was now giving him a taste of his own medicine. Something weird, even weirder than the dreams he'd had, had happened to him the other day. It was mostly a blur now but fragments floated around inside his head like pieces of a jigsaw puzzle, waiting to be fitted together. He had seen that man again, the one who had first come to see him inside the classroom. Billy shuddered to think about it. He had been standing next to a busy road, yes he remembered that part, and he had been looking at someone standing on the opposite side of the road. Then something had happened, the screeching of tyres, a car horn maybe, and after that everything had gone black. He remembered nothing after that. But why?

At least he had not dreamed for a few nights now, but there was still a weight on his mind though. He could not forget about The Tunnel, didn't want to in fact. He was determined not to run away from this, regardless of how scared he felt.

Outside the main assembly hall Billy sat on a wooden bench. He was watching all the other children laughing and enjoying the last day of school. Billy didn't feel like celebrating. He hated thinking it but the truth was he didn't enjoy life any more. He was thankful to have his best friend, Amy, but sometimes that just wasn't enough. He wanted what the children he was watching had. He wanted to enjoy being young. He wanted to be a kid again and to feel loved. His mind drifted back again to a happier time.

I won't let anything happen to you buddy ... I promise.

He wanted to cry again, had to wrestle back his tears.

The sounds of laughter and the look of smiles seemed so foreign to him lately. He couldn't remember the last time he had laughed, really, really laughed, to the point where you think you are going to piss yourself. It didn't seem fair, why should he be the one that was unhappy when it seemed that all the other kids he was watching didn't have a care in the world. Billy wished Justin was still alive because every little boy needs a hero to look up to from time to time. He closed his eyes and pictured his brother. After a few more minutes he got up from the bench and went inside. He no longer cared to hear laughter any more.

4

Billy had gone to the same spot on the disused railway line each day he had skipped school. It had been the only place where he felt less alone. He couldn't begin to explain why that was. The last time he had seen Amy was on the first occasion he had gone. That was when he knew he should have spoken to her instead of shutting her out, instead of being rude to the one living person that he could truly say that he loved. He needed Amy now, but where was she?

Every second of the day had thus far dragged along for

Billy Cooper, but the final bell of the school term was about to sound. Every kid in class was now watching the second hand of the clock like their lives depended on it. News of Billy's hallucination from the beginning of the week had provided the class with a little light relief on more than one occasion, but like most things at that age it would soon be forgotten about. However, one person had been paying particular attention to Billy that day, perhaps for a few months now.

The bell rang.

A loud cheer erupted, followed by sounds of many chairs scraping against wooden floors. Doors opened quickly and shoes echoed along corridors. Billy waited. When the herd of children had cleared he pushed back his chair. The scraping of his chair against the floor seemed so lonely in comparison.

Mr Harris paid attention when Billy stood up, his beady eyes peering over the tops of his glasses.

'Billy,' Mr Harris said, standing up. Billy stopped and turned. 'Do you have a minute please?'

A minute, Billy thought. *I have a lifetime...*

He reckoned he knew what Mr Harris was going to discuss with him. But he had been wrong. Mr Harris pulled up a chair next to his untidy desk, littered with papers he would no doubt be marking over the course of his summer vacation, and motioned to Billy to sit down.

He did so.

5

Billy liked Mr Harris. For a teacher he was all right. He was an overweight man, with grey receding hair. He was Billy's maths and form tutor.

Mr Harris looked at Billy for almost a minute before finally speaking. Billy just listened. He didn't feel like talking.

'Are you all right, Billy?' Mr Harris asked. 'You have missed most of school this week.'

Billy nodded sheepishly. 'I'm OK.'

'Jolly good,' Mr Harris said. He paused for a few seconds.

Billy looked at the wooden flooring as if it was suddenly the most fascinating thing he'd ever seen.

'But if you are having problems, Billy, then please know that you can talk to me.'

Billy looked up. Mr Harris was smiling, still looking over the rims of his glasses. His grey hair was all messy.

'OK Billy.'

Billy wanted to tell him. He wanted to tell him about everything. About how he had not slept properly since Justin had died a year ago. And about how he felt unfounded guilt about his death. He wanted to tell Mr Harris about his home life and about how his parents treated him like the same way a child does a new toy he or she has suddenly lost interest in. He wanted to tell him about how much he was hurting inside, how empty he was feeling, lost, and how he wished his parents would look at him like they once did Justin. He wanted to tell him about the strange man he had seen and the dreams. He wanted to speak of The Tunnel and hopefully get some explanation as to why he felt so strangely drawn to it. He wanted to ask for help. He wanted Mr Harris to explain to him why both his parents didn't love him any more, and why he felt guilty even existing. He wanted all the answers that a twelve year old boy couldn't ever begin to fathom. He wanted to know why life is so cruel and unfair, and why oh why his hero had to die.

Billy did none of this. Instead he did what he knew how to do. He smiled and put on a brave face again.

'I'm fine, Mr Harris,' Billy said.

He sounded convincing, almost believed it himself.

Mr Harris smiled again and then nodded his head slowly.

'OK then, Billy,' Mr Harris said. 'Have a great summer, son.'

'I will,' Billy said, standing up. He put his bag over his shoulder then turned to Mr Harris. 'You have a good summer too.'

Mr Harris smiled gently.

Billy started walking towards the door. His head was spinning. He felt like there was so much to do when he left school today, and there was. Most children were looking forward to a holiday of doing nothing but Billy Cooper was going on a journey of discovery and danger – a journey of his lifetime.

'Billy!'

Billy had just been about to leave the classroom when Mr Harris had called out to him.

He stopped and turned around.

Mr Harris removed his glasses and leaned back in his chair, making it creak a little.

'You know, Billy,' Mr Harris said, putting his glasses down next to a huge pile of paperwork on his untidy desk. 'I am fifty-seven years old next month and I have been a teacher for thirty-five of those long years.' He smiled.

Billy put his bag back down again. He suddenly wanted to listen.

Mr Harris continued. 'Over the years I have met and taught many children. And may I hasten to add that most of them have been wonderful to teach. Most of them by now have probably forgotten my name, and I in turn have probably offered them the same disservice.' He cleared his throat then picked up his glasses again. He dangled them from his right index finger and thumb. 'But you know what, Billy,' he continued. 'Sometimes you remember the names, and the faces of those children that for some reason or another stood out to you. And one of those names and faces that I will always remember will be your brother, Justin.'

In that moment, listening to Mr Harris as he spoke Justin's name, Billy looked at him like he was the most important man on Earth. He went cold, and goose pimples rose all over his body.

'Your brother was one of those few students I shall always remember, Billy. He was a wonderful young man and a joy to have taught. I liked him a lot and was saddened to hear about his death.' He paused and watched Billy, who did not speak. 'I just wanted you to know that, Billy.' He paused again and then finally said, 'And I hope whatever is troubling you sorts itself out soon, son.'

There was a short silence, shared by two people that had spent the entire year together but never really spoken, not until now anyway.

'Thank you, Mr Harris,' Billy said eventually, filling up a little.

'Not at all. Now have a great summer, son.' He smiled again.

Billy nodded then smiled, which was something he didn't do much of lately. He picked up his bag and walked out of Mr Harris's classroom. He was leaving tonight, going to The Tunnel. His long journey was about to begin and it was now time to find out who or what was calling out to him from afar.

5

Journey Into The Night

1

After school Billy went around to Amy's house. He didn't want to leave without first going to see her; after all he didn't know whether he would be coming back. If he played it cool, and maintained his composure, then hopefully she would not guess that he was planning their joint trip a day earlier than expected, and without her in tow. Of course Billy knew that as far as Amy was concerned they were still going to The Tunnel together. And at first Billy had wanted her to come, though he hadn't considered the dangers posed to both of them. After all, he had absolutely no idea of what was going to be waiting for him in that old dark, damp and empty tunnel. And as far as Amy was concerned he was going to lie to her. Tell her that they would go tomorrow, like they had agreed. He would then quietly slip away tonight. He was the one that had been dreaming about The Tunnel, it was calling out to him and not Amy. Yes, this was definitely going to have to be a solo journey. What of his parents though? Billy reckoned they probably wouldn't even notice he had gone.

Probably bring a smile back to the old man's face, he sadly thought. *Like how he used to smile when Justin had been alive.*

No time to dwell on that now though, he had to put his game face on.

Amy's house was close to Billy's. She lived in a slightly busier part of the town at the bottom of a main road. Billy liked Amy's house, it seemed ideal to him, the perfect house with the perfect family inside, with a long driveway and small garden at the front with a low white picket fence at the front. On a bright warm summer's day Billy thought that it looked like something out of a fairytale. Everything about Amy's house reminded Billy all of that his own lacked. Amy's parents, Carol and Mike, actually spoke to him and were interested in what he had to say. Carol and Mike's home had this welcoming feeling to it that was almost intoxicating. Billy loved their home, so different to his own, so full of life and possibility. And most importantly it made him feel like twelve again.

Before going to Amy's house Billy had been sitting in the park again. His time nowadays seemed divided between the threshold of The Tunnel and the park. He had thought a lot whilst sitting on the wooden bench in front of a slow running stream. He had mostly thought about Justin and the dreams he'd been having. He had also thought about Amy. When he had met her he had been at his most low, and Justin had not long been laid to rest. Amy brought him back to the surface, when he thought all he was going to do was drown in his own pain and sorrow, her friendship had saved him. The notion that he had been saved by a little girl should have been laughable to him at his tender age. But Billy knew; he always did. Amy was his pillar, she always would be. And even though he never told her, Billy loved her so much for doing that for him, helping him see a daylight that he thought would never show itself to him again.

Billy rang the doorbell twice before seeing a shadow appearing behind the stained patterned glass. At first he thought it was Amy. But it was Carol Johnston who actually opened the door. Billy was greeted with her usual warm smile that he reckoned could have melted butter. He went inside. It was time to be king again for the evening.

2

They talked for what felt like hours. Billy savoured the time spent with them all, but there was one problem, Amy wasn't in. Apparently she was around a friend's house doing some homework. Strange, Billy thought. He didn't remember seeing her at school and as far as Billy knew he was her only friend, and vice-versa. This wasn't good. He was now not going to be able to see Amy before he left. So where was she?

'I'll get you another Coke, Billy,' Carol Johnston said, her smile once again lighting up Billy's sad heart.

'Thanks.'

Billy started looking at some pictures on the side unit. Most of them were of Amy and her parents. They looked such a close family.

'You like those, Billy?'

'Yes,' Billy said, now turning his gaze over to Mike who was reading his paper.

Mike smiled and nodded his head.

Both Carol and Mike were early thirties and both good looking people. It would probably be a safe bet that Amy was going to be a stunner when she grew older. Carol had model looks accompanied with rich long brown hair that was almost down to her lower back. Mike was broad shouldered with swept back thick blond hair. Billy always thought that he looked like an action hero from a Hollywood film. And he could have been, because Billy couldn't recall Amy ever actually telling him what her father did for a living.

'You like photos, Billy?'

Billy nodded. 'Yes sir.'

'Come over here then son.'

Billy got up from his chair and joined Mike in the corner of the room. There was a white cabinet next to his chair. Mike opened one of the creamy coloured doors and pulled out a photo album.

'Here,' Mike said, handing it to Billy. 'Have a look through this.'

Billy took the album and opened it.

As simple a gesture as this was, Mike simply showing an interest in Billy, letting him look through one of their family albums made Billy feel happier than he had done in a long time. This is what families do, right? They talk, they sit down with each other and look at old pictures that rejuvenate old memories again from the circuitry of the brain that had been long forgotten. This was what Billy wanted. He sat back and enjoyed it.

3

Looking at the photos of Amy and her parents made Billy smile. It also saddened him. He wished he was as close to his parents as Amy obviously was with hers. He imagined himself in those pictures with his parents. They all looked so happy. Even Justin was in them. The picture then faded. Billy came back.

After looking through the album from cover to cover, Billy looked at his watch. It was getting late and was now time to go. He wanted to begin his journey tonight. It would be easier for him to disappear in the darkness.

'I have to go now,' Billy said, his voice sounding like this was the last time he was ever going to say it. He hoped not, God, how he hoped not.

'Come around anytime, Billy,' Carol said. Mike nodded as if to reinforce her words.

'We'll tell Amy that you came around,' Mike added. 'I really don't know why she is staying out so late tonight.'

After two slices of cake, and three glasses of Coke, Billy was now feeling a little stuffed. He wasn't too concerned about that though. After all he had a long journey ahead of him tonight and needed his energy levels to be high.

He was back outside now. The moon was full in the fading sky and lit part of the Johnston house. Billy looked at the house in wonder for almost a full minute then was on his way.

4

Amongst other things, Billy had concocted an imaginary list in his head of all the things he was going to have to take with him over the next couple of days. He didn't want to write them down just in case his mother discovered anything. And the list was long. He was going to require a large bag. But Billy was only small and didn't fancy carrying a heavy bag for ten miles.

It was dark when he finally arrived home. Billy liked the dark. He liked the notion of hiding and not being seen. He opened the front door and was greeted with the usual heavy silence. A morgue had more life to it.

Billy's parents were sitting in the front room again. He peered in between the gap around the partially open door. Good! They were both watching the television. Billy quickly went to his room. It was now time to get ready. It was now time to become a man and begin the journey of his life.

Get changed out of school clothes. Check!

Take blue zip bag from out of wardrobe. Check!

Now grab an extra top. Check!

Now for some spare underwear. Just in case. Check!

Billy was packing in a hurry. He wasn't sure what he should take with him so extra clothing seemed a logical place to start, and his watch, which had extra special personal value to him. What about food and bedding? He stopped, forgetting about the extra clothing. Food seemed the more important of the two now. But he was going to need decent bedding because even though it was July the nights were occasionally cool and unkind.

There was plenty of food in the pantry, crisps and chocolate – all healthy food groups for a growing boy. But there was a slight problem. Billy reckoned his sleeping bag was 'sleeping' in the garage next to his rusty old bike. He was going to have to get it, as the idea of sleeping on a cold dusty ground did very little for him.

Shit!

Billy knew that his father would have locked up the back door and garage by now so he was going to have to find the key to the garage door and sneak outside unnoticed.

Shit, shit…

Billy was now panicking a little. He had wanted this to be simple. It wasn't going to be.

He sat on the bottom of his bed and looked at his hands. They were shaking and his palms were all sweaty. He got up and hid the bag by the side of his bed, leaving his jacket on the bed. He then headed for the kitchen.

Shit, shit, shit…

He could still hear the television but the heavy silence between his parents strangely overpowered it. Billy sneaked past the living room door and then to the key rack on the kitchen wall just underneath the clock he had bought for his mother a lifetime ago. To be caught now would be disastrous. But it didn't take him long to locate the garage key. Billy took the key from off the hook and headed for the back door, which was unlocked.

The back garden was large. There was slab paving immediately outside the house and a healthy looking green lawn. Billy's father had even built a wooden archway at the divide. That had been a long time ago. That had been when he still smiled and the sound of him laughing was not such a foreign sound. He carried on walking past the side of the house. The outside light suddenly came on.

'Shit!'

No, no ... chill partner, it is only the censor you have activated.

'Phew ...'

He was now standing in front of the garage door, his reflection looking all distorted in the opaque glass. Billy placed the key into the lock and turned it.

Click.

He went inside and closed the door, leaving the key in the lock.

Alex Cooper suddenly remembered where he had to be. He got up from his chair, making his knees click, and then left the room without so much as looking at his wife. But Kate watched him, her bright, yet sad inquisitive eyes following him until he left the room. He went into the kitchen and stopped in front of the key rack.

Strange, he thought. *I could have sworn I locked the garage and hung the key there.* Alex spoke a lot more inside his head than he did out loud these days. He went to the back door. He went outside. The outside light was also on.

There were two parts to the garage. The back part was a spare room where items over the years just accumulated. Old bikes, kitchen paper, bottles of booze, an old stereo system, electrical bulbs, an old settee, coffee table, and of course a red sleeping bag, were many of the eye-catching delights.

Billy picked up the sleeping bag. It smelt a little musky, like old socks, and was dusty but would do. He suddenly froze on the spot, his blue eyes looking up, blazing with terror. The back door had just opened and closed again.

5

He didn't have long to find a place to go and hide.

First things first though, switch off the light. Check!

Now go and hide, for the love of God. Billy did. Check!

Now stop breathing and pray to God not to be seen. Check!

The garage door then opened.

Shit!

Billy's heart speeded up.

Alex looked lost, a soul trying to find its way home. Billy watched; his eyes flickering from side to side like flames in the wind. All Billy could do now was hope he wasn't seen.

To Billy's relief Alex went straight into the end room of the garage and closed the door. Billy, who had been hiding behind Justin's old red Peugeot 205 sighed, then slowly got to his feet. He picked up the sleeping bag and made haste, wiping his brow as he went.

Billy stopped by the door. He could hear something. The television in the end room was on. Billy hadn't realised it even worked any more. The volume was set so high that Billy could hear it with perfect clarity even from behind the closed door. He could hear a familiar sounding voice. It was younger sounding than he had remembered but still it was unmistakable to him. It was Justin.

Billy wanted to go, this was a perfect opportunity. Call it curiosity or even madness, but for some reason he started to open the brown wooden door.

The door was now ajar, no more so than the living room one had been when Billy had sneaked past. He could see what his father was watching. Billy saw everything.

It was Justin's birthday. He couldn't have been any older than seven. In the video he was wearing a yellow party hat and getting ready to blow out the candles on top of his huge cake. Occasionally the video moved onto other children that Billy didn't know. Hell, he hadn't even been born at that time. His father was sitting forward on the settee and watching with his hands on his knees.

Billy's mind momentarily went off to a place where dreams

65

can come true. He was now the one in the video with the loving parents holding him as he was preparing to blow out his candles in one single blow.

Go on Billy, blow out the candles ... One, two three ... Good boy ...

Billy had never heard his father sounding so excited and fused with energy before. In actual fact he sounded as excited as Billy looked.

But it was only a façade. He came back; the musky smell of the sleeping bag told him so.

Go on Justin, blow out the candles ... One, two three ... Good boy ...

Billy wanted it to be his name that he heard, but like most of his dreams of late concerning his parents it was never to be.

Justin blew out the candles. A roar of applause, laughter, a sound that was as stale as bread left outside to Billy's ears these days.

Did you make a wish Justin?

Yes Daddy – I did ...

Smoke from the candles floated away, carrying with it a little boy's hopes and wishes for the future. But it was a wish that was never to have been.

6

Alex was now crying into his hands and so was Billy. His little beady eye still peered through the gap around the door, red and puffy, showing too much hurt for one so young.

Alex sniffed a couple of times then wiped his eyes. 'I miss you, son.'

Billy heard him with perfect clarity.

Alex then got up and walked back over to the television and switched it off.

In that moment Billy wanted to enter the room, he wanted

to hug his father and apologise for everything and nothing. He wanted to tell his father that it would be all right. But Billy was not the parent here, and it was not his job to make everything better with a hug.

Billy knew that he should have gone by now. He was watching his father almost like it was the first time he was actually seeing the man, after hearing stories about him for years. Perhaps seeing his father showing emotion was just too captivating for him in that moment to leave.

His father suddenly turned. Billy trembled.

Before Billy had the time to either think or react Alex had already pulled open the door. He was now towering over Billy, not like a father but rather in a menacing, intimidating way, a towering shadow of mistrust and hate.

'What are you doing, Billy?' His voice trembled a little.

Billy was expecting a back hand not a question. But in a strange way he thought this was a weird kind of progress. At least his father was now speaking to him.

'BILLY!' He shouted this time.

'I … I …'

'Answer me, Billy. Were you spying on me?'

'No Dad.' Billy felt afraid. He hated him for that. He wanted him to die for that.

'I don't believe you; now get back inside you little sod and don't ever follow me out here again.'

Billy wanted to hurt his father, inflict the same pain and sorrow onto him that his father had done to him over the past year.

'Screw you.'

'What?'

'You heard me you miserable bastard. I'm not going to keep letting you make me feel like shit because you blame me for what happened to Justin.'

'Why you little shit!'

Billy suddenly saw a shimmer of white light then felt a

sharp pain on the left side of his face. He then fell to the ground, sharp pain tunnelling into the left side of his little face like a drill.

Alex was still standing over him but this time looking at his hand. Billy's cheek was already red and swelling. He wanted to cry but he was not going to let his dad have the satisfaction, not now, not ever again.

'Billy ... I ...'

'I hate you! I hate you!'

Billy scrambled to his feet, grabbing the sleeping bag and running back outside. He now had more reason than ever to run away tonight.

Alex didn't go after his son. He stayed put, still looking at his hand. Yes, he would remember doing this tomorrow all right. He eventually left the garage and locked it. He went back inside and put the garage key back on the hook where it belonged.

7

The night air was cool, sharp, biting at his skin. His cheek still throbbed, not that it had been hit particularly hard. It was more the thought that his dad had hit him.

Billy had been running for a long time. He was in shock. His father had never laid a hand on him before. It seemed like his family had now finally hit rock bottom.

Billy finally stopped running. He was breathing rapidly and a stitch had taken over his right side. Even though it was cold a light sweat had layered his skin. He wiped his brow, still breathing quickly. He then looked across the road. The beginning of his journey lay out in front of him. He had been guided to it like a heat-seeking missile. He crossed the road and walked over towards the brown wooden fencing. He dropped his bag and leaned forward, resting both arms over a section of the brown fencing. He looked up. The night sky was clear and a thousand stars twinkled down at him, like diamonds. The moon was full and a light breeze reminded him of the fact that he had also forgotten his jacket. But tomorrow would be warm and walking in the sun wearing a jacket made him thankful he had not brought it with him.

Just more shit to carry, he thought. *And I am carrying enough shit lately…*

He suddenly thought of Justin again and looked up at the night sky. Billy's grand-dad had once told him that each new star in the sky was an angel getting its wings.

'Are you up there?' he muttered angrily. 'Can you see what is left for me here?'

Billy looked away from the sky and at the dark path that lay ahead. It was an uncertain journey that would eventually lead to an even more uncertain fate. He thought about the stories again.

The Tunnel is haunted. The place is evil, Billy. There is a reason why it was closed. There is a reason why people do not venture out as far as you intend to.

The voice was not his own. It sounded as hostile as the path that lay ahead looked. A labyrinth of darkness surrounded him but the only path he was going to take was the one ahead. Billy dropped his bag over the fence. He climbed over to the other side. The journey had now begun and he was not afraid any more. He was now a man. All he had for company was the endless darkness. So he thought anyway. He heard someone coughing and spun around.

The light of the moon highlighted her pretty face. 'I thought we had a deal, Billy Cooper?'

'What?'

'We said we were going together, remember?'

Amy didn't sound annoyed at him for breaking their deal, she sounded hurt, let down. Billy could only say one word.

69

'Sorry.'

Amy had a rucksack over her shoulders that looked pretty full. Billy selfishly hoped she had brought some food. She nodded her head then climbed over the fencing. Amy was wearing blue jeans and black jacket and her hair was combed back into a single pony-tail.

'Did you forget your jacket?' Amy asked, looking at the red zipped-up cardigan he was wearing.

Billy nodded. 'I had to leave in a hurry. I didn't bring any food either.'

'Well I have more than enough for the two of us,' Amy said, looking really pleased. 'I even brought a torch, see.'

Amy pulled out a silver pocket-sized torch and shone it into Billy's face.

'Hey!' Billy shielded his eyes with his left hand.

'Serves you right, Billy Cooper,' Amy said. 'Serves you right for trying to go without me. You were supposed to–' She suddenly stopped talking and frowned. 'What happened to your face, Billy?'

'Nothing,' Billy said defensively.

'But it looks all bruised.'

'It's OK. I just caught it earlier on.'

Billy didn't give Amy any more time to continue with her interrogation. 'We'd better get going.'

Billy zipped his cardigan all the way up.

Amy was now standing alongside him.

'OK then, let's go,' Amy said. 'And trust me, Billy you will be glad that I was waiting for you.'

'Have you been home tonight?' Billy asked.

'Yes,' Amy said. 'And don't worry. I have taken care of our alibi.'

Billy wondered what she could have said, not that he cared about lying to his own parents, but he liked Carol and Mike, and cared about what they thought of him, and didn't think that they would look upon him too kindly knowing that he had taken their twelve year old daughter on a trip to a haunted tunnel where people had supposedly died.

They both followed the path that lay ahead, soon disappearing into the darkness. Two children walking together, both having their own reasons for going, but still sharing that same hope and innocence that only children can.

8

They walked along, sharing a comfortable silence, the torch lighting the way as they went. Billy was actually glad of Amy's company. Whether he knew it or not he was going to need her before this was all over. He loved Amy. And even though he had only known her for about a year now couldn't possibly imagine living his life without her.

The ground was uneven in places so they had to be careful of their footing. Billy tripped a couple of times but luckily never went completely over. Amy walked with an almost effortless grace. The air was still and the moon offered the occasional extra lighting where the surrounding forest cleared. Eventually their eyes adjusted and their surroundings revealed a little more to them without the need of the torch.

'How long have we been walking?'

Billy wasn't sure. He didn't even remember what time it had been when they set off. It could have been an hour or it could have been ten minutes.

'Not sure,' Billy said, looking at his watch.

'It must be getting late,' Amy added.

Billy stopped and shone the torch on his watch. Amy waited next to him looking around. It was almost 10.30pm.

'Let's find a place to set up camp,' Billy said. 'I need some sleep.'

Amy smiled, feeling the same. Billy had secretly wanted to go camping for as long as he could remember. It almost made the adventure that much more real.

Camping…

They carried on walking with Billy periodically aiming the torch at the sides of the track. They didn't want to spend the night sleeping on the dusty track so any space between the trees and bushes would suffice. The track was beginning to narrow in places the further they went along. The forest was much denser, spreading out across the path like huge ugly fingers.

'There!' Billy said. He noticed something in between the thickets. He walked to the side of the road.

Amy followed closely.

Standing at the top of a steep embankment they could now see it better. It looked like a bus shelter made out of old cobbled stone but obviously wasn't.

'Probably used by the workers on the lines,' Billy said, remembering what they were now walking on used to carry trains. It was easy to forget. 'Be careful,' he added, turning to Amy. 'It looks steep.'

Billy went down first, the idea being that he would then be able to catch Amy if she slipped over. The bag he was carrying made the descent even more awkward for him. The slope was about twelve feet deep and the cool moist air had made the grass damp and very slippery. Billy felt like he was walking on ice not grass.

'Steadily does it, Billy,' Amy called out thinking his descent was looking far too clumsy and quick.

'I'm OK,' Billy said, trying to sound like her concern was not needed. But he also knew he was about to go arse over head. It was then when he suddenly saw The Tunnel again. It was like he had temporarily returned to his dream. The image flashed through his head like an explosion. The archway was in front of him, eternal darkness now lay ahead. The fair-haired man was also there, standing in front of him. He was motioning for Billy to come inside, smiling inviting him with seducing hand gestures. The Tunnel opened up like a mouth. He suddenly lost his footing and went over.

'Billy!' Amy cried out.

Billy's efforts were in vain, he could not stop himself from falling. The moon and the stars rolled on by. Billy had gone over onto his right ankle before he fell. He landed awkwardly in some bushes, face down in the dirt.

Amy followed down the embankment. She did not slip, even though she went down much quicker than Billy. Once at the bottom she darted towards the bushes.

'Billy, are you all right?' Amy asked, moving the bushes out of the way.

Billy was already sitting up. He had twisted his ankle on the way down but his pride hurt a whole lot more. He knew very well that boys are not meant to fall over in front of girls. Boys are macho, fearless creatures, warriors.

Amy knelt down next to Billy and held his hand. Billy looked down at it like it was something alien to him, for someone to be actually showing him any human empathy. He was now going to have to be helped up by a girl, God could it get any worse?

'What?'

'Nothing.'

'Have you broken anything?'

Billy made sure everything felt all right before he answered. Arms, legs and wrists all present and correct. Good!

'I think I have just twisted my ankle.'

Amy smiled.

'What?' Billy asked, still feeling pretty stupid.

'I don't know, Billy Cooper,' Amy said, placing her hands down onto her hips. 'What am I going to do with you?' She giggled a little. It was pretty funny, Billy sitting on his ass, buried in a bush, face now a little dirty.

Billy smiled, he couldn't help it. Amy then helped him up. He left an arm around her waist for support.

'The shelter,' Amy said, looking ahead.

She bent slightly to grab Billy's bag then helped him towards the stone shelter. They would spend the rest of the night in there. Tomorrow they would leave early, The Tunnel was still calling.

6

The Stone Camp

1

The shelter was made up of two areas with a half-collapsed brick divide. There was also a small opening in the far wall looking like an incomplete window. The ground was cold but once inside their sleeping bags they were comfortable enough. Billy's ankle still hurt a little but the pain was beginning to subside. They were both laying long ways in front of the opening that probably once had a door to it, and staring out into the pitch blackness.

'You saw him again, didn't you?' Amy asked, referring to the fair-haired man.

Billy turned in his sleeping bag to see Amy. 'Yes – and the opening of The Tunnel.'

He paused, looking slightly frustrated. 'I just wish I knew what it all means, Amy.'

'You will,' Amy said. Her voice was as reassuring as always, calm and soothing. 'I have no doubt in my mind.'

In that moment, looking at Amy in the pale moonlight and listening to the wind howling against the old brick shelter, Billy realised that he was lying next to the most important person to him in the world. Amy would never hit him, or make him feel inferior. She would never hurt him or forget about him, she was his friend and no matter what happened she would always be there for him. So he hoped anyway. He also realised something else about himself. Even though his home life was as ruined as the shelter they were currently occupying, he was strong, he was a survivor. He was glad Amy was here with him, and thanked God secretly in that quiet moment that she had entered his life.

'Thanks.'

'For what?'

'I don't know, for just being here I guess.'

Amy smiled, almost lighting up the darkness. She reached over and took Billy's hand in hers.

They slept.

2

It was 2am when Billy awoke. Another dream about Justin had done it. Sometimes when he had almost convinced himself that he had nothing to feel guilty about the dreams would make it all come flooding back to him again. He couldn't cry now though, not in front of Amy. Surely falling over in front of her was bad enough. Yes – he would have to bury his guilt deep within for the time being, as well as his tears. He was getting good at that. But the burden was starting to get a little too big for one so young to carry. He wiped his eyes. No crying tonight.

A sound, only faint but it was there. He looked over at Amy. She was sleeping peacefully on her side. He climbed out of his sleeping bag and hopped to the entrance of the shelter. It was cold and he shivered a little.

He peered out into the darkness; the moon cast a dim light, making a yellowy shadow against the side of his face.

There, he heard it again.

He took a step outside, testing his injured ankle; he could put some weight down on it.

That place is haunted.

Could it be? Could it really be that they had already found them? They hadn't even got as far as The Tunnel yet and their journey was already over. They had been found.

The wind blew against Billy's face, a soft whisper. Kyle Jacob had come for them. He was no longer swinging in the mouth of The Tunnel. He had tired of swinging effortlessly in the air. He had now been sent to ward them off – they had no business being here and must turn around and go home now. Billy could venture no further. This place belonged to the dead, not the living.

'No!' Billy muttered. 'It is just the wind. I do not believe in …'

Ghosts!

The hairs on the back of his neck saluted.

He could not finish his sentence.

Shadows danced before him and the sound echoed through the night air again, Billy steadily followed it.

He hobbled to the bottom of the embankment. He was going to have to climb it come first light. He listened again. His heart thudded like a drum, his breathing rapid. The night air carried the sound again. Billy spun around, grimacing in pain, momentarily forgetting about his right ankle.

'No ghosts,' he muttered. 'No ghosts!'

The trees rustled and danced in the wind, Billy listened.

'Oh, God,' he said.

Billy now realised what it was he was hearing. Something was crying out.

Billy was now having second thoughts about coming here. He had absolutely no idea of how far they had come and with his ankle as it was at the moment making a run for it was out of the question. He was scared, mostly for Amy, his options few. Girls are afraid of the dark, every boy knows this. It was his duty to protect Amy, not to act like a big baby. He heard the sound again. It was closer this time, in front of him, behind him, it was everywhere. Billy's heart was now beating like ten drums.

'No ghosts,' he reminded himself. 'They do not exist!'

But did he really believe that?

'Amy,' he suddenly muttered.

He hobbled back to the shelter.

Amy was gone. Her sleeping bag was open and all ruffled looking like she had got up in a hurry, or been taken in a hurry. He quickly checked (as fast as he could anyway) the other side of the shelter. Apart from the odd broken piece of glass and stone debris there was little of interest. It was dusty, Billy sneezed. He went back outside again with the torch.

He looked up at the moon. The night sky was beautiful, peaceful looking, like a magician had cast a spell in the sky. Billy called out for Amy, there was no answer. He walked forward to where the trees became thicker, endless like a tragic fairy-tale. He called for her again.

No answer.

He started to panic.

Maybe she had to go for a whiz? Billy thought returning to the shelter. *She wouldn't leave me and go off someplace unless she had to.*

'AMY…'

Billy's awkward steps echoed against the cold stone flooring of the shelter again. He found the torch and shone it around. He was hoping Amy might have left him a note. How long had she been missing now, was it ten, fifteen, twenty minutes maybe? Shit! He didn't know.

Wait, he suddenly thought.

Why would she have left the torch behind? He looked down at the torch in his right hand. The very idea chilled him. Why would Amy leave the shelter in the middle of the night and not take her torch with her? A warm feeling gripped the pit of his stomach. It was fear, pure fear.

'AMY!'

Oh my God, someone has taken her…
Kyle Jacob, Billy, he has her…

One of Billy's earliest childhood memories was one of the few happier ones he could remember. And the circumstances surrounding that memory coupled by the fact that it was one of the better ones saddened him now. He had been five at the time and had gone shopping with his mum. He had always held onto the trolley whilst his mum loaded it. That had been the one rule.

'Don't move, Billy. Mummy has to go over there for a minute.'

Those words were still as fresh as the night air.

Billy had normally obeyed his mum but the picture of a toy on his favourite breakfast cereal looked too inviting to be ignored. He'd eventually found his mum but in that moment when he realised he couldn't find her he had felt more lost than he'd ever remembered. That same feeling was back again now, almost like it had travelled through time to join him again in this very moment and crept over him slowly like a maddening itch. Billy was lost and feeling all alone. He was scared and all by himself.

But this time there were no supermarket aisles or grown up people to see how scared and distressed he looked. There was no light accompanied with soft background music that was annoying yet strangely comforting at the same time. There was nothing. Still holding the torch Billy once again went outside. He would find Amy; there was no way he was going to lose her.

'AMY!'

He went to find her, following the echo of his own voice.

3

Billy entered the forest, a collage of menacing shadows, a maze of trees and tall grass, so dense it was almost impossible to see within the darkness too.

Billy occasionally shone the torch straight ahead, but mostly aimed it at the uneven terrain. He didn't want to fall again. The light from the torch looked like a glowing shield against the ground.

Billy's ankle started throbbing again, and a cool sweat caressed his skin. He wasn't warm, he was just scared. He walked on, negotiating dwindling tree branches and bushes that seemed determined to get in his way. He called out for Amy many times but there was no answer, just the distant echoing of his own voice and a soft breeze blowing through the trees. He now felt like he was walking down a slope. The ground was slippery. He aimed the torch forward and the beam penetrated the darkness then stopped on thick bushes in front. They were wavering, not caused by the wind. Billy stopped, keeping the torch fixed. They were rustling, something was behind them. Billy's heart pounded, his palms were all of a sudden sweaty. He gripped the torch tightly in his right hand. The bushes moved again.

'Something is watching me,' he muttered to no-one.

There was a scurrying sound and the bushes moved with more purpose. Billy was breathing faster, every shadow now his enemy. He looked up. The forest was thick and only a few stars were visible in the night sky. Angels.

The scurrying sound turned into a rustling. Billy moved the torch along the bushes, following the sound that was terrifying him. He swallowed hard.

'Amy,' he spoke in a voice that sounded the way he felt, a lost child in the woods. 'Is that you, Amy?'

Of course he knew it wasn't. The sudden urge to run gripped him, every fibre inside his body wanted him to get the hell out of there, all except for his ankle.

Ghosts, Billy ... Now tell me you do not believe ... The Tunnel is not the only haunted place up this here track. They are coming, Billy.

'No!' Billy said.

The ghosts are coming, Billy, they are watching you, waiting to ...

'No!'

Billy suddenly started to run, hobbling. The rustling sound seemed to follow him. His ankle hurt with every painful stride he made. He wasn't even sure which direction he had entered. He just ran, puffing and panting with only the instinct of survival helping him cope with his nagging right ankle, that and to find Amy, who was now surely lost forever.

The light from the torch danced around the forest as he ran; his little arms and legs pumping like pistons. The cool air made his eyes water. He wiped them, almost running into a tree at the same time, a branch scraped across his face. The forest seemed to close in around him, a huge menacing abyss of bark and shadow. Billy didn't stop running until he made it out of the forest. Trees seemed to be thinning out, and bushes no longer jumped into his path. He reckoned that he was just about in the clearing when he tripped on a root coming out from the ground and went hurtling forwards landing on his front. The torch left his hand and went flying in the opposite direction. He slowly looked up and saw an outline, mostly hidden by the darkness, standing in front of him.

'Oh, God.'

Yes, Billy they are here...

'Billy.'

To Billy's relief it was only Amy. She reached down and picked up the torch which was currently providing light for nearby pond life.

'What are you doing out here?' Amy asked.

Fright suddenly turned to anger for Billy. 'I was looking for you.' Billy got back to his feet. 'I couldn't find you and thought something had happened.'

Amy smiled. 'I'm sorry. I didn't mean to make you worry. I needed to pee.'

Anger suddenly left his body like a weight. 'You needed to pee?' Billy asked now sounding out of breath. 'You needed to pee?'

'Sorry,' Amy said, looking awkward in the dim light. 'I

81

didn't mean to make you worry. I left the torch for you, just in case you got scared.'

Steady on gal, boys don't get scared, remember?

'SCARED ... I don't' get scared,' Billy said, trying to sound like the big man in charge, but noticing Amy smiling anyway. 'Just make sure you let me know next time. I thought something had happened to you. I ...'

'You what?'

'Nothing,' Billy said, looking away. 'But you shouldn't wander off alone, Amy, not in a place like this.'

Amy looked at him. 'You were really worried about me, weren't you, Billy Cooper?'

'Not really,' Billy said, trying to look in any direction except hers. He noticed her still grinning at him. 'I wasn't ...'

Amy smiled then leaned forward and kissed Billy on the lips. 'Thank you,' she said, pulling away.

Billy blushed, and looked so red that for a second or two they didn't need the torch. He liked the kiss Amy had given him and smiled at her.

'You're welcome,' Billy said, still blushing.

Then a crazy notion of a 'Pissing Pass' suddenly entered the back of his mind.

Sign your name and time on the provided sheet. Then you can piss all you want ...

Amy wanted to laugh; she really did, seeing how red Billy's face still was, and knowing that her kiss was the cause of it. But Billy suddenly remembered the screaming sound that had started all of this off in the first place and the rustling sound in the bushes.

'Come on,' Billy said, looking around pensively. 'Let's get back to the camp now.'

Amy led the way back, the torch being their only guide. Behind them, in the thickets, the bushes were disturbed once again. Billy and Amy were watched the entire time by a pair of menacing eyes deep within the forest.

4

Back in camp the torch remained on, and two sets of young eyes stayed wide open, alert.

Two things occurred to Billy whilst looking outside into the cool night air. Number one was that Amy had just given him his first proper kiss. Number two was that the batteries on the torch were probably not going to last much longer. Billy had already noticed his torch beam had lost some of its glow now.

'We need to save the batteries,' he said, turning the torch off.

Amy never said anything. It took them both a few minutes to adjust to the darkness.

'What do you think we will find, Amy?' Billy asked after a couple of minutes had elapsed. Of course he was referring to The Tunnel.

Amy shuffled inside her sleeping bag and turned to Billy. 'I'm not sure,' she replied after careful consideration. 'What do you think we will find?'

Foul stroke, no points, answering a question with a question.

Billy sighed. 'Well I'm not crazy. The dreams and visions must mean something ... Don't they?'

'Of course,' Amy said. Her voice was comforting, believing. 'There is definitely something there, Billy. And we will find it.'

Hearing Amy saying that made Billy go cold.

Something there, but what was it going to be?

Was it going to be a friend, a long lost uncle perhaps? The realisation of the danger they were walking into hit him like a warm fist in the gut. This was not going to turn out nice.

'But whatever happens, Billy,' Amy said, now sitting up. 'We are in it together, right?'

Billy nodded. 'Right, we are in it together.'

That was a comforting thought for both of them in the darkness.

'The Tunnel here we come,' they both said in unison and then, laughing, they punched the night air.

There was suddenly a rustling sound outside that broke the calm again, Billy suddenly grabbed the torch and switched it on. The beam pierced the darkness, highlighting nothing but trees and bushes wavering in the wind.

They are dancing for me, Billy thought. *Waiting in the shadows…*

'It was just the wind,' Amy said in a reassuringly tone of voice, leaning back against the cool stone.

Billy wasn't so sure. He maintained the torch beam, moving it around the blanket of darkness, sitting up in his sleeping bag like a trooper on sentry.

'Billy,' Amy said. She waited until he turned to her before continuing. 'What happened to your face?'

The torch went out.

'You can talk to me, Billy,' Amy said softly.

Billy moved his fingers over the bruise on his cheek. He saw his father's hand again, swinging down at him like a huge mallet. In a funny way that punch was what supplied him with the fuel to go, made him forget about his fear. Running away wasn't easy at Billy's age, but any doubts that he had been feeling back at the house were soon forgotten after his dad's vicious attack. But was that what he was doing here? Was he really running away? Was Billy Cooper running away from something or was he running to something? Perhaps he didn't know himself. His thoughts returned to Justin again. A flash of light and Justin's face was once again inside his head, brilliantly. Billy began to feel a swelling inside his throat like trapped food. He shook his head and wiped his teary eyes.

'Billy?' Amy moved in closer to him. 'What is it? Please tell me.'

Billy looked at her. Even in the dim light she could see his face was washed with hurt and sorrow. A lost and tortured soul he looked.

No, no, Billy. Boys don't cry remember, not in front of girls. Come on, pull yourself together will you.

'My dad,' Billy said, struggling to get the words out. 'My bastard dad hit me.'

'Oh, God,' Amy said, putting her hands up to her mouth. 'Billy...'

'It's not good enough that he tortures me mentally by not speaking to me ... Now the asshole has to go one step further and hit me.'

Amy shuffled over to Billy and now had a comforting arm around him, leaning into him with her head. He looked at her, his tears looking like pearl drops in the darkness.

'I hate him, Amy ... I really hate him.'

He shook his head, trying not to succumb to hidden emotions and hurt he had kept buried within for so long now. But emotions always win out in the end.

No, no, no ... BOYS DON'T CRY, REMEMBER, BILLY? STIFF UPPER LIP TIME, JUST LIKE YOU DO AT SCHOOL AND IN FRONT OF YOUR PARENTS.

Tears rolled down his cheeks. 'I want my brother back, Amy,' Billy said, choking up. 'I really want my brother back.'

Little boys are not supposed to cry, especially in front of girls that they have a crush on. Boys are strong, Billy knew this. He knew the rules well, hell he'd written half of them. Boys do not cry. But tonight those rules went up in smoke. A little boy who had been pretending to be a man for such a long time now, had been forced to be, was now reduced to the child he really was, by a little girl who loved him.

Amy placed both her arms around Billy and held him as he sobbed against her shoulder. He put his arms around her too and let her take away his pain, a gesture he wished had been offered to him by his parents.

Tomorrow was going to be a new day, and Billy, although

slightly embarrassed by crying in front of Amy, would soon get the chance to prove his valour and honour. Their journey had not yet even begun.

7

An Unexpected Encounter

1

The next day they set off early. Before leaving they had something to eat and Billy tended to his ankle. It was still painful but not as swollen as it had been last night. Both had little sleep, their minds and bodies buzzing too much with the thoughts of adventure for them to relax. After all, wasn't this just that, a kind of adventure?

The morning was warm. Both felt the sun beating down on the backs of their necks. Billy was already sweating and finding it a little tough going, especially with his ankle. Amy was still walking with the same effortless grace that she had been blessed with, and seemed to be enjoying herself. She was humming, had been for most of the morning now.

'What is that?' Billy asked, turning to her.

'Just made it up,' Amy said nonchalantly. 'Like it?'

'Uh, ha.'

She carried on humming.

The track went on for as far as the eye could see. There were little bends here and there, but not sharp enough to hide the path ahead. There were tall trees running alongside and an embankment which led into fields below, which were empty with only blades of grass moving with the wind.

When Billy and Amy spoke it was mostly about The

Tunnel. Every step brought them closer, and with it the reality of where they were going, and perhaps more importantly what they may find.

It is a quest, Billy thought, walking along, still feeling the sun beating down on the back of his exposed neck. He had put his cardigan inside his bag and was now only wearing T-shirt and jeans, jeans a little stained after his fall last night. The bag was beginning to feel a little heavy, his right arm was aching. Billy glanced over to Amy. She was still humming. Billy threw his bag over his shoulder and carried on.

Stick to the rules, he thought again. *OK, I cried last night, but still … I have to at least pretend I can take the strain. I broke one rule, I cannot break another.*

Amy had tied her black denim jacket around her waist and was carrying her rucksack over her shoulders, and marching along like a proper trooper. Neither of them had any idea of how far they had walked. One mile, two miles, three who knew? Granted, they were hindered slightly because of Billy's ankle, but had been walking for what seemed an eternity. Still the road went on and on, never cornering, or going up or down hill, the horizon forever looking back at them, bouncing, shimmering, and reflecting in the heat of the Saturday morning.

Their feet scuffled along the dirt track, sending up little puffs of dust. The day was now even hotter, with shimmers of heat bouncing up from the road looking like gas vapour. Billy noticed a tree on his right. It was standing all alone. It was all twisted and without any blossom or leaves, unlike the other trees he had seen all morning. Billy had heard stories about such trees, that they were the remnants of some tortured soul that once walked the earth.

He shuddered.

'What time is it?' Amy asked. She then started humming again.

Billy instinctively looked down at his left wrist. 'Shit!'

'What?'

'My watch is gone. It must have come off last night in the forest. Damn it! Shit!'

'It's OK, Billy,' Amy said. 'We can tell the time using the sun. I'll show you.'

Billy suddenly frowned. 'No!' Billy said, sounding frustrated. 'You don't understand. Justin gave me that watch.'

Amy stopped. Billy did the same. She placed her hand on Billy's arm. 'I'm sorry. I didn't know.'

'It's OK,' Billy said. 'How could you. Sorry for snapping at you, Amy.'

Amy smiled. 'We could always look for it on the way back.'

Needle in a haystack, Billy thought. He wiped his brow and then looked back at the long stretch of road.

'OK.'

They walked on.

2

The reason for Billy running out of the forest was still unsettling him. Something had been in there, watching him. He occasionally checked both left and right flanks as he walked along. Could the thing that had been disturbed inside the forest last night now be following them? Could it now be walking alongside them, hiding in the fields down below, waiting to pounce? Billy tried to remove that idea from his mind, and quickly.

They were now in the middle of nowhere. They hadn't heard a car or encountered another person for ages. It was like they were the only two people left on Earth, survivors after a great war. The sky was clear blue, like a still ocean in the heavens.

The track was not that unfamiliar to Billy. He had seen it many times before in his dreams. He had not been walking, more like floating, and it had been dark, but still it had looked the same. A strong sense of déjà vu suddenly gripped him.

'I have been here before,' Billy remarked casually.

Amy looked across at him. 'Been where?' Amy asked, just catching what he had said.

'This place,' Billy said. 'I have been here before.'

'In your dreams?'

Billy stopped and looked around. Dreams? Was that really it? Was this place really just part of a bad dream? What did that make The Tunnel then? Had he really seen what he had seen? So if this really was just a dream then he wasn't really here, was he? He wasn't real and neither was Amy. Eventually people wake from dreams, Billy was pretty sure he was awake right now though. He hoped it was a dream. Perhaps when he really did awake from it, he would find out that Justin was not really dead and forever sleeping in a wooden box in Silver Gates Cemetery. If Justin was still alive then this also meant that his family was still alive too. Billy liked that idea, wanted to grasp it between his hands and never let go of it.

'Yes – in my dreams. Everything I want is in my dreams.'

Perhaps Billy didn't even realise he had said that last bit out loud.

Amy didn't say anything for almost a minute. They just looked at one another. Eventually she spoke, once again saying the right thing, as she always did. 'Sometimes dreams come true, Billy.'

Billy smiled. They walked on, still dreaming their dreams.

The pangs of hunger were beginning their call when Billy noticed something up ahead. Amy noticed it soon after. In the fields towards the right was a house. It was a strange place for a house, miles away from any other and at the end of a field. The closer they got the more hungry they felt.

'I wonder if anyone lives there,' Amy remarked.

Billy didn't like to comment. He didn't like this one bit.

The little voice in the back of his head was telling him to stop and turn around, and that voice was mostly right. But there was definitely somebody home. Smoke was coming up from the chimney, making clouds of grey in the blue sky which they hadn't noticed at first.

'I guess that answers that then,' Amy said casually.

Billy didn't hear Amy, as he was too busy listening to the voice in his head still telling him to run like the wind.

A house in such a desolated place was a strange notion. Billy firstly wondered why somebody would choose to live in so secluded a spot. But he reminded himself that occasionally people are victims of circumstance. Not everyone wants what they have, and sometimes most just want more.

The house was now only fifty metres away. A path ran down the embankment leading to a dirt track which was presumably the driveway. There was no car nor were there any overhead electrical cables. Billy hadn't seen this in his dream. Had there been a reason for that?

The tiny house they had seen some five minutes ago was now right next to them. It looked old. Slates were missing from the roof and two windows on the side were boarded up. The wooden door at the side of the house was partially open, occasionally banging in the wind. Billy looked down the slope and memories of his previous slip came back. The grass verge was worn down to cracked earth, obviously used regularly then. To the rear of the house was a long cracked Tarmac road, eventually leading to a metal gate, probably leading onto a country road.

Smoke still rose from the bricked chimney and Billy's stomach churned and moaned.

'Are you hungry?' Billy asked, his back now facing the house.

'Amy?'

'Yes,' Amy said.

'We'll carry on for a bit more and then stop to eat.'

'What's wrong with here?'

Billy didn't know where to begin answering her question. He loved Amy, but Jesus Christ sometimes she was such a girl. Billy had consulted the files inside his head on such matters. Twelve year old boys just know about this type of shit. These files are created through years of studying the opposite sex.

'Amy,' Billy said, sounding quite stern. 'Don't you think this is a little weird? I mean who would live in such a place?'

'Perhaps he's a hermit?'

Billy frowned and found it quite interesting that Amy would assume it to be a man living there.

'I was thinking more on the lines of a psycho, Amy,' Billy said seriously.

He then suddenly remembered the forest again from last night and one of the stories he'd heard. Legend had it that a werewolf stalked the track during a full moon, seeking victims for its carnivorous lunar activities, and hadn't it been a full moon last night? And thinking about it, the house wasn't that far away from where they camped last night either, so someone could easily have walked to where they had been sleeping and then changed, watched them the entire time, and changed back in the morning, and then returned back home. Someone or something.

Jesus Christ...

'I never told you, but last night I heard something moving around in the–' Billy suddenly stopped talking.

Amy appeared frightened, her bright brown eyes widening, her mouth opening just a little, bottom lip quivering.

'Amy, wha–'

Billy didn't finish the question. He turned abruptly and saw an elderly looking gentleman standing there wearing dirty blue overalls, with white top on underneath, and old brown hat on his head, and pointing a shotgun at them.

3

'Were it ya all?' the old man asked in a husky tone of voice. He must have been at least seventy years old.

The barrel of the gun went up and down as he spoke. His face was wrinkled and aged, like old worn leather. He had very few teeth remaining in his mouth and spoke with a rough slang.

'Well,' the old man said. The gun moved up and down again. 'Did ya not hear me? Speak ya all.'

Billy could not speak for Amy but judging by the look on her face she was just as shit scared as he was. He had trouble understanding the old man. According to the files Billy kept in his head, this type of man was called a 'Cletus,' or a 'Slack-Jawed-Yokel.' Other files suggested that this was also where the boy would protect the girl and be the hero of the hour. Boys do not get scared in situations like these. Boys keep cool heads, and say the right things, just like the rugged, handsome looking hero in the action movies. It seemed Billy's body was not playing ball though. A feeling like warm water was gushing around inside his bowels, and his heart was beating for two.

'Speak up, now.'

Amy then did something that Billy did not see until it was too late. She stepped in front of him so the shotgun was now aiming at her. She was shielding Billy.

'NO!' Billy shouted, quickly pulling Amy back so he was now the one with the shotgun aimed at him. 'Don't you dare hurt her.'

'No!' the old man said. He laughed. 'Didn't me think so... kids?'

Billy and Amy shared a very nervous exchange. This guy looked and seemed crazy, loopy.

'Didn't me ta scare ya all,' he spoke with the same deliberate slang. 'Me eyes ain't no good these days.' He lowered the shotgun. Billy's bowels let up a little and his heart relaxed. Amy sighed; her face was once again her own.

Billy remembered that he was the boy here, he was in charge. He took a deep breath. 'So why did you point the gun at us?'

Yeah asshole, you're lucky I don't break you in two for scaring me shitless in front of my girl. Now who pissed in your coffee cup you mean old bastard?'

The hero Billy wanted to be, and the hero he was were worlds apart. Billy's voice had trembled and his hands had shaken when he spoke. There was no air of authority, he sounded like he looked, a scared little boy.

'Tis a lot of weird shit happening lately,' the old man said. 'Thought yous were trouble when I first cast ya.'

'Not trouble,' Billy said, 'just passing through.' His voice was stronger now. Amy was still silent, staring at the gun.

The old man frowned, his wrinkled brow creasing ever more. 'Where's ya going? Tis nothing round here, not this far out.'

Billy glanced at Amy, who simply shrugged back at him. He didn't want to tell the old man too much. There was little point, this was their adventure and this old guy had no part of it.

'Nowhere,' Billy eventually said, knowing he did not sound particularly convincing.

'Yous too far out to be going nowhere,' the old man remarked.

Billy watched the old man with untrusting eyes. He wanted to leave now, get Amy away from this crazy old coot.

'We have to go now,' Billy said.

He reached back and took a hold of Amy's right hand, something that he had never done in such a casual way before, his protective instinct over her kicking in again. Amy liked it, felt like he was protecting her. She took a firm grasp of his hand and began to follow him as he walked.

'Not going to The Tunnel are ya?' The old man smiled,

revealing a lonesome decayed yellow tooth at the top of his mouth.

Billy stopped, keeping a hold of Amy's hand. That was what boys did. They looked after the girl who had come along for the ride.

The old man was still grinning when Billy turned back to him. His feet scuffed on the road. Amy once again stayed behind him.

'What makes you think we are going there?' Billy asked, sounding a little defensive.

The old man tilted his head in an attempt to highlight his right ear which was buried beneath a bush of white dirty hair.

'Ya said tunnel, didn't cha boy?'

The old man suddenly looked very serious. 'If ya goes there then we needs to talk ... Dat place is full of badness. Tis soil is sour in dat place, boy.'

Billy didn't realise at the time but he'd tightened his grip around Amy's hand.

'Come on ya all,' the old man said, walking along the path down the embankment. 'Ya need to hear this before's yoos go.'

Billy stayed where he was, as if glued to the spot, watching the old man limping down the grass verge, and amazingly not falling arse over tit as he went. He didn't want to follow but there was a burning intrigue deep within his stomach that could not be ignored. The Tunnel had Billy now, dangling from a noose.

'Why should we trust you?' Billy shouted.

'Aye,' the old man's voice spoke. He was now out of sight. 'Goes if you wants to, make no diff'rence to ma. Only trying to help ya' all.'

Billy turned to Amy. 'Wait here.'

'No way, Billy Cooper,' Amy said sternly, and giving him the eye. 'He has a gun remember. Let's just carry on. I bet there's nothing he can tell you that we will not find out for ourselves anyway.'

'I have to hear what he has to say,' Billy said.

'He's crazy,' Amy said. 'I bet he knows nothing.'

Billy let go of Amy's hand and smiled at her. 'I won't be long.'

Before Amy could argue any more Billy was already walking down the embankment. The wooden door of the old house was still banging in the wind. Billy stood in front of it. The old man then came out smiling, and brandishing his shotgun.

4

The old man led Billy around to the rear of the house. There were two windows there, one of which was cracked. The house was small and judging by the exterior the interior wouldn't be up to much either.

Moss was growing up on the lower bricks and the smell of damp and sweat was undeniable. Billy thought the house was like the track, forgotten in time. But the old man, well, he had his own story to tell. He had lived as a hermit for almost all of his life. He did not like people and since his wife and son had died he had been living here alone.

The rear garden was a tip. An old rusty bike leaned up against an oak tree with old pieces of furniture, and what looked like clothes and a rotten wardrobe lying next to a small pond. Billy could see midget flies hovering above the water, looking like tiny helicopters in the sun. The grass was long, and Billy wondered what could be living in it. Snakes!

The old man sat down on a wooden bench that creaked. It looked rotten to Billy's eyes and was probably infested with woodworm too. He tapped the bench slowly with an old wrinkly hand, motioning for Billy to sit. Billy did so. He no longer felt afraid even though the old man's gun was not far from reach.

Billy looked at the old man. He wasn't aware that his right leg was moving up and down like it was being pulled by an invisible wire. The old man sat motionless taking in the warm air the day had to offer. It really was hot and Billy had developed a thirst. His throat felt as dry as the bottom of his shoe. He fanned his top back and forth, waiting for the old man to begin.

The old man leaned back against the bench and pulled out a thin silver square case. He opened it and pulled out a cigarette.

'Want one, boy?' the old man asked, offering Billy the open case.

'No!' Billy said. 'Not right now, thanks.' Billy didn't smoke and never would. He thought it strange that a man of this age would offer a twelve year old a cigarette.

'Suit ya self, boy,' the old man said, putting the cigarette between his cracked lips. He struck a match and lit the end of it. The cigarette came to life and as the old man puffed on it, orange flames reflected in his tired eyes. He took two long deep drags then blew the smoke out like he had turned it into some kind of an art form. He then turned and faced Billy.

'So why ya wanna go to The Tunnel for?'

'I have to,' Billy said, surprising himself about how open he suddenly became with the old man. 'I think there is something there for me.'

'Ha,' the old man said, laughing as a puff of smoke seeped through his chapped lips and nose. 'Ma boy thought tis same ting...'

Billy hadn't heard the old man's last sentence clear enough to react.

'I see it in my dreams,' Billy said. 'Every time I close my eyes it is there, calling out to me.' His voice was once again weaker, like he was hoping the old man could offer him some kind of an explanation. 'I have no other choice than to go.'

'Has ya heard the tales of dat place?'

'Who hasn't?' Billy remarked, looking around the tip of the back yard again that looked as old and dirty as the man he was sitting next to.

'Does ya believe them?'

It all depended on which ones the old man was referring to as to whether Billy believed or not. The story of the vampire that lived in The Tunnel that only came out at night time to feed on the living then take their bodies back inside to rot. Billy forgot who had told him that one. But apparently you couldn't see the ground for all the bones that had been decaying there over the years. Or what about the werewolf that roamed the disused line every full moon. Holy shit! That one was now becoming more plausible. Billy suddenly remembered the sounds from last night, the rustling inside the forest. Most stories are believable at Billy's age. The ghosts, Billy believed in those. The visions of the young man dressed in old clothes, the dreams of The Tunnel. As for the vampire and the wolfman, well he would have to think carefully about those two, especially after last night.

'Some of them,' Billy said. 'I believe in some of them.'

'And ya still wanna go?'

The old man then got a dirty blue rag out from his overall pocket and wiped his creased brow.

'Me boy died at dat place,' the old man added.

Billy swallowed hard. He felt a shudder coming on and tried to fight it but there was no use, like trying to ignore your bowels when they need emptying.

'Died?' Billy asked. His voice trembled again, a whisper in the wind. 'What happened to him?'

'Come here,' the old man said, getting up. He stretched his awkward back and then walked over to a tree.

Billy followed.

There was a red stained white cover.

Blood, Billy thought. *And shit loads of it too.*

The old man took a final puff of his cigarette, savouring every second, and then discarded it by the small pond. He bent down and pulled away the red stained cover, sending several flies on their way in the process.

'Tis why I pulled the gun on yas all,' the old man said. 'Thoughts ya did this to ma Royal.'

Billy wanted to puke, had to close his mouth and fight it back down his throat. Royal had been the old man's golden retriever. The animal was a bloody mess, head hanging on only by muscle fibres and the odd artery, and its insides all in the wrong places.

'What happened?' Billy asked, now having to put his hand up over his mouth and nose.

'Facked if I knows,' the old man said. 'I's found him like this in da morning … Heard ya's all humming or something, and tis thought yous killed him.'

'No!' Billy said. 'We didn't kill your dog, sir.'

The old man frowned again. Perhaps it was the first time he had ever been called sir or maybe he just didn't believe Billy.

'We's didn't, right?' the old man spoke, 'whose might we be?'

'Amy and me,' Billy said.

'Amy and me?' the old mad repeated.

'Well my name is Billy, and the girl back on the track is my friend, Amy.'

The old man frowned again. 'Whatever ya says boy.'

Billy then started wondering whether Royal had been killed by the creature that had been making those noises last night, the werewolf. He suddenly wished he could take the old man's gun with him, but don't you need a silver bullet? He wasn't sure, he would have to consult the files in his head on that one.

The old man took out another cigarette and lit it.

'I think Royal twas killed by Legend,' the old man said, blowing smoke up into the air again. 'The Legend of dat Track.'

'What's that?' Billy asked, trying not to breathe in the old man's smoke too much.

'Never yous mind, boy,' the old man said. 'Just hope yas don't meet him on yas travels … Just hope boy.'

'I will,' Billy said in passing, but not really taking the old man too seriously. 'But please tell me about what happened to your son?'

The old man turned and smiled once again revealing his only yellow tooth.

'Kyle?' the old man said.

Billy suddenly realised he had heard that name before. The old man took another drag on his cigarette then began.

5

'Kyle dreamt of The Tunnel too,' the old man explained. 'Tes dream plagued him like d'sease.'

It had called out to him, enticing him to go. He had gone to The Tunnel one night after awaking from a dream. It had called out to him over and over again. The old man had gone into his room and had been greeted by someone he no longer recognised.

'Eyes all glazy, they was,' the old man added. 'Likes he was on drugs or some shite. Says he had to go.'

The dream had always been the same for Kyle. He would get to The Tunnel but always call out, then wake up prior to entering the darkness. But one night he did indeed go. The old man moved a calloused hand over his jaw-line, making a scraping noise. Whatever he found inside caused him to kill himself, the old man explained to Billy. Billy sat mesmerised, and hanging onto the old man's every word.

'Never saw me boy alive again,' the old man said.

'What did he find?' Billy asked tentatively.

The old man did not answer straight away; he deliberated

for quite some time. His old face then creased up even more.

'He finds his ghosts,' the old man finally said. 'Then hung himself from a tree. Tunnel is seven miles from ere, he walked all the way dat night.'

Seven miles, Billy thought. *Not far now then.*

The old man then started walking away from Billy, leaving him standing next to Royal.

'Mr Jacob,' Billy said. 'Why did he go in the first place? The Tunnel, I mean.'

The old man stopped then turned around very slowly; his old body looked stiff and painful.

''Tis same reason you are,' the old man said. 'To lay his ghosts to rest.'

'How do you know that is why I am going?' Billy asked.

'Eyes,' the old man said. 'Yous have da same look in ya eyes as ma boy did.' He then smiled again, Billy didn't like the grin he produced. 'Just remember,' the old man continued. 'Whatever yous take in there tis what ya will find ...'

Billy didn't know what the old man had meant by that, wasn't even sure whether he believed his story either. But something had killed his dog, and something was pulling him towards The Tunnel, that much was apparent. And the part about the dreams, Billy was all too familiar with, that part of the story had scared him the most.

'Watch out for tis Legend,' the old man warned. 'Dat will facking kill yous before ya all even get there ... The guardian of dis track, it is.'

Billy shuddered, thinking about Royal again.

The old man then went back inside his house and closed the wooden door. Billy never saw him again.

When Billy arrived back on the track Amy was waiting next to a tree. She had heard most of what had been discussed between Billy and the old man. But listening to Billy and the old man talking, she now reckoned she knew something that Billy didn't, but couldn't say so at that time. There was going

101

to be plenty of time, after all they were still seven miles away from The Tunnel. And once there, Billy would soon know what the dreams had meant and why he had to come.

'Ready, then?' Amy asked, walking towards Billy.

Billy nodded. 'Yeah, let's go.'

They walked on, the sun still bearing down on them, with Billy still thinking about The Legend.

The Guardian of this place...

8

The Other Side of the Track

1

Kate Cooper could hear the engine running but didn't pay particular attention to it.

It was Saturday morning and the house felt even emptier than usual. She was hot and bothered and trying to find any mundane job that would make the time pass by more quickly. It wasn't working. And Billy, where was Billy?

It was almost a year to the day since Justin had been killed, and Kate was still only just managing to keep her head above water. She was now seriously worried about her family and wanted to put it right again. But sometimes things are easier said than done. Kate loved Billy but since losing her first born she had become emotionally withdrawn from him. She was too afraid of loving and losing again. Kate found it easier to bottle her feelings up and let them stew in their own juices. It was just her way of coping, she guessed.

Justin's death had left a gulf between her and Billy, and a universe between her and Alex. It wasn't anybody's fault really it was just circumstance that had caused the rift. Some families pull together during crisis and some fall apart. This is just the way it is.

The problem was nobody knew how to fix the mess any more. Perhaps nobody was willing to make that initial first step. Maybe Alex and Kate thought that if they started enjoying and living life again then that would mean they no longer missed and loved Justin. And maybe it wasn't Billy they were really angry with. They both blamed themselves for that day and that was something that would never change. Billy was just a painful reminder of what they allowed to happen, and that was why they pushed him away. Not out of hate, but out of their feelings of failure towards Justin. And every time they looked at Billy they were reminded of that failure.

The silence had crept up on them all. Kate wanted to fix it, make it all right. But she needed help, she needed her husband. He was gone though.

The anniversary of Justin's death seemed a good place to lay all their ghosts to rest. There was no way of apologising or coming up with half-baked excuses. No! All they had was the future and Kate now wanted to mend her family. She was tired of the silence, she was tired of hating her husband and her herself, she was tired of upsetting Billy, seeing the hurt in his eyes when she withdrew from him, when all he was seeking was her love and affection. She was so tired her body ached.

Kate hadn't seen Billy all morning, which was strange. Even though she never made it known to Billy, she was always aware of him. He was always around at weekends unless he was visiting his friend. What was her name again? Kate couldn't remember. She had an idea it began with an A. Her mind was all over the place this morning. Alex was keeping out of the way more than usual too. It wasn't going to be easy (in fact Kate thought it was going to be one of the most painful experiences of her life) to make that first important step, but she would try.

Kate stopped day-dreaming, looking out of the kitchen window and then put her coffee cup down. It was cold now anyway. She looked at the clock on the wall. It was just after midday. And whilst Amy and Billy were carrying on up the track towards The Tunnel, Kate Cooper went outside to find her husband. Yes, it was now time to fix this mess. It had all gone on for long enough now. It was time to right all of the wrongs, put things right before the anniversary, and do it for Billy's sake, not their own. It's amazing how a night spent looking up at the ceiling can make you have that moment of decision.

2

Kate needed Alex for this; she needed him to help her mend their broken home. She couldn't do it alone. It was time to talk and make things right again. They barely even looked at one another these days, let alone spoke. Kate couldn't remember the last time Alex had even held her at night time, let alone made love to her. The man used to screw her brains out. That seemed a lifetime ago now though, almost like it hadn't been her. She missed the intimacy, the physical contact, she missed the shagging, she missed it all, and most importantly she missed her family.

Kate went outside into the warm sunshine thinking about what she was going to say. She knew that it was going to have to be good.

The sound of the engine was louder now that she was outside.

At first she thought it was coming from her next door neighbour, George Capall. That inconsiderate ass was always revving his car, tinkering with the engine until the early hours of the morning. When Justin and Billy had been babies they were woken many times by that man's heavy foot. K&N filter, boy racer exhaust, job done, baby! Kate Cooper had wanted to ram it up the man's ass on more than one occasion.

However, George 'Petrol Head' Capall was not responsible for the noise pollution bellowing out on this glorious Saturday afternoon. The sound was coming from the garage. Kate was pretty certain their silver estate was parked on the driveway, the keys safely hanging on the hook on the kitchen wall. The only other car they owned was Justin's old Peugeot 205 that Alex had fixed up after the crash. It was parked inside the garage, where it had been for the best part of a year now.

Kate wasn't in any way worried by the rough uneven idling sound of an engine that obviously needed a good tuning. That was until she opened the garage door.

3

When Kate opened the garage door she immediately found herself back at one of her high school discos, with the smoke machine obviously working on overdrive. Except this was not harmless smoke.

Kate coughed and immediately shielded her mouth from the poisonous fumes. Instinctively she pulled up her top over her mouth. The fumes saturated her, sticking to every fibre of her clothing and drying out her throat. It was like looking through a thick mist that had suddenly appeared out of nowhere. She coughed.

She smelt the fumes, tasted them also. It was horrible, disorientating, and to make matters worse somewhere inside here was her husband, most probably dead.

'Alex!' Kate called out in between coughing fits. 'Where are you, Alex?'

But Alex did not want to be found today. He had decided this morning, shortly after eating breakfast that this was going to be his last day on Earth.

She never comes inside the garage. It will be easy...

It had been a selfish thought by a desperate man standing on the edge, only being held there by the finest of wires. To end his own life inside his dead son's car with a tube running from the exhaust pipe through a gap in the window seemed the only option to Alex Cooper that morning. And it hadn't taken that long really, and had been rather painless. Light-headedness followed by the faint feeling of nausea, the nerve endings inside his body firing all over the shop, and lungs fighting a losing battle. It had all been quite easy to do really. Sleepiness had eventually crept over him and then he allowed it to take him away. A nice long deep sleep, just what the doctor ordered. The darkness had been quick in consuming him.

Suddenly Kate forgot about what their family had been through. She forgot that her husband had barely spoken to her in the last six months and how they had both pushed their only remaining son away like a child would an old toy. She had forgotten about how he had hit her the other day. In that terrible moment all she could think about doing was getting to Alex and saving his life. That deep buried love she had once felt for this man suddenly came scurrying back to the surface again, and gave her the kick start she needed.

She took three deep breaths and pressed her top (which already reeked of exhaust fumes) firmly up against her mouth again. She went inside the garage, determined to still mend her broken family, hoping beyond hope that this would be enough to save her and Alex too.

'Alex!' Kate called out again.

9

Justin Part II

1

Billy could hear Amy talking but he wasn't really listening. His mind was elsewhere, transported off to some other place in time that only existed for him. He went back again.

He was no longer walking on the dirt track that used to be a railway line. The sky was still crystal clear and the day humid, but Billy was back inside the car with Justin, speeding along. His breathing was shallow and a fine layer of sweat had now appeared on his brow. Billy looked distraught, was fighting to suck air into his lungs. The clamp had tightened even more, and he now thought that he really was going to die. He'd had asthma attacks before, but this was far worse than anything he'd ever experienced.

'Hang on in there, Billy,' Justin said, giving him an alarming look.

The car raced around another bend in the road, the tyres screeching as the car came out of it. Justin looked down at Billy again, his strong features now looking terrified as his little brother fought to do something that usually didn't even take any thought at all. Jesus Christ his little brother looked poorly, his little frame jolting awkwardly, trying desperately to stay alive.

The road ... Watch the road ...

Justin looked up again.

The film temporarily stopped inside his head. Billy suddenly stopped walking. Amy stopped also and turned back to him, he had started to dawdle behind a little. Billy looked like he was in some kind of trance, his body rocking slightly from side to side. His eyes were all glazed over.

'Justin,' Billy suddenly cried out. 'I can't breathe. Please help me.'

Billy suddenly clutched his chest like a man would if he were suffering cardiac arrest. He dropped to his knees. The lights went out.

'BILLY!' Amy screamed, running over to where he was crumpled over on the dusty track. 'What's happening to you, Billy?'

Amy watched helplessly as Billy fought to breathe. He made a horrible gasping sound like someone was strangling him.

'Billy! What's wrong?'

Amy turned Billy over, trying to determine what was wrong with him.

'BILLY!' Amy said, trying to get him to respond, by lightly tapping the sides of his sun-baked face. 'Please don't die, Billy.'

Billy opened his eyes and glared up at the sun. He could hear Amy, even feel her lightly tapping his face, but the hazy memory was what he remembered the most, it was just too beautiful to be denied, watching the sun moving through the window of Justin's speeding Peugeot, burning down onto his young face like a huge oven. His chest tightened, breathing became shallower. Billy Cooper then went back to the day that changed him and his family forever.

2

The tyres screeched again. Billy moved around in his seat. Every movement felt sluggish and lazy, like he had suddenly aged sixty years. He gasped again. Panic was now setting in.

Always stay calm during an attack. Panicking will only make it worse!

Nurse Taylor's advice might as well have been delivered in a foreign language for all the good it offered Billy in that moment. All he could think about was dying. All he could think about was how painful it was going to be. To hell with the not panicking advice given by a lady that obviously enjoyed her junk food a little too much.

Even if Billy got home and took his medication there was still no guarantee that it would be effective at this late stage of the attack. It was all in the hands of the gods now, and his brother Justin, who was speeding like his life depended on it. And Billy's did.

Billy tilted his head and looked over at Justin. His face was full of concentration, determination. Billy could see that he was not going to let him die, how hard he was trying to keep his little brother alive. Billy's head went all limp, like a drooping flower, and rested against the car seat. The horrible wheezing sound had become worse and every so often, with now slightly blurred vision, he saw Justin looking down at him.

'Hang in there, Billy Boy.'

The words lifted Billy, made him want to hang on tighter to his life. He couldn't die now; he still had so much to do and to see. Life had only just begun for him.

Justin wiped his brow then slowed down to negotiate an approaching chevron. Once safely around he floored the car accelerator again, the engine roared to life. Justin's fair hair was all sweaty looking now, and damp patches had appeared through his blue shirt. Not long now though. They were almost there … God they had to be.

Justin looked down at Billy again. His little chest moved up and down so quickly each time, making a wheezing noise that Justin had never heard before, didn't want to ever hear again. Was it even possible for the human body to make such a terrifying noise?

Billy maintained his stare on Justin, almost like that was the only thing that was keeping him in this world now, and every so often their eyes met and Justin smiled reassuringly. But underneath Billy knew Justin was shitting himself. He was still his hero though. Billy closed his eyes. He wanted to sleep now.

The car came to a sudden stop which knocked the life back into Billy. He opened his eyes and looked up through the window. The sun beat down on him, making him squint. He heard the opening of a car door, followed quickly by a thudding sound. He saw Justin running down the driveway, his trainers making a scuffing sound as he went. Billy watched until he disappeared inside the house. He closed his eyes again.

Justin ran straight to Billy's bedroom and grabbed Billy's Ventolin inhaler. The whole family knew which drawer Billy kept his medication in, just in case of emergencies like this one. Billy used the Ventolin as a relief when an attack came on. It worked by relaxing and opening the bronchial cavities of the lungs, which constrict during an attack. Billy also had another inhaler called a Becotide, which he used to prevent an attack from coming on. Later that night he threw that one away.

The passenger side door suddenly opened and Billy felt Justin lightly tapping his flushed sweaty face. His face felt warm, too warm even for a day like this one. Billy opened his sleepy eyes.

'Open your mouth, Billy,' Justin ordered.

His voice was firm, no messing around there.

Billy managed to part his dry lips which were starting to go blue in colour. It took a ridiculous amount of effort for him to do such a mundane task.

Justin pulled the cap off the inhaler, which was an 'L'

shape, and then placed the mouthpiece where the medicine was administered in between Billy's lips. Justin's heart skipped a beat. In that moment he really did think he was going to lose his baby brother. He started thinking that he should perhaps have taken him straight to the hospital. Doubt crept into his mind, seeping around like an ill mist, making him question his judgement of the situation.

'Now listen carefully to me, Billy,' Justin commanded. 'When I count to three I want you to breathe in as quickly and as hard as you can. Do you understand me, Billy?'

Billy, very slowly moved his head up and down.

'One ... Two ... Three ...'

Justin pressed the silver canister firmly down that sat inside the casing of the blue inhaler, and then Billy simultaneously breathed in as the spray of medicine entered his dry mouth.

They repeated this process twice.

The inhaler felt to Billy's lungs like water would to the back of a desert-stricken man's throat. And amazingly after the second puff of the inhaler, Billy's breathing became regular again. His colour was starting to return to normal, and that horrible wheezing sound had quietly subsided. When Billy came around properly he found himself sitting in the front room of the house. Justin was by his side. He smiled when Billy opened his blue wondering eyes.

'Welcome back, little brother,' Justin said, rubbing the top of Billy's head, messing his hair up.

Billy smiled then put his arms around Justin. He always felt safe with Justin. Nothing could ever hurt him when he was with Justin.

They held each other for almost a minute.

'You had me worried there for a little while, buddy,' Justin said, patting Billy's back, feeling relieved. 'I'm going to run you over to the hospital now, just to make sure you're OK,' he added.

Billy suddenly let go of Justin, his blue eyes burning with the urgency of a lost child.

'No!'

'It's OK, Billy,' Justin said smiling. 'I'll stay with you. I just want you to get checked out by Doctor Wilson. I'll call dad's mobile so he knows what's happening.'

Justin got up from the couch but Billy quickly reached out and grabbed his wrist. 'Wait.'

'What is it?' Justin asked, turning around.

'I needed to talk to you earlier on at Aunt Mary's. I still do, Justin.'

Justin was alarmed by Billy's tone and expression. It was obviously important to Billy, so that also made it important to him too.

'Well what is it?'

Billy took a few deep breaths. God that felt good to be able to inhale a full dosage of air again.

'I had a dream the other night,' Billy began.

Justin sat back down on the couch and listened, hanging on to his little brother's every word.

2

The present-day Billy had somehow been affected by the Billy from the past. That wasn't to say that some kind of time warp had miraculously intertwined them. Billy had been thinking about Justin all morning. He hadn't mentioned anything to Amy. Ever since the day Justin had been killed, Billy's asthma had been cured. He couldn't begin to explain why that was. The last time he had used his inhaler was when it had been administered by Justin. And considering Billy used to use it four times a day that was a pretty incredible recovery. The memories he had of Justin and of that painful day had spurred on the attack. Amy had been quick in reacting. She had rested his head down against his bag and kept his airway clear. But the part of the memory where Justin had administered Billy's medication to him was when the present-day Billy had recovered. It was strange. It never occurred to Billy that the memory of an asthma attack could actually trigger one off in the present, and almost kill him. But the circumstances were far from normal for Billy Cooper at the moment.

'Are you all right, Billy?' Amy asked, kneeling alongside Billy and holding his hand.

For a second Billy thought that Amy was Justin and they were back inside his front room again. After realising where he was, he sat up, looking a little disorientated.

'Slowly,' Amy ordered, standing as quickly as a soldier would on morning inspection. She brushed her jeans off, and did the same with her black trainers.

Billy consulted the files inside his head again.

File 2.1: Boys must not let girls fuss around them too much, especially when it is they that the fussing is aimed at.

P.S. Boys are strong, remember?

P.P.S. Boys don't cry.

'I'm all right,' Billy said.

But he was not as strong as he thought. Billy Cooper was learning a lot about that so-called rule book he had written in his head. He had learned that most of it was bullshit. But perhaps most importantly he was beginning to learn something about himself.

'You scared me, Billy,' Amy said. Her voice was weak, soft, her brown dazzling eyes all watery. 'I thought you were going to heaven.'

Heaven?

Billy just looked at Amy for a few seconds, his reddish, slightly dirty face holding hers. He didn't know what to say to her. He was too touched to speak, more so than ever, because he knew that Amy cared for him, but perhaps in that moment he actually realised just how much so. That the thought of him dying was enough to bring her to tears. Sometimes it was easy to forget that they were both only twelve years old.

'Heaven can wait,' Billy said.

Perfect! What a macho response.

Amy smiled then wiped her watery eyes. 'So where did you go, Billy?'

'I went back to Justin,' Billy explained, not quite understanding, but hey, he didn't understand lots of things these days. 'Back to the day he died, I mean.'

Amy looked curiously at Billy. She then said, 'Then you must go back and finish what you started.'

Billy nodded, immediately understanding what Amy had meant. If he was ever going to lay his ghost to rest then he first had to confront it. He had to go back and finish off that painful memory. It was the only way he could go forward and reach The Tunnel.

'Come here.'

Amy walked over to a tall tree and sat down in the shade it offered. Billy did the same. It was nice to be out of the direct sun. He looked over at Amy and smiled, he then closed his eyes, once again going back a year in time.

3

Justin kept a journal which he normally had with him at all times, and what Billy had just told him would have made a fantastic entry. He had put everything inside that journal, and wanted to give it to Billy before he went away. He had put all of his dreams, all of his fears, things that Billy would read and understand about and relate to in his own life, not just now, but also in the years to come. Justin was wise far beyond his years and the journal was a little piece of him, a

115

written reflection that he wanted to leave back just for Billy. Most of the entries had been Justin's inner-most personal feelings, things that he wouldn't have even shared with his girlfriend. But Billy was different. He was Justin's little brother and Justin knew he would always shine in his eyes no matter what.

'Here,' Justin said. 'Take this. I wanted to give you something else but this will have to do for the time being.'

He removed the watch from his right wrist, and gave it to Billy, then ruffled up his hair again. Billy's face suddenly lit up as if all his Christmases had come at once.

Every little boy needs a hero, someone to look up to and to admire when times get tough. Some little boys choose a footballer, a film star and sometimes their parents. As far as Billy was concerned he was looking at his hero. And the best part about it was he could actually talk to his.

'Your watch,' Billy said, feeling the cool metal against his skin. 'I can have it?'

'Yeah,' Justin said. 'It's yours, Billy. It might not fit you at the moment but you can grow into it I guess.'

The watch was gold, with a brown leather strap. Billy looked at it over and over, turning it this way and that. He thought that it was the most beautiful gift he had ever received.

'Billy,' Justin said, leaning into him. 'I know you are not too happy about me going away to college. And I'll miss you too, even though you are a pain in the ass.'

Billy smiled then looked at the watch again, it shone like a jewel.

'When you're missing me,' Justin continued, 'just look at this watch and know that I am not really that far away, OK?' Billy smiled again. 'OK … but what about the dream?'

'Dreams are just dreams, Billy,' Justin said. 'Nothing more and nothing less.'

Billy was starting to feel better. If Justin believed that then it was also good enough for him.

116

'Now will you let me take you to the hospital little brother?'

Billy nodded.

'OK, let's go champ.'

Billy jumped up on Justin's back and he gave him a piggy-back ride all the way to the car.

As the car pulled away the phone rang. It had only been just over forty minutes since Billy and Justin had left Aunt Mary's. It was Alex Cooper on the other end. It was the strangest thing really. In all honesty he hadn't even noticed that Billy and Justin were missing. He was staying over at his sister's tonight so was pleasantly merry. He was sitting down in his sister's large front room, next to Kate and taking long gulps out of a can of lager when out of the blue he'd had the sudden urge to phone home. It was like an unseen force deliberately took control of his body, guided him over to where the telephone was and made him dial it. With a finger that he was not controlling any more he dialled the phone, not really knowing why. But surely there was nobody at home. They were all at Aunt Mary's, right?

The phone rang and rang.

Billy and Justin were long gone.

4

The sun reflected down onto the watch making it gleam. Billy looked at it with fascination. He then looked out of the window. Trees and fields he had seen a thousand times passed by in time, looking even more beautiful for some reason today. Billy looked over at Justin who was looking much calmer now and driving at a safer speed.

Billy leaned back in his seat and pressed his right hand against his jacket pocket. Good! His inhaler was safely secured. Billy now felt content again. The world was right again and he was riding shotgun with the person that he loved the most. The day was still, and humid, so Billy wound down his window. He welcomed the cool breeze against his young face.

Everything seemed to happen in slow motion. They were both aware of what was happening but powerless to do anything about it. They were coming up to the great lake, which was about two miles around and on the outskirts of town. Justin had taken the back roads deliberately to avoid all of the traffic. It was nearing rush hour and he was afraid that the combination of humidity and engine fumes would cause Billy to relapse, not if, but when they got sandwiched between every car in town. All Billy remembered before they crashed was hearing what sounded like a small explosion. It was after this when he saw Justin frantically wrestling with the steering wheel of the car. Justin's face looked panic-stricken again, like it had earlier on. Billy could hear the screeching sound of tyres and an irregular thudding noise.

'Shit ... Hold on, Billy. I've lost it ...'

I've lost it?

Justin had the sound of desperation in his voice that meant he was no longer in control of the situation, that he could no longer stop what was about to happen to them both. That terrified Billy, and chilled him to his core.

'Christ!'

Billy could see the fence they were approaching. Even though the car had lost the front nearside tyre it wasn't slowing down. Billy called out, as did Justin when their car smashed through the fence, leaving behind splinters, then over the drop that would send them straight down towards the glistening water below. Billy closed his eyes and felt Justin's arms wrap tightly around him. It was a selfless act that cost Justin his life.

The car crashed into the lake, sending up an explosion of water, crashing over the entire car and the bridge above. Billy lunged forward from the impact and opened his eyes. Justin was gone.

Water was filling the car fast, pouring in through Billy's window and the huge hole in the windscreen which Justin had left behind. He had removed his seatbelt before the impact to shield Billy and the impact of hitting the water had sent him straight through the glass and to his untimely death.

Billy spat out some water then saw Justin's lifeless body floating.

'Justin!' he shouted out.

He sucked in some water and started coughing. He retched, managing to spit it back out. Billy shivered, looking around – he didn't know what to do. The car began tilting forward under the weight of the water and engine housing. Billy could feel it sinking. He panicked. But all he could do now was watch Justin, who was still floating in front of him face down, with blood pouring out from his head, turning the water red around him.

The car was sinking fast. The water levels had now almost reached Billy's chin. Survival instinct began taking over, but fear was what he felt the most. And that fear was not for himself any more, but for his brother.

He could still see Justin through a haze of water. Maybe, just maybe if he could get out of the car, get to Justin then swim them both to shore.

Yeah sure, Billy, you weigh what, seven stones, and that is after a big meal and with your heavy shoes on. You are not even on your way to being five feet yet. Justin has at least four stones on you and totally towers over you and you are still weak after your asthma attack. You might as well try to swim with a slab of concrete attached to you.

'I have to try,' Billy muttered, almost gargling, spitting out some more water. It was now almost over his lower lip.

My turn. My turn to save Justin. I will not leave him to drown. I cannot do that.

Billy still had the wits about him to undo his seatbelt. He

reached down and pressed the red release button. The belt suddenly felt loose and retracted back a little. Billy closed his mouth – he could now only breathe through his nose. His eyes flickered from side to side as he felt the water moving higher up over his terrified face, the car was now being taken under. He didn't have long.

OK, Billy OK. You need to open the door now and swim out of the car. Can you do that, Billy?

He could have sworn the voice telling him what to do was Justin's.

'Yes.'

Billy found the door handle and pulled it. The door opened but there was a surprising amount of force pushing back on the other side. The fact the Billy's window had been open probably saved his life because it evened out the pressure. He quickly took in one last breath of air.

The water was underneath his eyes. He closed them and pushed on the door with every ounce of strength he had left. All he could think about was getting to Justin.

Billy escaped through the door just as the water was about to swallow him completely. He surfaced and began breathing rapidly. The thought of another asthma attack suddenly made him panic again. Did he even have his inhaler any more?

I have to be quick now, go under and bring up Justin. No time for an attack, must save my brother.

Billy looked to his right and caught the roof of the car sparkling underneath the sun before it went under. It was now gone. Only the broken fencing and scattered pieces of wood floating on the water offered any reminder of what had happened. He took three long deep breaths and then went under.

Underneath the water Billy could see Justin and the car both dropping like stones. Swimming in his clothes reminded him of the time he had gone swimming with the school and had to pick up the brick whilst wearing his pyjamas. But this was harder, there was nobody around to jump in and rescue him should he find himself in any sort of difficulty. Billy was all alone.

Focus, Billy…

Billy felt like he was trying to swim through thick cream, not water. He had almost reached Justin when the need for another breath of air imposed itself upon him. But he could not resurface now, just for his body's own selfish needs. Could he? And Justin was only in touching distance now, and if he did go back up for air, there was no guarantee he would ever find Justin again. The water was not as clear underneath as it had looked on the surface. No! He could do this, he had to do this. It was going to have to be a case of mind over matter. He was not going to leave Justin. Breathing would have to wait.

Billy reached through the murky water and grabbed Justin around the wrist. The water had turned to blood around him. Justin's eyes were open and his head tilted to the side.

Billy gasped, blowing up bubbles through the water, using up precious oxygen. The look of death on his brother's face horrified him.

Now with all your strength, Billy Boy, you have to swim and get to the surface. It must only be a couple of metres after all.

Billy had to stay on point here, get Justin out of the water and then see what needed to be done for him. He kicked out with both legs and pulled through the water with his one free hand. He didn't go anywhere. He felt like he was trying to swim with an anvil attached to his ankle. The need for air had become greater and his lungs couldn't last much longer, his strength was all but sapped.

Billy opened his mouth, sending out a jet stream of air which blasted bubbles through the water again making a gargling sound. He desperately kicked with his legs, and was almost grabbing at the water with his free hand. But Billy could not do this, as much as he tried, as much as he wanted

121

to, he just couldn't, and he began sinking to the bottom of the lake with his dead brother.

His chest hurt, felt tight, blocked. He took in another mouth full of water and danced around frantically. He released Justin but it was too late. His frantic dance ended quickly. Billy was now lying at the bottom of the lake with his brother.

5

There was silence all around him. Billy couldn't see or hear anything any more. He could still feel though. There! Something touched his wrist, he didn't know what. He was lost some place in the darkness where no light could ever reach. But the feeling, he was aware of, the same way that a person in a deep sleep might be aware of someone talking to them or touching them.

Touch, someone is touching me ... Am I dead?

Billy thought he had died, Justin most certainly had. He had died almost immediately after fracturing his skull against the windshield of the car. But Billy, how could he still be alive? The dream continued, because this was what this had to be. Justin wasn't dead. Their car hadn't plummeted off over a bridge then crashed into the water below. No! The tug Billy felt on his right wrist was his mother obviously trying to wake him up or Justin messing around as he often did.

I am being pulled now ...

Billy began floating off the lake's bottom, and being moved upwards through the water, leaving stream-like trails behind. This dream, like a trance, still held him as he moved upwards through the water held by an invisible hand.

Light, I see light now. The sun, I can feel the sun on my wet face ...

Light, there was so much light, an orchestra of angels played. Billy, still sleeping, was laid on the rocky shore of the lake. The light was bright then gradually disappeared. Daylight had returned to normal, the music and dream ended. Billy rolled over onto his side then emptied his body of water. He hated vomiting, it hurt like hell. A little puddle of water lay next to his mouth. Billy opened his eyes. Someone placed a blanket over him and then there were singing sirens and dancing lights all around him.

'Steady lad,' the black paramedic said with a hand on Billy's chest. 'Stay calm, help is here.'

He pulled me out, Billy thought. *This man saved me. But what about Justin?*

'Is he all right?' a female paramedic asked, running over with an orange bag.

'I think so,' paramedic number one said shining a torch into Billy's wet face. 'I don't know how long he has been lying here.'

Lying here? Then it wasn't you that pulled me out of the water.

It was then that Billy closed his eyes again and went back to sleep. And it was then that he realised Justin was really dead.

The paramedics placed Billy onto a stretcher then carried him off to a waiting ambulance. Inside Billy had dreamed again, he had saved Justin, and that they were both now sitting in the back of the ambulance with the red blankets around them, together, like they always were.

6

Billy saw Justin when he came back to the present. Every memory, every moment they had ever shared together.

'It's OK, Billy,' Amy said. 'It's over now.'

Billy had told his story and re-lived his agony again. The first time he had told it was for Amy. That time had been for him.

123

'How long was I asleep?' Billy asked, rubbing his tired eyes.

'Quite a long time,' Amy said. 'But you are back now, Billy.'

And it had felt long to Billy. He remembered the day looking really bright before he slept; it had now faded a little and was not as warm either.

'Here,' Amy said passing Billy a sandwich. 'Eat this.'

'Thanks.'

As the sunlight faded around them they remained underneath the tree and ate, not talking much. It was only the first day of their journey and already it had brought with it so much uncertainty and danger. After they had finished eating Billy and Amy just leaned in against one another and watched the sun going down. It was the first time they had ever seen a sunset together. It would be their last one.

10

Legend of the Track

1

Remembering that day again made Billy recall the strange circumstances surrounding his own rescue. Who pulled him out of the lake? And why wasn't Justin saved as well? That night those burning questions were not as easily put to the back of his mind as they had been before. Billy could not sleep and was simply looking up at the night sky, staring at the milky coloured moon. Amy was fast asleep next to him. It was a warm night that made sleeping outside pleasant. Billy hated the hot summer nights back home in bed. He was always too hot. It didn't matter how wide his window was or how many times he pushed his bed covers down.

Billy didn't know what time it was, didn't particularly care either. It was a peaceful night and all he wanted to do was watch the moon, hoping to get inspiration from it. He needed answers, not sleep. So he watched the moon with an almost fascinated look running across his young face. So far away yet so near too, almost in reaching distance. He thought about The Tunnel. How far away were they now anyway? He didn't know. All he knew for sure was that if they followed the track they would eventually come to it, and then he would find the answers he had been seeking.

Amy stirred. Billy looked down at her. He had laid his red cardigan over her as she slept. Not that it was cold, rather because he thought it was the right thing to do.

File 2.2: Always act like the perfect gentleman.

Billy watched Amy for a few seconds more. *My best friend,* he thought.

And she was. Billy didn't have many friends. He had always been a bit of a loner at school and mostly hung out with Justin when the opportunity arose. But Amy was different. Billy felt a connection with her that was something he never thought he could share with another person, save for Justin that was. In short, he liked talking to her, liked her company, and she was perhaps the single most important person to him in the world right now. He watched her sleeping for a little longer, finding her steady breathing soothing.

Billy looked back up at the moon. A cloud was partially covering it now. He leaned back against a tree and waited for the cloud to move. When Billy had been younger he thought the moon looked like a pie in the sky. He smiled at that notion now.

His thoughts shifted again. The Tunnel was obviously reaching out to him for a reason but would it be able to answer all the burning questions that he had? What if it didn't? What if when he finally reached it he found it to be nothing more than crumbling rock with a bad case of moss? That idea scared him a little, made everything feel so final. The Tunnel had to hold the answers for him, it just had to. Doubt was creeping into Billy's mind again.

I know what I saw … the dreams … the man dressed in old clothes … I didn't imagine it. Amy believes me. There has to be something there.

It was a fair argument, but along side the voice of reason was the voice of doubt.

Yes, Billy, but did you really see those things? You have been through so much over the past year. Justin died, your parents stopped talking. Is it possible what you experienced was just the emotional response to a horrible situation that a little boy could have?

Billy considered the possibilities for almost a full minute.

No! It can't be. I saw The Tunnel and the man in class. I saw him when I was crossing the road, when I was ... You know ... Anyway, Amy believes me.

There, argument settled, perhaps?

Yes but, Billy, Amy is your friend and of course she is going to believe you. She would believe anything you said. The question is do you really believe, Billy? Well, do you?

Billy shook his head. A wave of frustration swept over his face, partially highlighted by the pie in the sky.

Yes I know. But I also know what I saw. I may only be a little boy, but I know what I saw.

Case closed. The jury will now leave and decide its verdict.

But nobody else saw what you did, Billy. The other children in the classroom, your teacher or the drivers on the road that night, nobody saw it but you, Billy.

'I'm right,' Billy muttered. 'There is something to find inside The Tunnel. And I think it has something to do with ...'

He stopped digressing and suddenly stood up. There was a noise, a twig snapping maybe, coming from the bushes and trees on the opposite side of the track. Billy scrambled for the torch and shone it where he thought the sound had come from, whilst Amy slept peacefully on her side.

2

The torch beam moved across the bushes then highlighted the trees in the background. There was another rustling sound but Billy couldn't see anything so tried convincing himself it was only the wind. This was no good. He would have to get closer for a better look. He looked down at Amy, she was still sleeping. He walked forward to where the first sound had come from.

The trees danced in the wind. He was now standing at the

top of the embankment directly in front of the bushes. It was darker in the thickets – the light of the moon only partially lit up the dusty track, making it look like gold. There was a small drop, similar in height to the one that they had come across on the first night. Billy was scared, really scared. All he could think about was the old man's dog, Royal. Something had ripped that poor bastard's head off. And that something was waiting for him, inside the bushes. He looked ahead; the trees were still, like something was going to happen.

The werewolf…

'Please no.'

The Legend…

'Perhaps?'

Which is it then?

'Shhh.'

Billy looked back over his shoulder, Amy was still sleeping. Satisfied she was OK, he made an opening in the bushes with his left hand and aimed the torch into the space for a better look. The beam moved slowly over the once-hidden trees, shaking a little. Billy tried to keep his wrist under control but it was like he no longer had any control over himself. The beam revealed nothing but a rabbit and what might have been a rat.

Are they heavy enough to snap a twig?

Billy didn't think so. The light carried on moving over trees and down to the bed of the forest and into the clearing.

He suddenly became aware that his heart was beating at a ridiculous rate, thud, thud, thud, thud. He pressed his hand against his chest and could feel the pumping action. He swallowed hard, his throat was dry and palms all sweaty. He was beginning to get the same feeling he had felt on the first night that he was being watched, *stalked.*

The beam of light moved around the forest, penetrating into the vast darkness that went on and on.

'Billy.'

Jesus Christ.

Billy spun around, almost losing his footing and slipping down the embankment again.

Amy was standing there, wearing his red cardigan.

'Sorry,' she said, noticing how quickly Billy was breathing. 'I didn't mean to scare you.'

'You didn't,' Billy said, trying to sound as cool as a cucumber and praying to God at the same time that he had not just shit himself.

'What are you looking for?'

Billy smiled, still trying to pretend Amy had not just scared him. 'Thought I heard a noise, that's all,' he said in manly voice. 'So I went to investigate to make sure everything was cool.'

'And is it?' Amy asked with a smile appearing in the corner of her mouth.

'Yeah,' Billy said. 'No sweat. Everything looks in order.'

Yeah, baby, no need to panic now, Billy The Kid is here.

'OK,' Amy said, nodding her head. 'That's good to know. Thanks for looking, Billy.'

Billy smiled, and of course wanted to tell her about the noise, and that it was probably caused by the same thing that had been stalking them last night, and the same thing that could rip the heads off dogs with one snap of its huge saliva-dripping jaws, and if Amy hadn't scared him so shitless then he probably would. But as Billy's late grandma used to say, 'Boys will be boys.'

'Are you sure everything is all right, Billy?' Amy asked folding her arms, and looking around.

'Yeah,' Billy said, starting to walk back towards the track where Amy was waiting. 'It's late. Let's get some sleep.'

Billy followed Amy back to the tree where their makeshift camp was. Two bags, each with a sleeping bag inside (it was too warm tonight) and spare tops for each of them, Amy's black jacket lying against the tree, a blanket, a two litre bottle of lemonade, some sandwiches, crisps, a jumbo-sized packet of biscuits and a water flask. It was a good job Amy came.

'Are you OK?' Amy asked as they settled back down again for the remainder of the night.

'Yeah,' Billy said. 'Let's get some sleep. We leave early in the morning.'

'Billy?'

'Yeah?'

'Thanks for the cardigan.'

Billy smiled.

They both closed their eyes and were soon asleep. Tomorrow they would see The Tunnel, and as they both slept shoulder to shoulder, dreaming their dreams, something came out from behind the thick bushes and watched them again, which it did for most of the night.

3

The morning was fresh enough to make your eyes water, with a low mist floating above the ground.

Billy and Amy packed up camp early then set off. Billy estimated they were still some five miles away from The Tunnel. It was funny though, because as much as he wanted to go, the closer he got to The Tunnel the further away he wished they were. The day eventually warmed, and the mist slowly burned away underneath the relentless sun.

They talked, joked and laughed together. But they knew each step brought them closer to the end of their journey. It was starting to become real to them, where they were going, and seemed more serious than it had done a few days ago on the walk to school. But one thing was certain and that was turning back now was not an option now. They had come too far for that. The Tunnel was now becoming a reality to them, something tangible, and not just a place Billy spoke about and only visited in his lost dreams. They were going, and would soon see it, but what then? They could only speculate.

After an uphill stint the path began to level out much to the relief of Billy. He couldn't even blame his ankle any more. He just wasn't as fit as he thought. Amy coasted along, still talking and laughing without a care in the world.

The path narrowed again in places then widened out again. Trees and fields were all Billy could see when he took notice of his surroundings. But the path went on and on, always in a straight line never cornering once, only shimmering in the blazing heat. Always chasing the horizon, they were. Billy then noticed something in the distance.

Ahead of them was a small wooden platform by the side of the track standing about eight feet in height, looking like a makeshift veranda. To the left of it was a large puddle of muddy water that ran all the way across their path. It didn't look that deep from where they were at the moment, but the closer they got the deeper the water started looking, and less like a puddle, rather more like a small river.

The puddle of water definitely did not look like a puddle of water when they arrived at it. It was about twelve feet in length and fifteen feet across. Seeing the water up close reminded Billy about the day of the crash. He stared into the murky-looking water and remembered.

He could taste the water again, feeling it crashing down into his lungs, drowning him. Then the water started bubbling and little ripples began moving across the once-still surface. Justin's body was coming up and started floating on the surface. His face was all swelled up, like it had been pumped full of air. His skin was pale, blotchy and perished like skin looks when exposed to water for too long. Billy didn't want to look but felt powerless to turn away. The head of the body moved. Billy stepped back suddenly, almost losing his footing. Justin's eyes suddenly opened, looking right up at Billy. There were black holes where his eyes should have been. Billy felt his chest tighten again and wanted to be sick. Why was he seeing this?

'Billy!'

He came back and looked at Amy, then back at the murky water again. There was nobody there this time, only muddy water with dead insects floating on the surface.

'Where were you then?' Amy asked.

'Sorry,' Billy said. 'What did you say?'

'How deep do you think it is?'

It didn't look that deep, but Billy wanted to be sure before he answered her question. The last thing he wanted was for them to start crossing it and then to disappear completely underneath the surface. Billy was sure that he had a file on this somewhere inside his head.

He looked around the grass verge running alongside the track. 'Back in a sec.'

Billy had noticed a wooden stake, probably left over by track workers from years ago, lying on the grass verge. He dropped his bag and walked over and picked it up. He walked back over to where Amy was waiting for him. The stake was roughly the length of a metre stick, and pointed at one end.

'Hold tight,' Billy said placing his free hand in Amy's. He reached out as far as he could without falling in and dragging Amy along for the ride, and then sunk the stake into the murky water. He hadn't even reached a quarter of the way over and already the water had reached up to his wrist. Amy helped pull Billy back to the side.

'It's too deep to walk in,' Billy noted. 'Unless you have brought some stilts.'

Amy smiled then said, 'Sorry, didn't think we would need those.'

'Well,' Billy said now looking up at the wooden platform, 'we have to pass somehow.'

'Right,' Amy agreed. 'We have come too far to turn back now because of a little water.'

Billy smiled. The idea of turning back because there was a little water on the track was an amusing notion.

That's right Billy Boy, we have to turn back. Ghosts', haunted tunnels, and a crazy old bastard with a gun is not a problem, but you never said anything about muddy water, buddy.

'I guess we have to climb then?' Billy said, looking up at the platform.

Amy looked up at the platform too, squinting a little because of the sun. 'It looks pretty high, Billy.'

'No problem,' Billy said, looking and sounding confident. 'I will help you over.'

A round of applause, and thank you very much. Rule 2.3: Offering the damsel in distress a helping hand. Good job Billy ... Good job. Clap, clap ... clap. Echo to fade...

'Once I'm up pass me the bags then I will help you up.'

Amy nodded. 'But how are you going to get up there?'

It wasn't that high really, but at Billy and Amy's age it seemed more than it was. Billy examined the platform like a builder would a house that was in need of some serious renovating.

'Tell you what,' Billy said. 'I will help you up first. Here.' Billy dropped the stake and then lowered his hands and grasped them together, making a step for Amy.

'What about you?'

'I will be OK,' Billy said reassuringly. 'I'll be able to pull myself up.'

Amy took off her backpack then placed it down next to Billy's bag.

'Just take a good step and I will bunk you up ... Amy?'

Amy still had her back to Billy standing next to the bags. She didn't answer or move. Billy looked up slowly and saw why.

133

4

When he swallowed he heard his throat clicking, when he farted sneakily he almost followed through.

'Don't make any sudden movements,' Billy said, slowly gesturing with his hands.

The sounds that Billy heard inside the forest on the first night had been made by what was now looking right at them. They were being watched by something large, with thick black mangled fur with traces of mud visible. It was sitting down on its hind legs, large head tilted to one side, ears pricked. It was big, perhaps too big to be any kind of dog, certainly any kind that Billy was familiar with.

'What is it?' Amy asked.

Billy didn't know. From where they were standing his best guest would have been a large cat, perhaps puma, but he also thought it resembled a big wolf.

The Wolfman.

Billy shuddered when something occurred to him. *Royal,* he thought. *Is that what killed Royal?*

'What do we do, Billy?' Amy asked in a surprisingly calm voice.

Billy gave her a nervous glance, and then looked straight back over at an animal that was no more than fifty metres away.

The animal stood up on all fours. Billy could just make out a tail looking like it was swatting at flies. The animal looked strong, a powerhouse of muscle. Its head was low to the ground, nose sniffing at the track that Billy and Amy had not long ago passed. The animal raised its head, ears pulled back, sniffing the air, perhaps catching the scent of its next meal.

'Billy?' Amy said, trembling, her voice not sounding so calm that time.

'On the platform,' Billy said. 'I'll help you up.'

'I'm not going to leave you, Billy.'

'Don't worry about me. Once you are on top I can pull myself up.'

Before Amy could say another word Billy had already grasped his hands back together again, making a step for her.

'Go on,' Billy said. 'As soon as you are up I will follow…'

'Promise,' Amy said.

'Yes.'

Amy passed Billy, giving him a nervous look.

As Billy helped Amy up onto the platform the animal started walking towards them, sniffing the air again. It was hungry and hadn't eaten in a long time. Billy glanced over his shoulder and could see the animal getting closer, ears pulled back now, and muscular frame moving slowly, with the sole purpose of killing.

5

At first the beast had been weary; scared just like it had been on the first two nights it had seen the strange-looking visitors. Not now though. The animal was growing in confidence with each and every step, drawing closer to a potential meal. The track had been quiet of late. The last meal had been another animal, but even then it hadn't had the opportunity to feast properly. A man with a long stick, that seemed to emit a loud banging sound had scared it off. But this potential meal didn't appear to have any such loud device.

The stick the boy was holding made the animal hesitant at first but once satisfied there was no danger it pressed on. It had been aware of a stranger on the first night inside the forest but hadn't been so hungry then, so it had let the meal escape. But now the hunger pains were not going away, and there was only one way they could be sated.

The animal was old now, very old, but wise, still strong and ferocious. Its pink tongue dripped thick chunks of elasticised saliva down onto the dirt track, leaving little wet spots behind. But what was this? It appeared the meal was trying to escape. The animal couldn't have this, so the energy it was intending to conserve for the kill would now have to be used a little sooner. It started running, muscular limbs making easy work of the short distance, wind blowing back its thick black fur coat. Instinct would always win out in the end.

6

'BILLY!' Amy screamed. 'It's coming, Billy.'

Billy had managed to push Amy up on top of the platform before the animal charged. He quickly glanced over his shoulder and saw the large beast running towards him, panting, tongue dangling at the side of its mouth, picking up speed fast.

Billy now reckoned it was a big wolf, but wasn't certain, because he thought wild wolves had been extinct in England for ages.

The Legend, he thought. *It has come for us – The Guardian of the Track.*

'Quickly Billy,' Amy pleaded, reaching down. 'Just reach up and grab my hand.'

Billy jumped up, managing to grab a hold of the platform. Amy immediately reached forwards, grabbing his wrists. The animal was now at the bottom of the platform, snarling and revealing some rather nasty dirty-looking teeth. Billy managed to raise his legs up and support his feet against the wooden pillar of the platform just as the beast jumped up trying to take a bite out of his left leg. There was a snapping sound as the animal's teeth closed against themselves.

Fear pulsated through Billy's little body as the animal continually jumped up, snapping at the air. It was quite poetic really. Firstly the animal distributed all of the weight on its back legs then pounced up in one smooth swift motion, snapping as it went.

'Leave us alone!' Amy screamed out. 'Just go away and don't come back.'

This beast obviously did not do requests. It continually jumped up, snarling and trying to bite a piece of Billy's flesh.

The third time the beast leapt it came close to Billy, far too close.

'Piss off!' Billy shouted down at it. 'Go on … get the hell out of here.' His voice trembled, fear had seized him. He could move no more, and he was slipping.

'Billy,' Amy sounded desperate. 'You have to help me. Use your legs to push up with.'

Billy did not hear her. All he could do was watch the animal dancing around in the air, trying to tear him apart.

The animal snapped, once … twice … three times. It was relentless, it was hungry and in its eyes Billy was no more than a piece of dangling meat on a hook.

'Billy, please,' Amy said. 'You have to help me. Billy!'

The animal jumped again.

'Leave us alone!' Amy screamed, tears running down her cheeks.

Billy felt sweat running down his back, it tingled all the way down. He was not going to be able to hold on any longer. His feet were starting to slip down the wooden pillar and Amy was losing her grip on his wrists.

Billy's eyes widened as he dropped nearer to the animal, its eyes were burning with hunger, mouth dripping with saliva. It jumped up and caught Billy's right shoe. He fell.

7

Billy landed hard on his back, making an imprint in the mud below.

The animal had temporarily retreated as Billy fell. It was smart enough not to get hit and possibly injured by such a succulent looking piece of meat.

Billy was dazed, and as he looked up the beast started towards him, teeth at the ready, ears pulled back again. Billy wanted to stand and run but fear froze his joints, cancelling out the signals of danger being sent from his brain. He felt a warm sensation gushing around inside his gut, fear, pure fear. So Amy had to think fast. She needed something, anything. The platform must have been a guard house of some kind because there were bracings and fixtures fastened into the wooden base. It must have been a shelter with walls and roof, dismantled, or vandalised after the line was made redundant all those years ago. There were loose nuts and bolt heads but nothing more. But they would do, steel against flesh would hurt, no matter how small they were. And Amy intended to throw hard. She grabbed frantically what she could find then moved over to the edge of the platform.

Billy was cowered up against the wooden pillar. The beast was only metres away. It was going to kill him so Amy had to act fast, she had to act now. The biggest bolt she found was an inch in length and had some weight to it.

'Hey!' Amy shouted as loud as she could.

It worked, she got the animal's attention just as it was about to leap and rip Billy's throat out. The beast looked up. Amy threw the bolt as hard as she could and hit the animal between its raging eyes.

Amy heard a little thud. The animal whimpered and backed away from Billy giving him time.

'Now go away!' Amy shouted, throwing more ammunition

at the beast. Three of the other bolts hit the animal in the side, making it retreat further. The fourth hit its head again, making it whimper.

'Leave us alone!' Amy shouted. 'Leave us alone!'

With the few remaining bolts she held in her hands Amy jumped down from the platform. She slipped and fell on her bum when she landed in the soft mud, but quickly got back up and was now standing next to Billy who looked like he was gasping in terror.

8

The animal retreated to a safe distance. It thought that it had a meal for certain when all of a sudden it was hit by heavy flying objects.

Nothing too alarming though but it had fucking hurt just the same. It wasn't as serious as the old man's loud stick but it was still an inconvenience. The animal sensed the person throwing the objects was angry and not such easy bait as the one lying in the mud. Time to regroup, it was still hungry and leaving now was not an option. It could wait, for a while. The beast sat down on its hind legs and watched, tongue panting up and down and still dripping with saliva on the track below.

9

'Billy!'

Amy held Billy by the shoulders and tried lifting him up.

'Can you move, Billy?'

Billy nodded. His pride was hurt more than anything else. Surely every little boy knows that girls are not meant to save them?

Billy got to his feet, Amy helped support him. They both looked at the animal. It was watching them with an almost twisted fascination.

'Why doesn't it go away?' Amy said.

Billy remembered the stake that he had checked the water level with so reached to his side and picked it up.

'We'll have to swim across,' Billy said, looking at Amy.

Amy looked at Billy, then at the water, then back at the animal. What other option was there?

'I guess,' she said uncertainly.

'You go first.'

Amy looked unnerved. 'No! We go together, Billy Cooper.' She said this holding his hand like she never wanted to let go of him again.

'We can't,' Billy said, feeling touched by her compassion for him again. 'I need to stay here and keep it away.' Billy raised the stake in his right hand. 'Go on, Amy,' he added. 'I'll be all right.'

'No,' Amy said, gripping Billy's hand tighter. 'I am not leaving you again, Billy Cooper.'

It was then that the animal charged again.

10

The beast made ground fast. Billy saw it first. Amy then saw it. She turned quickly.

'Get behind me,' Billy ordered. He surprised even himself by how calm and commanding his voice sounded.

Billy stepped in front of Amy giving her no opportunity to argue this time. He raised the stake and brought it down in a clubbing motion just as the animal jumped.

The piece of wood hit the animal on the side of the head. It was a sturdy strike but only fuelled its anger more. The animal danced around Billy like a boxer, snapping out with powerful jaws and swiping with its front paws. Billy stood his ground and carried on clubbing at the animal with the piece of wood. Amy could only look on.

The wood struck the animal's head again, making it retreat this time. It growled, snarled, mouth dripping, and eyes burning with red hatred. It was going for the kill this time. No more Mr Nice Beast. It was a large animal, so one more long hard leap should knock this irritatingly evasive meal onto its back.

But Billy read what the beast was going to do next. He positioned himself at the ready. This was it, the buck stopped here. It was going to be him or this fucking beast that was determined to make a meal out of him and Amy. Billy was now a knight of old, and this beast was a dragon that needed slaying, and Amy, the damsel in distress.

The beast pulled back its ears and leapt through the air in a graceful motion for one so large and menacing. Billy quickly pushed Amy aside and held up the stake, thrusting it forward with every bit of energy his small frame could afford. The beast landed on Billy sideways, knocking him back into the muddy water.

The beast followed Billy into the water. There was a huge splashing sound then they both disappeared.

11

Unfinished Business

1

Kate held his hand, cold as it was.

She didn't know what else to do … He was her husband.

She had phoned work earlier on to tell them that Alex had been taken ill, giving no details of why. After all, he was her husband. It was the right thing to do. There is nothing like a tragedy to bring a family together. The very thought of that made Kate smile. Wasn't it a tragedy that had pushed her family apart in the first place?

The plastic chair was starting to feel a little uncomfortable, reminding her of her days from school. But she was not going to leave his side. Alex should be dead, so should she for that matter.

There was so much left to say, so much damage to repair. Was this a second chance to do that? Billy was missing, of that much she was sure. All Kate could do in that moment, as she gripped Alex's hand, was hope that she got a second chance with Billy too. Where was he now? Who was he with? Was he in any kind of danger? These questions banged around inside her head like dodgem cars. She wanted her son, she wanted her family back. Kate was a realist, and knew sometimes to wish is not enough.

Why the sudden change of heart? Simple really, they could

not go on like this, hurting one another. No amount of blame would ever bring Justin back. Kate had been blinded by her loss and was now starting to open up her eyes a little bit wider and see what was in front of her. She had a son who needed her right now, a son she barely knew anymore, God, how she was going to put that right given the opportunity. And sometimes when people lose something that they didn't think they really needed, this is when the true meaning of that loss is realised. It certainly had for Kate Cooper. Billy was missing, and she now realised just how serious this could be, and the thought of something happening to him, especially since they had parted on such terrible terms, to know that could be their last encounter together filled her with unimaginable sorrow and regret.

Kate watched Alex like a mother would watch her new born baby. She thought she had lost him, thought she had lost herself. But sometimes miracles can happen and God only knew their family needed one.

It was Sunday afternoon. The sun was shining outside and every so often Kate caught a light breeze against her face blowing in from the open window. She looked outside as the nets blew inwards. It reminded her of when she had been a child herself, lying in bed on a summer's night with the window wide open and curtains moving with the warm breeze. Back then she couldn't have imagined that one day her life would have turned out to be so complicated and messy. It saddened her to think like that.

Alex's hand moved in hers. She looked away from the window and down at him. His eyes were open and looking at her. Kate lifted his hand and kissed the back of it. Alex smiled.

'Sorry,' Alex said.

His voice sounded dry, like a man who had spent days walking in the desert. Kate smiled and shook her head. It was now time for them to talk.

2

Kate didn't know where to begin explaining to Alex how she had got him out of the garage. It had been close, very close.

Kate had collapsed before reaching the car. Lying on the garage floor tasting the toxic fumes inside her mouth, she suddenly felt angry. There was no way in hell she was going to let her husband take such a cowardly way out. There was no way she was going to have to look Billy in the eye and tell him that Dad decided to take a nose dive, and a permanent one. She had already lost a son, and there was no way she was going to lose her husband as well.

Unfinished business, she thought, forcing herself up onto her feet. *If he goes to the grave with all the hurt he feels within then he will never be at peace. Neither will I and neither will Billy.*

Kate wobbled to the open door. If it had been closed then she would have surely died. Outside she collapsed onto the lawn, coughing and vomiting. Her head ached, like it was suddenly going to implode, her body floating on air. This was scary, Jesus! What was happening to Alex? God only knows how long he had been in there.

Move!

Kate hurried back inside the house and found the key for the overhead garage door. The key was hanging from a hook, always in the same place, and in that moment Kate was thankful that her late mother had drilled her so much to be tidy when she had been a kid.

Always know where things are Kate … Then you will never lose them.

Her dead mother's words had sounded inside her head like she had been standing right next to her.

Before going back outside Kate grabbed a cloth from the kitchen sink and ran it under the cold tap.

Kate was outside again now. She unlocked the overhead door and pushed the lever in. The large garage door slid up into an open position. Clear smoke poured out, engulfing

144

her. She shielded her face but the smoke overpowered her.

'Alex!' she called out, stepping back, trying to escape the cloud of fumes.

Kate moved the damp cloth up over her mouth and went inside the garage again. She could barely see the side of the car for all the smoke, let alone anything else.

The first thing she did was pull out the tubing Alex had placed into the open car window and dropped it outside. Next job, turn off the engine and then get Alex outside. The thought that he was probably dead already never even entered her mind.

Keeping the cloth against her mouth with her free hand she tried the door. It was locked. She quickly went around to the other side of the car and pulled on the passenger side door.

'Jesus!'

The handle flicked back down. She was going to have to break a window. What was there to use? Kate looked around hopelessly.

The steady clearing of smoke helped Kate's cause. She found something. Standing at the side of the garage next to an old set of cupboard doors, and a well used dartboard, was a wheel jack. Kate picked it up and banged it against the passenger side window. The glass smashed with ease, Kate felt a feeling of triumph creeping over her, but the work wasn't over yet.

She tapped away the rogue glass from around the door frame then reached inside the car and unlocked the door. Kate opened the door and moved what pieces of glass she could see off the passenger seat with her foot.

Kate was no longer looking through fog, the smoke had cleared. But the smell and constant pounding inside her head was enough of a reminder for her to be quick, and even more so when she saw that Alex was leaning forward onto the steering wheel.

Shouldn't the horn be sounding? Isn't that what always happens in the movies?

It was going to be easier to get Alex out on his side, so Kate reached across and unlocked his door then quickly got out of the car and ran back around to the other side.

When she opened the door and Alex flopped out, like he no longer had a spine, it was then that she convinced herself he was dead. His eyes were closed and his body had all the life of a stone. But undeterred, Kate took a hold of Alex under both arms and then dragged him outside.

Kate's neighbour was out for the day so she was all alone. Remembering the days when she had taken first aid at school, she began giving Alex the kiss of life. She fought for him, she fought for their family. She had fought for everything in her life so far, so she was not going to stop now. In that moment Kate took control of everything. Yes – everything depended on Alex waking up.

3

'You came back to me,' Kate said, still gripping his hand. 'I fought for you and you came back to me, Alex.'

Alex looked at Kate. After listening to her explaining how she saved his life you would have thought that there would have been some kind of response. Alex looked as uninterested as he used to look when Kate would tell him that they had no ham at the local supermarket.

'Please say something to me, Alex,' Kate pleaded. 'For God's sakes won't you just talk to me?'

Alex looked away and swallowed. 'What do you want me to say, Katie?'

Katie.

He hadn't called her that in years. Kate couldn't remember the last time, probably a lifetime ago, when they had first met at college.

'Well to start with, why, Alex?'

Alex never answered.

Kate suddenly felt angry. She wanted an explanation. What gave Alex the right to take the easy way out anyway, and leave her head high in shit? Isn't marriage supposed to be a partnership, after all? She waited for Alex to speak but that did not happen.

'Alex,' Kate said. 'Please will you talk to me? I am right here.'

Alex simply stared at the white unit next to his bed like it was the most exciting thing he had ever seen. He heard Kate all right, but was not ready to talk, yet. He wanted time to think, to come to terms with what he tried to do to himself. He had been at his lowest yesterday, even more so than the early days after Justin's death. He didn't mean to be so selfish, that had not been his intention, and he didn't mean to cause his wife more pain. But he was a selfish man, he accepted that. Over the past year he had put his grief over Justin ahead of everything else. He was the only one that missed Justin, he was the only one that loved him and shared that special bond with him. He was the one whose life fell apart when Justin died.

That was just Alex's own selfish way of thinking. Of course the rest of the family missed Justin as much, but in his own short-sightedness and colossal yearning to hang onto a son that was not coming back he had failed to notice. Work colleagues, friends, everyone had been pushed away to the point of almost no return. But one person it seemed, had held on for dear life, and she was sitting next to him.

'Alex,' Kate said sternly. This time he looked at her. The bed creaked as he moved the rest of his body. 'We all miss Justin, and I think you know that. But I need you right now, Billy needs you right now. I mean.' She lowered her head for a few seconds then looked up again. 'Jesus … What has happened to our family?'

'Billy,' Alex muttered.

'What?'

'I hated myself so much for what I did to him.'

Kate leaned in closer to the bed. 'What are you saying?'

'I hit him,' Alex said rubbing his tired eyes. 'I hit him, Kate.'

'Oh, Alex,' Kate said moving her hands up over her mouth.

'I hated myself so much afterwards ... I–'

Kate quickly motioned with her right hand for him to stop. She didn't need to hear any more. A single tear drop ran down Alex's cheek. He wiped it away quickly. It was the first time Kate had seen him crying in ages. He had been stone faced at Justin's funeral, bottling up all his feelings. As a matter of fact Kate couldn't remember ever seeing him crying and that scared her a little.

'Is Billy here?' Alex asked, wiping his eyes again and looking around.

Kate didn't answer. She rubbed her forehead, shook her head and then rested both elbows down onto the bed. She felt drained, like the past year had suddenly caught up with her, squeezing down, pressing her, preventing her from breathing.

'Katie?'

'Billy's run away, Alex,' Kate said, her voice breaking up a little. She began to sob. 'He's missing.'

Alex's stomach suddenly tightened. He sat up in bed and watched Kate. All that could be heard was a light breeze blowing in through the window and her gentle sobs.

4

The phone call, Alex always remembered that phone call. And it was strange because he hadn't remembered making it. Not long after Justin had been killed Kate Cooper checked for messages on the phone. It was just a ritual of hers. After Kate had pressed the various key strokes the computerised voice said, *Thank you for calling. You have one new message. To hear the message press three.'*

Kate's original thought had been that it was going to be a friend or some family member she had not seen in ages just offering their condolences over Justin. But that had not been the case, and after hearing the message she dropped the phone receiver down onto the floor. That message stayed with her, haunted her. It was chilling, made her wonder why on earth Alex wouldn't have told her about it. And more importantly, how the hell he knew about it in the first place. There lay the problem. Because when Kate had asked Alex about it he couldn't remember ever making the phone call. Alex's first assumption had been like Kate's, that the message had been left by his elder brother, Bryan. It wouldn't have been the first time those two had been mixed up. But Bryan would not have said, 'This is Dad ...'

Alex listened to the message over and over again. Kate sat at the kitchen table watching, lost in that terrible moment of total bewilderment.

Justin, Billy. God, I hope I'm not too late. Listen to me, this is Dad. I know what's happened with Billy but you both must stay put. Do not leave the house. There's going to be an accident. Just stay put and wait for me. I love you.

The message then stopped and the line went dead.

Alex had felt the same chilly feet walking down his back as Kate had felt. It wasn't bad enough that they had just buried their first born, but now this as well. It was just too much.

'What is this?' Alex blurted out. 'I did not make that call.'

But Alex had. The force that had taken over his body had just made him forget.

Fragments of that day slowly started coming back to Alex. Scattered memories, like fallen leaves in autumn. And two weeks after Justin had died Alex remembered something that was a key point in understanding the strange phone call he had made. He had seen it in a dream but after waking he realised it had been remnants of what he had actually done in real life.

149

After making the phone call, Alex ran outside to his car. He was way over the drink driving limit but the force controlling his body would not let any ill harm come to him. Hands that were no longer his own gripped the steering wheel of his car and he raced off to try to prevent a moment that every parent dreads. Kate, and everyone else inside were still too busy drinking and having the time of their lives to hear the screeching tyres of his car going down the long driveway.

The force controlling Alex could sense it was too late. It couldn't save both of them and it couldn't risk endangering the body it was currently occupying any more either. Too many rules had already been broken for this boy. There was no time. The force quickly left Alex's body, leaving just enough behind to send him safely back to Aunt Mary's with no memory of what had just happened. Alex arrived back and parked. It was then that his body became his own again. He went back inside the house with no memory of what had happened. The party went on, and outside the faint sound of sirens could be heard carried along with the wind.

Later that evening Alex and Kate received another phone call they both would never forget.

5

Timing, everything is always a question of timing. Alex knew this; Kate knew this and so too did Billy.

Everything that had happened to Billy lately was all to do with timing. It was the right time for the dreams, the visions and the sudden yearning for The Tunnel. It was all part of the same plan that he was being forced to follow, a plan that would inevitably lead him to what he most wanted. Billy had not told his parents about his dreams or The Tunnel. The only person that knew was Amy.

Right now Alex and Kate were faced with a bigger dilemma. They both had no idea where Billy was. They knew about Amy though.

'Do you think he is staying at Amy's house?'

Alex nodded. All he really wanted to do in that moment was disappear off the face of the Earth. By his own admission his actions had been cowardly and selfish and the fact that he'd forced Billy away by hitting him only made it worse.

'Alex,' Kate said. 'Do you think we should speak to her parents?'

Alex didn't know what to say. He hadn't offered any advice on Billy's life over the past year so it felt a little hypocritical to start doing so now.

'I don't know, Kate,' Alex said, sounding like a man on his final chance.

'We're a pair of selfish bastards,' Kate snapped. 'We never once asked if he was all right, or if he needed anything. We were so caught up in our own grief. I mean ... Just take a look at our family will you, Alex.'

Alex didn't need to. The picture was crystal clear and he didn't want to look at it any more.

'I am going to fix this family,' Kate said, sounding determined. 'And I need your help Alex. I can't do this alone.'

Alex nodded. 'I know.' He reached out and took Kate's hand.

Kate wiped her eyes. This was the first time Alex had shown her any affection in a long time. A hug at night, a kind word, Kate would have opted for either. But instead she got a pair of cold shoulders to sleep next to, the shell of a man she had once known and loved so much.

'He'll come back to us, Katie,' Alex said.

'Will he?' Kate asked, beginning to cry again. 'Would you, Alex?'

Alex didn't even want to consider what he would do if

placed in the same situation. If he was ever going to make it up to Billy then the thought of it was too scary for him to even comprehend. He had too much to lose. He had to keep some hope alive that Billy could one day forgive him. One day! Alex Cooper certainly had a lot to mull over.

'Do we call the police?' Kate asked tentatively, wiping her eyes.

And tell them what? Alex thought. *That my son ran away because I socked him one.*

'I don't know,' Alex said.

'Well I do,' Kate said after careful consideration, knowing that involving the cops could complicate things further. 'First thing I'm going to do is go and see Amy's parents.'

She moved her chair back, making a screeching sound, and then stood up.

'First thing's first then,' she said, putting the chair up against the wall. She walked back over to the bed. Alex watched her the entire time. 'I know that I would never win mother of the year for the way I have behaved towards Billy, Alex … but you crossed the line with him. And if you ever cross that line again then there will be no second chances. Do you understand me?'

Alex nodded then said, 'For what it's worth you couldn't hate me anymore than I hate myself right now.'

'I don't hate you, Alex,' Kate quickly said. 'I just want this family put right again. We all miss Justin and that will never change, but…' She stopped and looked out of the window. Maybe she was surprising herself at how strong she was suddenly sounding or maybe what she was about to say was really more for her rather than Alex. 'We will always love Justin and he will always be a part of us all, but life goes on, Alex. We have another son who needs both of us. Now please let's just start acting like the parents here and not the kids.'

Kate walked over to Alex and kissed the side of his face. As she tried to leave he grabbed her right arm.

'I'm sorry,' Alex said. 'For everything.'

They shared a hug.

'Tell that to Billy,' Kate said, releasing him. 'Our son needs us now more than ever, Alex … Do you understand?'

Alex nodded.

Maybe this family could be fixed but Billy was still on his way to The Tunnel and at that moment didn't share his parent's optimism. He was closer now than ever, but as his parents had been debating the future of his family, Billy was now involved in the fight of his life.

6

After Kate had left the room Alex was left with a lot to think about. It was going to take time for him to make amends with Billy but maybe, just maybe? But the problem was he still wasn't sure whether when he looked at Billy he would see his son or a person that Justin died for. And he wouldn't know the answer to this question until he actually saw Billy again. If he ever did, that is, because right now nothing was certain for any of them, especially Billy.

12

Billy and Amy

1

Billy dreamt about Amy. The first time he'd met her, that is.

The day was warm with the scent of freshly mown lawns filling the air. He had felt lost, a stray who no longer knew his way home. Home; that was the last place he had wanted to go. For almost two weeks after Justin had died Billy visited his grave every day. It didn't matter what the weather was like outside he went without hesitation. Home was hard at the moment. His parents had become terribly withdrawn since the funeral and had hardly spoken to him or each other. Billy was starting to get the impression that his father blamed him for what had happened. It was a bitter pill to take, but one that Billy swallowed just the same. His father had also started drinking. He would either hit a pub straight after work and come home completely wasted or pick up a bottle of Scotch on his way, whatever helped him to forget, Billy supposed.

Billy's mother had also changed. She didn't talk so much or laugh any more. Billy used to love hearing her laughing. It really had been quite infectious. Billy also had to live with the fact that he was never going to see Justin again, his brother, but far more importantly his hero. As time passed by the lines of communication broke down. Billy's father had been the worse affected. He couldn't even bring himself to look at Billy any more. His mother still cooked meals and washed his clothes, but the part about her that Billy loved the most seemed to have been buried along with Justin. Their family had been left in ruins since Justin had been laid to rest, and it seemed that Billy was the only one who noticed, and cared, and as time passed by things gradually got worse. Alex and Kate stopped talking all together, there wasn't even any small talk between them any more, and Billy had been totally shut out, just spending what time he wasn't at school either inside his bedroom or by Justin's grave. He wanted answers; he wanted to know why his once happy family was now nothing more than a shipwreck lying at the bottom of the ocean. And why, most importantly his parents didn't love him any more. He was lonely and scared. He was a child of eleven years old.

When Billy was five he had the same nightmare for almost a week. In the dream he was sitting at the breakfast table with both his parents and Justin. It had looked and felt like any other morning in the Cooper household. There was a problem though. The people sitting around the table looked like his family but weren't really. Stoned faced expressions, black holes where eyes should have been, emotionless voices. Billy would ask his mother to pass the sugar. She would stare at him blankly, and then Justin would look at him, and then finally his father. A sense of loss gripped Billy. What had happened to his family? Sure these people looked like his family all right, but the essence inside of them that made them who they were was missing. They were shells, and that was all. Billy would ask over and over again where his real family was. There were never any answers offered from any of them. They just continued staring at Billy, like he was some kind of freak that they had never seen before, but had heard existed none the same.

By this point the dream started turning nasty. The black holes where eyes should have been started dripping with a thick black substance looking like tar. Billy then pushed his chair back but could not get away. It was like his feet were shackled to the floor by an invisible chain. He called out, started trying to run away again, but it was hopeless. Hands with long ugly fingers started reaching out to him like they do in zombie movies, trying to pull little pieces of his flesh away to eat. It was then that their heads exploded like balloons and drenched Billy in that awful looking black tar. Billy would always wake up at that point screaming, expecting to find his face covered with tar.

And standing in front of his brother's grave he started remembering that dream again. Billy was scared that the dream was starting to come true, that his family were leaving him one by one, and that he was going to be left all alone; and his parents were becoming like they were in that dream too, distant and unloving towards him. Sure they both looked like Alex and Kate Cooper but inside they had changed, they had become full of black tar; empty, emotion-less shells that scared Billy shitless. And seeing Justin's name carved in stone with the words 'Rest In Peace' underneath made Billy realise this was final. It wasn't going to be like in a film when the hero always comes back at the end, and everything turns out to have been just a horrible dream. This was real, this was life, and he was going to have to face living his without his brother any more. Billy could feel a lump swelling in his throat. He didn't think it was possible to cry any more and surely he had no more tears left to cry?

He would go to Justin's grave after school every day and just sit there talking about the kind of day he'd had. Sometimes he could even hear Justin talking back to him inside his head, like a soft voice echoed from the heavens. Billy would picture Justin inside his head as he spoke to him. He hated the idea of talking to rotting flesh and dusty old bones so that helped a lot. He had never really considered the possibility of an afterlife before, at eleven years old why should he have? But Justin's death had made him question this. He wanted to believe in a heaven and hoped Justin was there, because if there was one then Justin deserved to be there more so than anyone. And that was the only way that Billy could accept Justin's death, knowing that his essence had moved on to a better place made it almost bearable.

A week after Justin's funeral Billy was once again at the cemetery. He was late going because someone had let off a stink bomb in class and everyone had been given detention. Billy knew it was a boy called Mark Jenkins that had done it but didn't mind staying late after school. Anything was better than the deathly silence that was waiting for him back at home these days. Meal times had become almost a chore. Nobody spoke, and there was just the occasional lonesome sound of a knife or fork scraping against a plate.

Billy had gone to the cemetery straight from school and was once again telling Justin about his day and about the ripper that Mark Jenkins had let off in class. It was then when Billy noticed her again. He had first seen her two days before but she had been with her mum and dad. But today she was alone, and two graves along, sitting down on the grass with her legs crossed. Billy stopped his conversation with Justin, feeling a little embarrassed, and started watching her. She had been doing the same thing as Billy had, talking to a slab of concrete, hoping the message would be relayed on somehow. The little girl's head had been bowed down almost in dismay. Billy wondered whether she was talking to her brother or sister. And in that moment, speaking to his dead brother seemed less ridiculous to him. The idea that some other person, a child, was doing the same thing made it more acceptable for Billy to be doing it too. He started thinking that maybe this was the normal way living people communicated with the dead. Billy hadn't heard what she had been saying, but that didn't matter. She looked about the same age as him and had been doing the same thing he had been doing. There was no reason to feel embarrassed about talking to his dead brother in front of her. Anyway, she was just a girl when all was said and done. Billy knew the rules about boys and girls, all right.

The little girl, with the blue ribbon in her long brown hair, acknowledged Billy by smiling. She then got up and walked over to him. Billy smiled and watched her walking over. She was wearing a white dress that was almost blinding.

'Hello,' she said casually, stopping next to Billy with her hands by her sides.

Play it cool, play it cool.

'How's it going?'

Bravo, bravo ... ten out of ten there, Billy Boy. Round of applause please...

'My name is Amy Johnston,' the little girl said enthusiastically.

'I'm Billy ... Billy Cooper.'

She nodded and smiled. 'Can I sit with you, Billy Cooper?'

Billy didn't even have to think about his response. He even moved over for her and let her have the flattened area of grass his ass had been occupying.

From those simple words a friendship and a great bond had been born. Billy had felt an instant connection, as had Amy. You might say that something good had come out of the tragic circumstances that had placed them both together in the first place. Amy sat with Billy for quite sometime. Billy told Amy all about Justin. Amy then told Billy all about herself and her family. Amy had made Billy smile for the first time since Justin had been killed, and he smiled even more after he found out that Amy was going to start attending the same secondary school as him after the summer holiday was over. He loved her smile and her laugh, and she loved the way he was so open with her about Justin and his family. They talked for hours, right up until sunset. Billy had then walked her home, and they had been friends ever since.

Maybe things would be all right after all, now that he had met Amy, someone that offered him a little light in his bleak life. But that was all a long time ago now, and Billy and Amy were together in a different place right now. The Tunnel was close, too close.

2

The Legend...

He remembered it leaping at him.

He then remembered falling backwards into water that looked like someone had used it as their own personal shitting pool.

But wait; there had been something else too.

The stake, he remembered doing something with the stake.

'Billy.'

He heard that, and that had to be a good sign.

Fast moving images played through his mind. He saw the beast snarling and snapping with thick chunky saliva running from its mouth like it was infected with rabies. Billy saw himself, which was weird, pushing Amy out of the way as the beast lunged at them, and then thrusting the stake up into the air to meet it. It had all happened so fast. But he remembered his strong instinct to protect Amy, which was still as strong as his desire was to stand.

He felt wet and his body ached but he could still hear...

'Billy!'

The voice still sounded a little muffled but he reckoned it belonged to Amy. And indeed it had, because when Billy Cooper opened his eyes the first person he saw standing over him was Amy. Her long brown hair looking wet, her pretty face now a little dirty too. Amy had tied her hair back into a single pony-tail. She smiled when Billy opened his eyes.

'Welcome back, Billy Cooper,' Amy said, still smiling.

Billy coughed then looked around. For a brief moment he felt completely disorientated. But after he saw the water and the high platform again he realised where he was.

'Shit!' Billy shouted sitting up. 'The Legend.'

'The what?' Amy asked, trying to prevent him from moving too soon. 'Careful.'

'That monster, wolf thing,' Billy said, frantically looking around. 'Where is it?'

Amy smiled.

'Don't panic, Billy,' she said calmly. 'It's gone.'

'Gone?'

Billy's eyes scanned the track and surrounding forest, expecting the fucking thing to come leaping out from somewhere again.

'You killed it, Billy,' Amy said, looking proudly at her knight.

'I did?' Billy asked, looking puzzled. 'I killed the Legend?'

'Yes,' Amy said. 'You are my hero, Billy, my knight in shining armour.'

She smiled and held his hand.

Billy looked down at his clothes and thought. *Your knight in muddy shit, more like.*

But this was good.

File 2.4: The boy always rescues the damsel in distress.

Jesus! This couldn't have been better if scripted.

Billy smiled so wide it made his mouth ache. He was a hero. This was a moment all little boys should have and Billy was having his right now.

The problem was Billy couldn't actually remember much about the hero part that Amy had kindly mentioned. He remembered feeling scared and nearly shitting himself. He remembered the beast jumping up at him. After then everything went a little blank. He suddenly felt like a man awaking from a coma and finding out that he had missed the past ten years of his life. Amy was going to have to fill in the blanks for him here.

'You don't remember, do you?' Amy said, after seeing the puzzled expression on Billy's face.

'Not really,' Billy said.

Amy sat down next to Billy and told him the story. Billy thought it was great, it was like a fairytale, like the ones his mother used to read to him when he had been a little boy, except this time the fairytale was about a boy called Billy, a little boy who slayed a beast. It was magic, and the best story Billy had ever been told. The beast was dead and the pretty girl would become his bride. He would ask Amy to marry him, she would say yes and then they would live happily ever after. Billy liked that story even more. Perhaps one day he would even get to tell it too. It was a magical fairytale that every child should get to hear about.

Amy explained the story in every detail, making Billy hang onto every word. It was Billy's quick thinking that had saved them. The animal (that incidentally neither one of them still knew what it had been) was preparing for one final leap. It was hungry and desperate. Roaming the track for days, maybe weeks or even months, hell who knew, but it needed a substantial meal. Old Royal had only been a side dish, perhaps, if he had been killed by the Legend, and the beauty of human beings, as it had heard they were called, is that they have less hair on them making them easier to devour. After Billy pushed Amy out of the way he was left toe to toe with the beast. As it was flying through the air he had raised the broken stake. The beast landed on it and the weight and momentum of the animal had subsequently caused its own demise. The stake had buried itself deep into the beast's chest cavity killing it instantly. Billy hadn't heard the yelping, or rather the screaming that Amy thought sounded like it had come from the beast as it landed on Billy and knocked him backwards into the water. Amy had thought the scream eerily human-like.

'Well how long was I under for?' Billy asked.

'Quite some time,' Amy continued. 'I was really scared at one point…'

Billy suddenly saw the word 'HERO' written in the air. The words were made of stone, each one beginning to crack and send down tiny dust particles.

'How did I get out of the water?'

Bigger cracks appeared in the letters, more dust fell to the ground. Dare he think it, dare he even say it, had Billy Cooper been saved by a girl?

The words began breaking up.

Amy could see Billy losing his glow here, that the thought of slaying the Legend then being helped out of the water by a girl was taking away his moment. Amy wanted Billy to have his moment, wanted him to always remember it until he was an old man. A story he could tell his grandchildren about some day. Billy needed this moment and at this point in his life more than ever, and Amy was not about to take it away from him. And which ever way Amy looked at it Billy was still her hero.

'Amy?'

'You swam out, stupid,' Amy said. 'How else do you think you got out? Not aided by me I hope.'

Billy smiled – his glow was starting to come back a little.

'I couldn't even pull you onto the platform so there was no way I could have pulled you out of the water, Billy Cooper.'

'Well, yeah,' Billy said. 'But you tried…'

'Of course I did,' Amy said. 'You're my best friend after all.'

Billy suddenly felt a little embarrassed. He wanted to consult with the files, but what the hell. 'You too.'

He looked at Amy's clothes, they were damp. 'Why are your clothes all wet?'

'Oh,' Amy said. 'Well … After you got out of the water I think I must have fainted … shock … and must have fallen into the water. You got me out too. When I came around you were sleeping.'

Billy stopped his interrogation there. If Amy told him that

was what happened, then that was good enough for him. He was a hero, period.

'Well, I guess I should feel tired after all that,' Billy said.

Amy nodded in agreement and then reached inside her bag and pulled out something wrapped in tin foil. She opened it and handed Billy a sandwich. Billy scoffed it down quickly, not even thinking about his dirty hands, and then burped. He wiped his mouth and then smiled. He hadn't realised how hungry he felt until he saw the sandwich in front of him, and even though the bread was a little stale now it still filled a nice gap. Billy then had a swig of water. He now felt ready to fight another day.

'What about you?' Billy asked, stuffing his face.

'I ate when you were sleeping,' Amy said.

'Are the supplies all right?'

'They're fine,' Amy said looking at what she had left inside her bag. 'We haven't even opened the biscuits yet.'

Biscuits?

Billy felt his mouth watering like a dog looking at its favourite bone. He reckoned he had space left for a couple of biscuits.

'Should even be plenty of food left over for the journey back,' Amy added.

In that moment something strange happened.

The journey back...

Billy hadn't even thought about the journey back. For some reason he had always assumed that this trip was a one way ticket. That was partly because he didn't know what he was going to find inside The Tunnel. And whether the force that was calling out to him was only bringing him there to a certain doom. There had to be some reason The Tunnel chose to call out to him, and haunt his dreams with ghostly images. But it wasn't just that either. The thought of going back home filled Billy with even more dread than facing the cold dark mouth of The Tunnel.

The Tunnel was uncertain, and whatever was going to happen would be a new experience. Home however, was stagnant and old. Billy didn't want to go back. As far as he was concerned there was nothing left for him there any more. Justin was gone, only an empty room with Justin's belongings offered any reminder that he once lived there. A room that Billy sometimes slept in when he wanted to feel a little closer to Justin, on those nights when he missed him so much that he felt like he couldn't breathe. A room where pictures gathered dust and school trophies looked lonely. No! For Billy this was a one way trip. He was not going back home. He would reach The Tunnel and walk through to the other side, then keep on running just like Tom Hanks in the film *Forrest Gump*. As long as Amy was with him then nothing else mattered. There was no going home, Billy had known this when he started his journey. That posed a question though surely, one that Billy had asked himself on more than one occasion. Was he running away to something, or was he simply just running away? Billy didn't have the answers yet. The cauldron of emotions he felt boiling within, contemplating that question, were just too much to cope with to reach a satisfactory conclusion at the moment. That posed another question. Why hadn't he told Amy any of this yet? She would understand though, she had to. It was easy to keep moving forwards when there was nothing keeping you back. Yes, this was definitely a one way trip. There was no going home for Billy Cooper.

'What is it?' Amy asked.

'Nothing,' Billy said. 'It can wait...'

Amy suddenly looked suspicious of Billy. There was no way she was going to allow Billy to keep on running. As far as she was concerned once they reached The Tunnel and found there what they needed to find, it was then home time. She had a family to get back to, a family she had told to expect her back in three days max.

'I'll be at Billy's for the weekend. Oh yeah, his parents are fine with it …'

But Amy hadn't realised that Billy's mother was planning a trip to her house pretty soon. It was a plan that only a child would think they could get away with. Whatever happened, Amy was not leaving without Billy.

Billy turned his attention back to the platform that had almost certainly aided them in slaying The Legend of The Track. He put down the bottled water and stood up.

'Billy,' Amy said, watching him walking over to the platform like the rotten pieces of wood had suddenly called out his name.

'Billy … What is it?'

Billy didn't answer her. He was too busy running back towards the platform.

3

It was Sunday, two days into their journey, which had already delivered so much more adventure than they both had expected.

Neither one of them had any idea of the time. It didn't matter here. Time was irrelevant out here. All that mattered now to both of them was reaching The Tunnel. Speaking of which …

Billy climbed up the platform. He slipped a few times, but made it to the top eventually. His arms ached like hell and with his trousers still wet each movement of his legs delivered a farting sound. Billy almost felt inclined to pardon himself as Amy looked on. Amy had the sense to bring the bags with her so when she reached the bottom of the platform Billy was almost on top. One more pull now, heave ho …

For a moment Amy lost Billy. She looked up at the top of

the platform, and after hearing it creaking she knew he was up there. It suddenly dawned on her that it might not be that safe. She had found an alarming amount of loose bolts and screws that she had used as makeshift bullets. There was another creaking sound followed by the heavy thudding of feet.

'Billy?'

No response, just the occasional shuffling of feet.

'Billy Cooper?' Her voice was louder that time with a hint of desperation.

Billy's head suddenly appeared again. He looked down at her and smiling. 'Throw up the bags.'

'The ones you forgot about?' Amy reminded.

Billy shrugged.

Amy threw up each bag, watching Billy disappearing again each time.

'Come on up,' Billy said, reappearing again.

'Are you sure it's safe?'

'Oh yeah,' Billy said, confidently jumping up and down on the spot.

The man who built his house on sand, Amy thought.

'Use the side pillar and push yourself up … I will do the rest …'

Billy still sounded confident, and excited, but why?

Amy jumped up and held one of the supporting rafters, then did as Billy instructed. She moved herself up and when she was close enough to the top Billy reached down and pulled her up.

Amy looked and felt like a novice rock climber who was just finding out that they are absolutely terrified of heights, which incidentally she was. The last time she had been on top of it there had been more important things to think about than her fear of heights.

The top of the platform looked larger than they initially thought looking up at it from below. It was roughly the size

166

of a snooker table making it about twelve feet long by six feet wide. After Amy had finished sorting herself out Billy was waiting for her in the far corner. Amy had a quick glance down. It looked higher all right. She carefully walked over to where Billy was waiting, constantly looking down at the space between the beams and at the ground below.

'We'll camp here for the night,' Billy said. His voice sounded like a man now in charge, all grown up.

Amy apprehensively looked down between the creaking wooden beams, sounding like they were alive, protesting at the sudden increase in weight.

'They will hold,' Billy said watching Amy looking at the beams. 'Don't worry.'

'How do you know?'

'I just do.'

Billy stared off into the distance again, making Amy curious as to what he was looking at. It was getting dark and they had missed the sunset so it wasn't that. But Billy continued with his mindless gaze.

'What can you see?' Amy asked inquisitively.

Billy turned to her and smiled. 'Come and see.'

His voice was soft and he reached out, taking her hand.

At first all she could see were tall trees all lined up. Then she saw birds on the branches getting ready for the ever threatening darkness. Fields, there were vast fields. There were no houses or roads to be seen, it was like they were the only two people left on the planet. Amy strangely liked that idea.

'Look more to your left,' Billy said in the same tone.

Amy did so. Her eyes widened when she saw it and just like Billy she stared for a long time. Over the far hills, slightly veiled through all the trees and growing darkness, they both saw it, a solitary sight that was the reason for this adventure in the first place. Billy felt a chill shooting down his back, like one of those you can feel coming and try to fight off but never quite manage. In the bleak distance, waiting for them, was The Tunnel.

4

They were both glad of the height, just in case the beast wasn't dead. Amy seemed comfortable lying down on her back, resting her head on her bag. She looked up at the moon, thinking about nothing and everything.

Billy was a little more restless. He was looking down into the water, half expecting to see air bubbles rising to the surface. The idea that the beast was only holding its breath and waiting for them to fall asleep before attacking again hadn't quite abandoned his mind yet. He too was watching the moon, the reflection in the murky water, looking like a floating pie in the sky. It was a peaceful night though, and Billy and Amy were grateful for the rest. They were both tired and the past couple of days had been crazy for both of them. But thus far they already had enough stories to tell their grandchildren about and the adventure was far from over. They hadn't even arrived at The Tunnel yet.

The water rippled, Billy paid close attention as the moon shimmered, looking all distorted. Was the beast coming back up? In that moment Billy felt like his heart had jumped up into his throat. He looked on, wishing the platform was higher.

'Billy,' Amy said, still looking thoughtfully at the moon.

Billy watched the water until he was satisfied nothing was surfacing then turned to Amy.

'What do you think we will find?'

Billy didn't even have to ask, she was of course referring to The Tunnel.

They were so close now. They had watched The Tunnel

until the growing darkness had made it impossible to see. And the fact that they were so close was another reason for Billy feeling a little on edge tonight, as something that he had only ever seen before in his dreams – something that he had heard so much about, was now so close he could almost taste it.

Billy thought about Amy's question. Putting aside his own supernatural visions and expectations, haunting dreams, he remembered something that the old man had said to him.

'I think we will find whatever we take in with us.'

Amy looked confused at such a profound sentiment. So was Billy, he felt rather stupid really, like a boy trying to impress a girl he liked. Wait a minute ...

'What does that mean?' Amy asked, turning to face Billy. She placed her right elbow down onto the wooden beams and rested the side of her face on the palm of her hand.

It was obviously a night when Billy was going to have to think long and hard before answering.

He thought about Justin and the ghostly figure of a man he still did not know. He then thought about his parents and how they had pushed him away for the past year. The only good thing he had taken away from the last year was Amy.

'I guess what we carry inside of us,' Billy explained. 'Our hopes, fears, what we want back again but can't have. Our own ghosts perhaps ... I don't know.'

'Justin?' Amy said; her face full of wonder and hope in the pale moonlight.

Billy smiled. 'And my family... I just wish ...'

Billy stopped, suddenly feeling what was like a tight cord wrapping around his throat.

Amy thought she saw a lonesome tear-drop in the corner of his right eye.

Billy turned over and looked up at the moon, hoping it would take away his hurt. There was no way he was going to cry in front of Amy again. Once was bad enough, but twice?

In that moment Amy wished that she had a magic wand that could take away all of Billy's pain. But as magical as childhood can sometimes be there wasn't enough to do that, yet?

'It's OK to wish,' Amy said. 'And you know, Billy sometimes wishes can come true.'

'Can they?' Billy asked hopefully, wiping his eyes but still looking up at the moon. He really hoped Amy was right, but whatever happened he was just glad she was with him.

'I believe so,' Amy said softly. She reached over and held Billy's hand as they watched the low moon together until the moment they could no longer fight off sleep any more.

Billy needed Amy right now, and he wanted his family back also. But the need to reach The Tunnel and then to carry on running far outweighed his desire to go back home. Everything would soon be revealed to Billy, and when it felt to him like nothing could ever get any worse, then everything really was going to come crashing down all around him again.

They were waiting ...

13

Drawings

1

It was Sunday night and Kate Cooper now had a lot on her mind, more so than usual. It had been three hours since Kate had left the hospital and Billy was still not home. His room had not changed since Friday night when he had arrived home and dumped his school bag down onto his bed, and the night he had disappeared.

Alex should be out of hospital tomorrow, pending a meeting with the hospital shrink that is, but Kate wasn't thinking about his suicide watch right now, nor was she thinking about how close they had both come to dying the other day. Kate was still thinking about Billy and where he could be.

Amy's, he has to be at Amy's.

The problem was Kate didn't know where Amy lived. Billy had spoken about her and probably mentioned a hundred times where she lived over the past year, but Kate hadn't spent much time listening to Billy. But she would put right that wrong, it wasn't going to be easy, she knew that, this was real life, not like one of those family dramas on TV where the end scene always shows everyone smiling and hugging. That was bullshit. Kate knew that more than most. Real life is real life, and families have real problems, and this happened to be theirs.

The same questions still played on her mind like a broken record now. How could she fix this awful mess? And how could she ever get Billy to forgive her? Kate had been blind, Alex even more so, but she was now going to repair what a few days ago seemed un-repairable, unimportant to her, that was now as important to her as the air she breathed.

Staring at a turned-off television set offered Kate little in the way of inspiration. She had reached one conclusion though and that was bringing the police into this would only complicate matters further. After all, from Kate's standpoint Billy had done a runner because of a back hand from Alex. She didn't know about The Tunnel or the strange dreams that plagued Billy like a swarm of locusts. She didn't know his real reasons for going, and perhaps Billy didn't either. Either way, the solution, she thought, was to go and see Amy's parents; they would surely know where Billy was. What scared her a little was thinking about how much Billy had told them. He would need to speak to someone. Over the last year had he been opening his heart up to complete strangers, telling them about his horrible home life and the no-good assholes he lived with that were once called his parents. Kate wouldn't have blamed Billy if he had. Jesus, it wasn't like he had anything good to say about either of them. But Kate hated being judged, and the idea that she was being judged and told all about to a family she knew jack shit about terrified her to the core. Yes, this is real life all right.

Kate got up from the chair she had been occupying for the past hour then left the front room catching sight of a photograph of Billy and Justin hanging from the wall as she went. She passed through the kitchen then made her way up the hallway which led towards Billy's bedroom. The room had not changed. The curtains were still partially opened, allowing a soft light to enter from one of the street lamps outside. Kate walked over and pulled the curtains fully. The light faded, dimming out her lost, lonely face.

172

She switched on the small lamp standing on the side unit then sat down on the end of Billy's bed. Billy's school bag was next to her. Kate needed something, anything to help her find Billy. She needed Amy's address. Billy must have written it down somewhere. It wasn't in any of her address books of that much she was certain. She had madly searched all through those as soon as she had got back from the hospital. She unzipped Billy's school bag and began to search through it. All she found was an empty lunch box and two school books that had seen better days.

Kate looked despondent as she got up from off the bed. She sighed, looking around for anything. She looked in front of her at a brown desk with a small television sitting on it. Kate had a look through all the odds and ends Billy had left lying around but found nothing that resembled an address of any kind. She was now going to have to look through the other drawers. She didn't want to but as she saw it there was no other option. To find out where Billy was, for there to be any chance of finding her son, she had to speak with Amy or at the very least Amy's parents.

The top drawer was full of old books and loose pieces of paper. Kate was hoping she would find what she was looking for. She pulled the drawer out and placed it down onto the bed. There was an A4 pad that apart from some scribble on the first sheet had nothing useful, no address at least. Billy wasn't very well organised, Kate knew this much about her son, what twelve-year old is? She hadn't been expecting to open the drawer and see a nice organised set of folders and one of them reading 'SECRET ADDRESSES TO KEEP FROM MUM.'

Kate carried on sifting through the drawer with most of its contents now on Billy's bed. Any folded piece of note paper she came across raised her hopes, temporarily. After emptying the drawer Kate had found nothing useful. She repeated the same process with the other two drawers, finding no details about Amy's address. Perhaps Billy had never written it down, just memorised it. Kate didn't think so. The reason Billy's drawers were so crowded with paper in the first place was because he had to write everything down. Ever since he had been a little boy he had felt compelled to scribble every little detail down. People's birthdays, sometimes what he did at school and what he liked and disliked were amongst a few of the other things. He also wrote stories, mostly about himself being the main character in the prose. Kate never read any though. Billy never let anyone, all except for one person. He had stopped writing after Justin had died. There was nobody left to read them after then.

Kate once thought that Billy would become a writer when he grew up. That was a long time ago now though, and before things had turned bad for all of them. Right now she would just settle for getting him back home in one piece.

Kate slid the drawers back in the unit then started searching Billy's shelves. There were three shelves and the top one was only holding two speakers for Billy's hi-fi system. Then something standing next to the left speaker suddenly caught Kate's eye. Within reason, a mother normally knows where everything is in her son's bedroom but Kate didn't have a clue. She reached up and brought down the brown folder. It was quite thick, with tattered pieces of paper peering out of the side. She sat down on the bed again, flicked a piece of her long brown hair around her left ear and then held the folder in her lap. There was one word on the front of the folder written in Billy's handwriting which was strangely familiar to her. The word, all in upper case was TUNNEL. Kate ran her right index finger across the letters then cautiously opened the folder, looking more like a woman defusing a bomb rather than simply opening a tatty-looking piece of brown card.

A single elastic band held all the tattered pieces of paper together. The first piece of paper was blank. Kate removed the elastic band and looked at the other pieces of paper. Her initial thought was that she was holding in her hand one of Billy's story folders. Where he had kept it on the top shelf, almost concealed by the speaker, made it seem the more plausible. But what Kate was holding in her shaking hands was not a story written with words, it was a story written with pictures. Kate crossed her legs and flicked another piece of her brown hair behind her left ear again. She looked at the page immediately after the blank sheet.

'Drawings,' she muttered.

2

There were pages and pages of the same individual drawing. The pictures were very detailed and professionally done. Kate had no idea that Billy could sketch so well.

It was true, the drawings Kate was looking at had been pencilled by Billy's hand but he had not drawn them, really. His body had merely been used as a communication device by a force that had made him draw what Kate was now looking at, pages and pages of the same drawing, but all varying slightly the further she went along.

The pictures were mainly from dreams, over the past month or so they had become more intense and so had the drawings. Billy couldn't stop them. After each and every dream he was compelled to draw what was still floating around inside his subconscious, like a dusty old memory that had somehow returned. The first time it happened Billy woke up with the pencil still in his right hand. He didn't remember going to get it or drawing on the pieces of paper that were scattered all over his bed in the morning. There must had been nearly twenty sheets, some of them fallen on the floor. Then the visions had started, and the undeniable desire to go to that place hidden in his dreams. That place was like a top secret code that he dared speak of to only one other person, Amy.

The Tunnel was drawn with a hand guided by a force that wanted Billy. And Billy had come, just like it knew he would. Kate couldn't believe how expertly Billy had drawn the pictures. She didn't think she was looking at drawings done by her twelve year old son, more like a professional artist who had turned his craft into a way of paying the bills. They were that good.

Some of the drawings were of a path, or perhaps disused road. Of course Kate was familiar with the old railway line, she had lived in Market Harborough all of her life, but still, she had no idea as to why her son would be drawing it and made no connection. She carried on turning the pages then suddenly shuddered, back and arms turning to ice.

After ten pages there was another picture of The Tunnel. This one was without the trees and the sky and surrounding fields. It was a sketch of The Tunnel opening, with a little boy standing in front of it.

'Oh my God,' Kate said. 'Billy…'

She turned the next page, each picture showed the pencilled figure drawing closer to the mouth of The Tunnel. She carried on turning the pages until the last picture showed the figure gone, disappearing into the darkness. The little boy was gone.

Kate didn't understand why Billy would draw something like this. They scared her immensely. If Billy had gone to The Tunnel then at least she now knew where he was, but why had he drawn so many pictures of it? And why had he gone?

She looked closer at the last picture, her long hair falling forwards again, partially hiding her distressed face. The picture seemed to move in front of her. Kate flinched and moved back quickly like a person suddenly realising they are in immediate danger. For a second she thought she saw something else in the darkness of the drawing, looking back at her. She shuddered again and quickly put the drawings back inside the brown folder. She had seen enough.

'Wait,' she muttered, stopping next to the door.

Something occurred to her. This was not the first time she had seen The Tunnel. There were other pictures of it in the house. Kate suddenly realised she was sweating and wiped her brow then went to find them.

3

Monday morning...

Whilst Billy and Amy had been getting ready to set off on their quest again Kate Cooper was on her way back to the hospital. She reckoned she knew where Billy was and why he had gone. She had not slept at all last night. Images of The Tunnel were now haunting her too. She could not get the pictures out of her head and she was scared, scared for Billy and what he was getting himself into here. She may not have paid much attention to Billy's life over the past year or so, but she knew he was not capable of producing the kind of drawings she had seen last night. There was just no way he could have drawn those.

Kate had found what she had been looking for last night, and that made the whole situation a lot worse. She had violated her son's privacy, but if that meant she could bring him home safe then so be it. She was no stranger to the stories about The Tunnel. Even when the line had been active there was talk of night workers seeing and hearing things that couldn't be explained, terrifying things. Sure Kate had heard the stories. But that's all they were, stories to scare people, like the bogeyman or alligators in the sewers. But there was no denying the fact that people had died on the track. Everyone had read the stories in the local papers over the years. From workers accidentally killed to the people that had deliberately thrown themselves in front of an oncoming train to the young man, Kyle Jacob, who had hung himself from a tree standing over the entrance to The Tunnel.

The more Kate went through all the stories she heard the more she hoped she was wrong about where Billy had gone. There were closer places he could have gone to, like the park, Amy's house. Hell, it didn't matter really, she just wanted him home. But if she was right about the connection with the drawings and what she had found last night in the house then maybe Billy had gone there. That would make sense. But the drawings, she could not stop thinking about the drawings, and the way in which Billy had somehow been used as a conduit for strange forces.

Kate had even been tempted to go to The Tunnel last night. But number one she wasn't a hundred per cent certain that was where Billy was, and number two, she needed to talk to Alex first. If they were ever going to be a proper family again then it seemed sensible to discuss it with her husband first. It was a no win situation though, because if Billy was in danger then all Kate was doing was wasting valuable time.

It had started to rain when Kate parked up. She grabbed the brown folder and got out of her car running towards the hospital entrance.

4

Alex studied the drawings, looking like a man staring into one of those magic eye puzzles waiting for the hidden image to appear and surprise him.

'Well,' Kate said. 'What do you think?'

'I don't know.'

Kate frowned. 'Is that all you can say after all I have just told you, Alex?'

'Maybe Billy didn't even draw these,' Alex said.

'He drew them, Alex.'

'How do you know that? They could belong to somebody else that he is just keeping them for.'

Kate suddenly felt angry. It was true she couldn't be certain that Billy had drawn them, but the more she thought about it the more it all made sense to her.

'Billy drew them, Alex,' Kate said assertively. 'I know he did.'

Almost a minute's silence held them both. They simply looked at one another trying to determine what was really happening to their family here. Could it really be that some supernatural force had entered Billy's life?

'OK,' Alex said finally. 'If you are right, then what has he gone looking for?'

'Looking for?' Kate said, looking confused.

'Well yeah,' Alex said in a simple tone, as if she was missing something so blatantly obvious it was criminal. 'The Tunnel is what, nine, ten miles from here? He wouldn't walk that far if there was nothing to find at the other end, would he?'

That did make sense to Kate, so maybe she had missed something. But she still wasn't convinced.

'I don't think Billy is going there to look for something,' Kate said. 'I think something is looking for him.'

Now Alex looked confused and suddenly felt a little scared too.

'So what are you saying,' Alex asked, 'that he is being forced there by something?'

'No, not forced, but enticed,' Kate explained. 'I think he feels that he has to go there, and it has to do with these drawings.'

Kate held one up in her hand as if to reiterate her point.

'But enticed by what?' Alex asked still looking confused.

Kate didn't want to say, not yet anyway.

'I don't know,' she said.

'Kate ... this all sounds a little ridiculous to me,' Alex said. 'I think we just have to accept that our son has run away because of what I ...' Alex stopped.

'Because you hit him?' Kate harshly finished.

'Yes,' Alex said, but only just daring to.

'Well I don't,' Kate said. 'Billy must have spent weeks drawing these pictures.'

'So what?'

'Well the point being that he was going to The Tunnel regardless.'

'But you don't think he drew them really, do you Katie?' Alex asked.

'Oh yes I do,' Kate said, 'but something made him, something that was channelled through him.'

Alex ran his fingers through his messy looking black hair and then sighed, his face now showing at least two days worth of unshaven shadow. He also had bags underneath his eyes.

'Are you talking ghosts here, Katie?' he asked tentatively. 'Is that where we are going with this?'

'Would that be so wrong?' Kate asked deliberately, not answering yes or no. 'Would it, Alex?'

Even if she had answered yes Alex wouldn't have laughed at her. He was starting to remember an incident from his past that was never explained to him. Perhaps he hadn't wanted it to be, and was too afraid of what that explanation would be.

'No,' Alex said. 'Sometimes things just can't be explained, can they?'

'The phone call you made,' Kate said as if reading his mind, like Amy sometimes did with Billy.

Alex nodded. 'I still don't remember making that call.'

Kate suddenly had an idea that made her shudder in her seat. Could it be? God she hoped not.

'What is it?' Alex asked, suddenly looking concerned.

Kate looked at Alex, her eyes wide and burning with

questions. 'What if the same force that controlled you that day is now somehow controlling Billy?' Kate suddenly felt scared again, scared for Billy. 'God,' she said bringing her hands up to her face. 'What have we done to our little boy, Alex?' Her voice sounded muffled behind her hands. 'What is happening to our family?'

Alex watched as she sobbed. His family was a mess. This really was rock bottom. He had no answers to offer Kate in that moment. He got out of bed and walked around to where Kate was sitting, body trembling as she cried. He held her hand and told her everything would be all right. She looked at him with teary eyes and wanted to believe what he said, God, how she wanted to believe him.

14

Going Home

1

Billy watched the sun coming up, held in awe by the brilliant, beautiful spectrum of colours, and with it the new day brought the final stage of the journey.

Billy hadn't slept much again last night. His little body was buzzing with too much excitement to have slept properly, like a child on Christmas Eve. Except it hadn't all been excitement that prevented Billy from getting next to no sleep. The realisation of how close he was coming to finding out what was waiting for him was now a reality, and it was like a sucker punch of terror that he had not seen coming. The truth was in reaching distance, but the problem being Billy wasn't sure whether he wanted to know it any more. He didn't want to turn back nor did he want to press on. He was caught somewhere in the middle, in a lost void of curiosity and terror.

The pull was undeniable, his desire to go inside like a thirst that could not be quenched. The Tunnel was less than a mile away, had to be. It hadn't looked that far away last night even in the fading light. He hadn't even told Amy the truth yet, but once they reached The Tunnel he told himself that was when he would do it. The Tunnel, what would be waiting for him inside The Tunnel?

Billy breathed in the fresh morning air, contemplating his question. Ghosts, the un-dead, do such horrors really exist? Billy didn't know.

He wanted to believe, but once again started disputing what he had seen already, and with it came a familiar feeling in the back of his tired head. Had he really seen what he had seen? Was it just images created by the over-active imagination of a lonely twelve year old boy or had they been real?

'Bullshit,' Billy muttered. 'The whole thing is just plain old bullshit.'

There had been no dreams over the past few nights or sightings of that creepy-looking fair-haired man with the stare that made Billy's bones want to leave his body. And there was absolutely no denying that something had made him walk all this way. He could certainly have thought of better ways of spending his summer holiday. And then there was Amy. She believed him. She never called him crazy or looked at him like he needed throwing into a padded cell. That must count for something, it simply had to.

Aren't you forgetting something else, Billy?

Billy flinched at the voice. It was his own but sounding off inside his head like an adviser of some sort.

'Something?'

Yes Billy … The drawings, remember the drawings. We both know you couldn't have drawn those by yourself. What made you draw those, Billy? Tell me…

It was a just question that was starting to tip the scales again. Billy couldn't put the drawings down to an over-active imagination. Seeing things was one thing but waking in the middle of the night and drawing twenty or so pictures of a place that he had never seen before, and in perfect clarity too, was a little harder to dismiss. All Billy remembered feeling was like he had been in some kind of trance, like someone had slipped him a hallucinogen of sorts, or like he had been possessed. A force had entered his body, made him grab a pencil and paper from inside his school bag then start drawing. He had drawn the pictures without even looking at the pages. He heard the pencil scraping against the paper and that was all. And if he required further proof his fingers had been black at the ends with lead the next morning. Billy had hidden the pictures inside a brown folder and had lost track of how many nights he had awoken in a dreamy state, because that was what it had felt like, a dream, and if it weren't for all the pictures lying on his bed sheets and his blackened fingertips in the morning then he probably wouldn't have even remembered. Billy hadn't even told Amy about the drawings. But soon he would, maybe.

Billy was terrified to admit this to himself, but there was no denying that something had possessed him and then made him draw those pictures, and the very idea of possession scared him shitless. To think a force entered his body then made him do something against his will really did stretch the boundaries of a reality that seemed to be growing further and further out of sight these days. Then the dreams and visions started. It was a spiral of events that had led him to where he was now.

Billy looked down at his arms – they were covered in goose pimples. Yes, there was something to find, and yes what he had seen and dreamt about had all been real. He breathed in deeply, and then out again, as if expelling any doubt he had about what he had seen. Yes, he believed all right.

Amy stirred; she was going to wake soon so Billy had to get his game face back on and quickly. He couldn't act like the scared little boy he felt like inside in front of Amy any more. They were too close now for him to start making her want to turn back too. He looked down at his clothes, they were dirty, and the dried mud on his jeans had started flaking underneath the heat of sun, but at least it had stopped raining now.

Billy brushed his trousers then looked at his hands. They

too were dirty, and as a matter of fact he had never seen them looking so unclean. Billy liked cleanliness. He wasn't obsessive about being clean but would have liked a sink and bar of soap right now. But suddenly there was a more imminent problem, Billy could feel it bubbling up inside his stomach and moving around. He wanted to fart and it wasn't going to be one of those you could simply control and let out in stages so little or no noise is made. No, this one was going to be a real bastard of a ripper, one of those that feels warm as it departs the gateway. Billy was in pain and his stomach was grumbling and the urge to fart far outweighed his urge to eat. Normally he would just let the beauty out without thinking twice about it. He probably would have smelt it too, to see if it was worthy and all. But he was less than two feet away from Amy's head, and she was down wind. And judging by the pain in his left side this one was going to give off enough force to ripple the wooden beams they were currently lying on, and possibly remove Amy's head.

Billy squeezed his arse cheeks together and got up. It was rather comical looking really. For one thing he was walking like he had just shit his pants. The ripper almost slipped out when he placed his right foot over the side of the platform but luckily the goal keeper up his back passage made a diving save just in time. But this baby was going to extra time. The whistle blew.

This was now getting serious. Billy was getting pretty emotional about the whole thing and was now sweating for Christ sakes. But it then hit him, in the most unfortunate of ways. What he was feeling was not just a fart. Billy needed to be sick too. His stomach churned and gurgled, the pain he felt in his side was now more centralised. He had not really eaten that much over the past couple of days so it couldn't have been the food. He then remembered the unclean water he had fallen into. He had got a mouth full of that shit when the Legend had knocked him under. He quickly lowered

185

himself down over the platform then dropped to the ground below, once again almost following through and being sick at the same time, it was a miracle really that he hadn't done either, and then made haste to the bushes behind the platform.

2

Billy hated being sick. It had only ever happened on three separate occasions before; the last time being almost a week ago now, another time when he had picked up a bug from school and when he decided to try some of his father's bottled whisky.

Billy leaned forward into the bushes. The fart didn't matter now. He was too focused on the watery sensation inside his mouth. The back of his head felt warm, like someone had placed a warm lamp there. It was coming, he could feel it; he didn't want it to because he knew it was going to hurt. The first one always does. Then the body kind of relaxes and lets loose what else needs rejecting. Billy's stomach felt like it was being squeezed from the inside. He was sweating and could feel it running down the insides of both arms. His pulse rate was rapid. It was going to happen and there was no use in trying to fight it.

Billy retched, making a horrible sound that seemed to echo through the morning air. Nothing came up. His heart rate increased and a fine layer of sweat appeared on his brow. He breathed in and out quickly, preparing himself for another attempt to empty the shit his body had refused to accept. He retched again, making a deep straining sound, then vomited up a disgusting brown liquid. There were pieces of food he had consumed the previous day, but most of it was a dark brown soup. He was sick three times in total then collapsed on the ground barely missing the puddle of vomit he had just left alongside his beaten up trainers.

Billy wiped his mouth and spat out the remaining pieces of vomit. He felt better now but unfortunately his aim had been a little off. Strings of vomit had clung to his T-shirt. He then heard a rustling sound behind so turned around. It was Amy.

Billy, feeling slightly embarrassed stood back up straight.

'Are you OK, Billy?' Amy asked.

Billy looked down at the front of his top. It was a mess and there was still a faint taste of vomit inside his mouth.

'There must have been something nasty in the water,' Billy said, looking back at Amy, slightly embarrassed. 'I've been sick, Amy.'

'Here,' Amy said, walking over to him. 'You'll need this.'

Billy saw her holding his T-shirt but for some reason hadn't recognised it as his own at first, and for a horrible second thought it was one of Amy's. He was glad he had brought it now though. Amy handed Billy the red top with a white stripe running across both shoulders.

'Thanks,' Billy said.

He stared at her, looking and feeling uncomfortable.

'Oh,' Amy said as if suddenly coming back to life and getting the message. 'I'll wait by the platform.'

When Amy had left, Billy changed his top, leaving the dirty one in the bushes. It felt good to be wearing something clean and fresh, it still smelt of his room and made him, very surprisingly, think about home. What was happening here? Two days ago he wouldn't have gone back home for all the money in the world. But it seemed the closer he got to The Tunnel the more he missed, well … his family. That was bullshit though. It had to be. He hated his parents, didn't he? The truth was Billy Cooper didn't have the wiring to hate anyone. He was a good kid who had been dealt the hardest of blows a person could receive in such an early stage of life.

But death doesn't mind how old you are, does it? And perhaps Billy had learnt the most important lesson and the cruellest one in life at too young an age. That the people he loved would not always be around. That life is like a sand glass. Eventually it runs out, and unfortunately cannot be turned over again no matter how much we want it to be. He also realised walking back towards Amy that there was a difference between him hating his parents and hating the way in which they had treated him. Maybe that was where the confusion lay. There was no time to think about home now though. They were a mile away from The Tunnel and every time Billy closed his eyes he could see it, looming, waiting for him to come.

They were both now standing back in front of the wooden platform that had been home for almost a day.

'Help me back up?' Amy asked looking back up at the platform.

'Sure,' Billy said with a cheeky smile.

Once they were safely over to the other side of the platform it was onwards towards another chapter of their journey, and when he was back on top of the platform Billy had one final glance at the water, just to be safe, just to be certain.

3

They hadn't been walking for that long when Amy suddenly stopped. At first Billy assumed the laces on her trainers had come untied, but when he looked back, Amy was just standing still, looking like someone's lost little girl, which Billy supposed she was. He had no idea where they were now and was pretty certain Amy didn't either. The road, the trees and the fields, there was just a feeling in the air that Billy and Amy were the first people to come out this far in a long time.

They were like two lost ships on an uncharted voyage, accidentally discovering new land. It felt like everything was new and being disturbed for the first time. Of course it wasn't, trains used to run this route daily, but in that moment, as they looked at one another they both felt it. The place where they were standing, the place where they were going to was theirs, it only existed for them. It was something waiting to be discovered by them for their own personal reasons. And perhaps those reasons wouldn't become apparent until their journey was finally over.

Billy's feet scuffled across the dirt track, sending up little pockets of dust as he ran back to where Amy was still standing. She looked frightened, which in turn made Billy feel frightened. For one horrible second he thought the Legend had returned.

'What is it?' Billy asked, standing in front of her. 'Amy?'

Amy didn't answer him; she just carried on looking with the same expression that Billy found difficult to read.

'Amy … what's wrong?' Billy's voice was soft, his tone understanding. He had never seen Amy like this before, she looked, well, blank, expressionless.

'Amy?'

Amy then focused onto Billy. 'Don't you feel it?'

Billy wasn't sure what she was referring to here. Sure he felt something, but judging by Amy's expression it wasn't quite the same thing as she was.

'Feel what, Amy?' Billy asked.

Amy's face was pale, just like Billy's had been before he had been sick.

'I don't know exactly,' Amy said, 'but there is something wrong here. I can feel it.'

Billy frantically looked around, half expecting an anvil to fall out of the sky and crush them both like flies, like in some crazy cartoon.

'It's all around us,' Amy continued. 'I feel it … everywhere.'

Billy was lost now. Whatever was giving Amy the spooks had not placed a cool hand on him, yet.

'I want to go home, Billy,' Amy said assertively. 'I shouldn't be here with you. I shouldn't have come. My mum and dad will be so mad at me when they find out what I have done.'

Of all the things Amy could have said that was the one furthest from Billy's mind. It had completely taken him back.

'Amy,' Billy said, but Amy was quick to cut in.

'You don't need me here, Billy,' she said. 'You were right to have wanted to come alone.'

That crushed Billy a lot more than he let on. Of course he needed Amy here, and not just for The Tunnel, he needed her wherever he was.

'It was a mistake for me to come with you,' Amy added.

'Don't say that,' Billy said. 'I'm glad you are here, Amy.'

'Billy … don't you understand?' Amy started, sounding frustrated, like a person showing something they believed to be incredibly simple to a person who just couldn't seem to grasp it. 'It is time for me to go home now. I need to go back to my family.'

Billy was left dumbfounded. He knew he should have said something but in that moment it was like he had lost his ability to speak. For the first time since he had known Amy, he was terrified he would lose her too, just like he had Justin and, in a different way, his parents.

'I'm sorry, Billy,' Amy said, as if reading his mind. 'I didn't mean for it to be like this. I thought that I was doing the right thing, but I think this is something you have to do without me now.'

'But we are so close, Amy,' Billy said. 'I thought we were going to do this together. Billy and Amy.'

Bingo…

Billy thought he had done it with that. And Amy did seem to be affected by what he had said. They had set off together and as far as Billy was now concerned they would reach The

190

Tunnel together, maybe. But Billy still couldn't understand where this sudden outburst was coming from. A few days ago he was going to The Tunnel alone but Amy had sensed his betrayal and waited for him on the threshold, so why all this now? None of this made any sense to Billy, why Amy would suddenly want to go home this far along. Hell would have to freeze over before he went home. But then looking at Amy, as the cool summer's wind blew rogue pieces of her brown hair across her young pretty face, Billy realised a significant difference here. Amy's parents loved her, and treated her like she was the most precious stone in the world, maybe even like a princess. They talked and went out, shared breakfast and meal times, and watched television programmes together. Billy had never felt as envious of anyone in his entire life as he did of Amy in that moment. He could understand why she wanted to go home, he really could. Maybe he was being a little selfish, or maybe the little voice in the back of his head telling him that if he let Amy go now then he would never see her again, was what spurred him to try to make her stay.

'It's twelve miles back, Amy,' Billy said. 'Do you really want to walk that far alone?'

Amy didn't change her mind. 'I'm sorry, Billy,' she said. 'I have to go home now. My parents will be worried. This is the best thing for me to do, Billy. In the long run, this is the best thing for me to do.'

Best thing? Billy thought.

But Amy was already starting to walk away in the opposite direction.

'But they think you are with me, Amy,' Billy shouted.

Amy carried on walking.

'What about the old man? He had a gun remember. And his dog, you should have seen his dog, Amy. It was horrible.'

Amy carried on walking.

She was moving away quickly and Billy knew he was grabbing at straws trying to get her to stay. He watched on helplessly, feeling like a little piece of him was leaving with Amy, like he was being dragged along the beaten-up track by the scruff of his sun-baked neck.

'Amy,' Billy shouted walking forwards a little. 'Amy, wait.'

She marched on.

'Please don't tell anyone where I am going,' Billy shouted. 'Please don't say anything, Amy ...'

Billy suddenly returned to that time when he had been five again. He was in the supermarket watching his Mummy getting further and further away down one of the aisles. The need to go after her was pulling at his body like an invisible hand, but he stayed put. His legs wanted to run after her, his mouth wanted to call out her name. Nothing happened though. His body was aching again, the need to call out to Amy or run after her was overpowering, but all Billy could do was watch as the distance between the two of them increased. Amy would soon be a speck on the horizon and Billy Cooper would be left all alone again.

Pride can be a strange thing. Perhaps that was what made Billy stand and watch Amy as she got further and further away. There was now about fifty metres between them, Amy didn't even look back once.

The files inside Billy's head would never had told him to say what he was about to say. 2.5: _Boys don't show emotion and all that shit, remember?_

That was obviously an important rule because it had even been underlined. But Billy was not going to speak from his head, or recite some shit he had taught himself over the years that was un-cool for boys to say or do. He was going to speak from the heart.

'AMY!' Billy shouted, running forwards and then stopping, his voice hinting on desperation echoing into nothingness. 'I don't want to do this without my best friend, Amy. If you don't come to The Tunnel then I don't go either.'

Amy stopped and waited. She then very slowly turned

around, her young face looking both lost and afraid. She was crying too.

Billy stayed put, breathing rapidly, like everything now rested on what Amy did next, and counting the heart beats drumming inside his chest.

1,2,3,4,5,6,7,8…

They looked at each another. The day was still, like time had now all together stopped. Billy looked on longingly.

Amy wiped her eyes, and then started walking back. How could she not? She never told Billy this but she considered him family now as well, and she always wanted a brother. But going back was only going to make it harder for them both in the end, and Amy knew this. So too did Billy, but all that mattered to him in that moment in time was where they were going and what it was they had to do, and Amy knew how important it was for Billy to go to The Tunnel, he had to, he simply had to go.

Amy was back. Billy had his hands inside his pockets, nervously swaggering from side to side looking like a drunk, his bag lay by his scuffed trainers.

'What did you say, Billy Cooper?' Amy asked, smiling a little, tears still rolling down her cheeks.

Billy smiled. 'You came back to ask me that?'

Amy's smile widened and she nodded her head, but she had heard him loud and clear the first time.

'Are you coming?' Billy asked tentatively.

Amy smiled. 'After you, Billy Cooper.'

She wiped her eyes again.

And off they went.

4

Monday mornings at school were shit, as Billy would have so elegantly put it. Monday mornings walking along an old railway line weren't much better. The day was warm again and the heat floated up off the road in a hazy dance. After a slight quandary earlier on they were now back on track. Billy still wasn't sure what to make of Amy's little outburst and sudden change of heart from earlier on and didn't really think it mattered now either, Amy was here, and that was all that did.

When he had seen The Tunnel from the platform he had guessed it was one, maybe two miles away tops. But in this heat it was beginning to feel like a lot more. But maybe The Tunnel had been further away than Billy had estimated, it wasn't like anyone had actually walked this far out since the line had been destroyed and survived? That's what Billy thought anyway.

Holy shit!

Billy suddenly had a disconcerting thought. Maybe they were never going to reach The Tunnel. Maybe it was some supernatural place that was always just too far away to reach? Kind of like a watering hole in the desert. Billy soon dismissed that idea, but they must have walked two miles by now, they simply must have.

Amy stopped again and removed her bag from her shoulders. Billy was glad of the break, his mouth felt dry and sweat running down off his brow was beginning to sting his eyes. He wiped his face and had never felt so relieved in his life when he saw Amy holding the bottle of water, even though it did taste a little warm now. Suddenly his senses came alive again, the very thought of a drink seemed like heaven.

'This is all we have left of the water,' Amy said. She handed Billy the bottle. Billy took it without hesitation and gulped the water down. He wiped his mouth afterwards and felt rejuvenated once more.

'Here,' Billy said, handing the bottle to Amy. Amy drank some more then put the bottle back inside her backpack.

'The food should last,' Amy said peering into her bag. 'But we shall have to be careful with the water.'

Billy nodded, not really caring after having a drink. 'We have lemonade, don't we?'

Amy nodded. 'Yes, but I wanted to keep that for the trip back.'

The trip back again…

The bottle of lemonade held two litres, not much really for two people, and also taking into consideration the humidity and that the journey back had not even begun yet.

'We will only drink when we really have to then,' Billy said, once again feeling like he was taking charge.

Amy smiled a little, but her eyes still looked a little red.

Billy thought it was nice to see, the smile.

'What?' he asked, noticing Amy now smiling and shaking her head.

'There's always that water back there,' Amy said.

'No thanks,' Billy said quickly. 'I've already had a stomach full of that crap.'

They shared another moment. It was nice and things were beginning to feel like they once did.

Amy picked up her dusty backpack and then threw it over her shoulders. She flicked her pony-tail back then started walking again. Billy followed.

5

The day was now warmer still. Billy felt the sun burning down on the back of his neck. He wanted another drink. But the water amount, he kept thinking about the water amount. It was low and they would have to ration it. The more he thought about rationing the water though the more he wanted another drink. The thought of that glorious wet liquid touching his dry lips was becoming a distraction. It was a vicious circle. Amy was managing so he was going to have to as well.

Billy and Amy were in mid conversation when they both noticed something they had not seen before up ahead. In fact it was so foreign to this journey that they both stopped. The track, about fifty metres ahead, actually turned a slight bend.

About time, Billy thought.

The sense that this part of their journey was drawing to an end was strong for both of them. It was like spending hours in a car or on a plane only to realise you are about to reach your destination.

'Around the bend,' Billy said, staring off ahead, unaware that his hands were shaking. 'It has to be there.'

Amy felt the chill too.

They carried on …

6

They got closer and closer to the bend, unaware that they were actually slowing down. Both shared an anxious look on more than one occasion and were no longer talking. This was it; this was what they had come for. All the answers Billy had sought lay beyond that bend which seemed a lifetime in coming.

The trees, bushes, everything seemed to pass by in slow motion. Billy focused on the bend whilst listening to his own footsteps that seemed to be getting louder. Amy stayed close by his side. She never said anything but Billy thought he could hear her breathing.

The path narrowed down to fifteen feet, trees and bushes invading it. They were both now walking in darkness, like a solar eclipse was suddenly happening. It really was hard to believe that trains used to operate on this route. There was a rotted wooden gate on the right side of the track, half hanging off its hinges. But at least the forest temporarily blocked out the sun and provided them both with well-needed shade.

Billy thought a huge plane had gone overhead because everything suddenly went dark. Huge shadows stretched out across the path in strange formations. They reached the bend.

The abrasive sounds of shoes walking on rough track abruptly came to an end. Amy and Billy had arrived. Ahead of them, waiting, looking like a huge gaping mouth, was The Tunnel. A steep embankment full of trees and tall grass surrounded it. Billy thought the trees looked like guardians of this place and half expected them to come to life.

They walked slowly, fixated with the entrance up ahead. On top of The Tunnel were more trees and other vegetation. One tree stuck out in particular, overhanging the top of The Tunnel. The black bricks were full of green moss and damp patches. There were cracks in the walls, and some of the archway had crumbled away, leaving behind a rough looking outline that looked like huge teeth. There were sounds of running water and coolness to the air that they had not felt before that was refreshing. It really did look like a place that time had forgotten, lonely and miserable, just as Billy had seen in his dreams. The entrance was roughly twenty feet with a sign hanging at the top that was no longer visible enough to read any more. For the first time, Billy noticed two parallel white lines outlining where the tracks used to be.

They both suddenly shuddered again, the vibe, they both felt the strong vibe The Tunnel was giving off, and it was nasty, malevolent, making them both want to turn tail and run.

A cool wind blew out across their faces and in it Billy heard his name. Something inside the darkness was now watching them, waiting patiently as it had been doing for so long. The

197

hardest part was now over, it had done enough to entice Billy here and it was now time. In the darkness Billy heard his name whispered again, echoing all around. He started walking forwards, towards the entrance. Amy waited; she could go no further. Her face suddenly looked pale and afraid again. She wanted to shout out to Billy but couldn't. Her mouth opened but there was no sound to come out. Something was wrong here, Amy could feel it. She suddenly felt dizzy, like she was floating off the ground. Maybe she wasn't allowed to venture any further, maybe what there was to find inside The Tunnel had to be found by Billy alone. She closed her eyes and collapsed into a heap, going into a darkness of her own.

Looking like he was in some kind of trance, possessed, Billy reached the entrance and went inside, the voice was guiding him and he could do nothing but follow it. He disappeared, splashing up puddles as he went, swallowed up by darkness that seemed never ending.

15

Secret Writing

1

Alex ran his fingers through his black hair. 'I admit, there is something weird going on here, but I am not ready to call in the ghostbusters yet, Katie.'

'Don't make light of this, Alex, don't you dare make light of this.'

That was then, and this was now, Monday afternoon, and Kate Cooper had a plan. Get some clothes together and then go to the hospital to collect Alex. They would then go to The Tunnel together and bring home Billy. It sounded so simple really when she went through the plan inside her head. But Kate Cooper knew that in reality it was going to be like trying to jump a canyon on a push bike.

Kate was a realist and knew it wasn't going to be easy confronting Billy, let alone trying to convince him to come back home. But she would try, she had set out two days ago to fix this family and that was what she intended to do.

Kate had managed to keep a low profile over the past few days. The neighbours were already talking about Alex's incident so she didn't feel like seeing any of them today. She'd had enough of all that when Justin had died. The last thing she wanted today was some nosy bastard trying to get every single sordid detail about what had happened just so it could then be recited inside every gossip circle in town over and over again. Their family had been discussed enough over the past year. And if people found out that Billy had run away too then the gossip mongers really would have something juicy to get their talons into.

Alex had an appointment with Dr Morgan, the hospital shrink, this afternoon, to determine whether Alex was still a danger to himself. He was however, (unknown to the hospital) going to have to miss this appointment because Kate needed him today. Did Kate still think Alex was a danger to himself? The truth was after talking with him over the past two days (which incidentally was the longest conversation they'd had all year) she didn't think so. Alex had fucked up, on more than one occasion, and Kate knew he was aware of this. The only doubt she had now was whether he had it inside of him to fix all of his wrong doings concerning Billy.

It was 2pm when Kate arrived back home from the hospital. It was now time to get things moving. Make some sandwiches, grab some spare clothes then go back to the hospital and collect Alex. Neither one of them had reached a satisfactory conclusion regarding the drawings and probably never would. Kate had considered the possibility that something had made Billy venture to The Tunnel and that that something may not want him to leave once he was there. But she would worry about that if and when the need arose. Kate still wasn't sure whether she believed in the supernatural, but when this was all over she would feel differently. There was a force at work here, there always had been, and it was no longer lying dormant between worlds. Billy knew about it, and soon enough Kate and Alex would too.

Kate parked at the top of the driveway then ran to the door. George Capall, their neighbour, was in because his car was parked so she didn't waste any time letting herself inside the house. George was a little too inquisitive for his own good at times. Kate liked him, sometimes, but the guy had this interfering way about him that sometimes gave Kate the urge to want to slap his shiny bald head over and over again.

Inside the house Kate ran to her bedroom to get some clothes for Alex. The house felt very cool today. She grabbed a blue bag from out of her wardrobe and then put Alex's clothing along with some spare clothes of her own inside the bag. Kate knew The Tunnel was a fair old trek by foot but Alex reckoned he knew a short cut. He had told her that if they drove straight up the A508 to Northampton then they would eventually pass The Tunnel on the way, and apparently two miles after that there was a beaten-up track that would then take them to the other side of it. That sounded good, because if Billy was planning to press on once he reached The Tunnel – then maybe, just maybe they could cut him off at the other side. Kate knew that would be a long shot, but if they acted quickly, then maybe, maybe … And at the moment if this was all she had to hold onto, then fine.

Kate picked up the bag and walked out of the bedroom. She closed the door then proceeded to walk down the hallway that led back into the kitchen. She passed Billy's room on the way, and then for some reason, felt the urge to suddenly stop. Not knowing why, Kate dropped the bag and peered inside his room.

The room felt cool, cooler still than the rest of the house. The curtains were still closed just like they had been for the past couple of days. The room smelt musky and old, like someone had been sleeping in there for days without any fresh air getting in. Kate slowly looked around the room, still not knowing why it had grabbed her attention. Her eyes wandered over everything then suddenly she saw it. She had been warm earlier on but now goose pimples rose on her arms making her shudder. It was cold, it was really cold, and Kate Cooper watched on not quite believing what she was seeing.

2

The notepad rose up into the air like it was suspended on invisible wires. Kate watched, her eyes burning with denial. This wasn't happening, it just couldn't be. She blinked, blinked again, and looked on not accepting what was still happening in front of her. The curtains blew inwards and Kate caught an ice cold breeze across her face. She shuddered, wanted to run, knew that was the right thing to do, but this was unlike anything she had ever seen before and she was strangely intrigued. She just had to watch.

The room was now so cold she could see her own breath in front of her. Kate was still watching the notepad which then opened all by itself, the pages making a flickering sound. She heard a tapping sound and looked down at Billy's desktop. A pen was moving across the top of it floating about an inch in the air. The clip of the pen occasionally dipped and tapped the wooden desk. Kate simply shook her head in disbelief then moved her hands up over her face as the pen floated through the air and stopped next to the blank paper of the hovering notepad.

The pen clicked and started writing on the sheet of paper. The invisible hand worked quickly, writing a message intended for Kate to see. She studied the message, trying to read it, but couldn't. Whatever was writing it was writing the message backwards. The force didn't have much time now, Billy had now reached The Tunnel and was inside.

The faint scribbling sound of pen writing against paper then stopped. Kate looked at the message, still not able to read it. The pad and pen then dropped down onto Billy's bed. Kate gasped as they did this, stepped back a little too, her eyes shining bright. She was scared and intrigued at the same time. The cold breeze she felt moving across her face then passed by, making her shudder again. Kate could have sworn that she had felt a hand touching her shoulder, knocking her out of the way so something could leave. She heard two words as the presence passed her by. And it was somebody's name. The room and house then returned to normal temperature.

Kate wanted to go over to the pad to see what was written but couldn't. She dropped to the floor and leant back against the bedroom door and sobbed like a child.

3

After Kate had stopped crying she slowly got back to her feet. She didn't really know whether she had cried because she was scared or that fact that some supernatural force had whispered a name she knew so well. But what had just happened could not be simply dismissed. There was a world outside the one she saw every day, and there were forces inside it that had a will of their own. It was looking more and more feasible that Billy was in danger, which made Kate want to get to him even more. Was it even an accident that she happened to be inside the house the very moment that some supernatural being decided to communicate? Kate didn't think so. Whatever was seducing Billy towards The Tunnel, and whether it meant him any harm or not, had just left a message for Kate to read.

Kate took a couple of steps towards the bed, her legs suddenly feeling like they were made out of rubber. She reached the bed and had to steady herself so she didn't collapse down onto it. She then reached forwards with a hand that was still shaking. The cover of the pad had closed again so she could not see what was written. She took two long deep breaths then picked up the notepad. She steadied herself again before opening the pad, trying to prepare herself for what the message might say. Could it be a message about Billy, could it be telling her that he is −

'NO!'

After she was ready Kate Cooper turned the cover over and looked at the words.

> Leave him alone. You
> must leave him alone
> The truth is his to find.

Kate couldn't read the words. If she really wanted to then she could have deciphered the message backwards but there wasn't enough time for that. With the pad in her right hand she ran to the bathroom.

4

Kate stood in front of the mirror and slowly raised the pad. After she had read the words in her head she then had to read them aloud too. She was hoping this would help her make better sense of them.

> Leave him alone. You
> must leave him alone.
> The truth is his to find.

Kate didn't understand what the 'Truth' part was about but she now understood the message. Something wanted her to stay away and let Billy find The Tunnel and what was inside there, waiting for him. She then remembered the name she had heard the spirit whispering to her as it had left the room and suddenly started realising what this was all about. Could it really be? She was then forced to make the hardest choice of her life. She was going to have to leave her son to an uncertain fate.

16

The Tunnel

1

When Amy opened her eyes Billy was gone. She had to find him now so didn't have the time to process what had just happened to her. She fainted, so what? It wasn't the first time she had ever done so, and on a day as warm as this one who could have blamed her? But there was another possibility that she hardly dared consider. Perhaps she was not allowed to pass into The Tunnel, maybe she had come as far as she was allowed. Where did that leave her, and more importantly where did that leave Billy? Amy shuddered to think about it.

She got to her feet and dusted herself down. The Tunnel was not twenty metres in front of her and Billy was inside there somewhere, lost in the darkness.

She slowly walked forward.

A noise, like a bird screeching, made Amy look up. It had been loud, almost deliberately making her look. The trees on top of The Tunnel were where her gaze rested, and on one in particular. Amy stopped, her eyes fixed on the lifeless body dangling from the rope. At first she thought it was Billy and almost screamed out for him. But it wasn't Billy. The pale looking corpse, wearing blue faded jeans and scruffy brown top was Kyle Jacob, the boy who had hung himself. His head was drooping to the side, looking like a dead flower, and his eyes were open, staring at the ground below. Amy could hear the rope snagging in the wind, gently swaying Kyle Jacob's lifeless body side to side like a giant pendulum. His eyes bulged out, as if the force of the rope tightening around his neck was enough to pop them out of their sockets. Amy watched, almost hypnotised by the gentle swaying motion of the man's body that had apparently committed suicide many years ago. Hadn't it been twenty or so years ago now? So why was Amy seeing him right now? She didn't want to see, that much she was sure of, and only hoped the train that eventually came along and popped him like a balloon would not appear as well.

Tentatively, Amy continued towards the entrance, keeping her eyes fixed on the swaying body above. The body occasionally banged into the crumbling side walls of The Tunnel, sending down tiny dust particles, moved from side to side, and even spun around, making the corpse look like it was doing some kind of mid-air dancing routine. There was a dripping sound coming from within The Tunnel that Amy could hear also. The closer she got the more she wished Billy was with her. She stopped in the entrance and peered through the darkness. It felt cold and damp, and the cool vacuum made her eyes water, forcing her to step back a little.

Right now seemed like a good time to get the torch out but Amy suddenly realised she had left her backpack lying on the ground next to where she had collapsed. She quickly ran back, trying not to look at the body as she went. But it was impossible, like when there is an accident on the road and a car is lying in a ditch, you don't want to look but that little bit of curiosity always makes you.

Kyle Jacob was still swinging in the wind, dangling from an old rope that looked like it could break at any moment. Amy noticed his eyes were now looking at her. He had been staring at the ground before, she was sure of this, but it now seemed the position of his head had shifted, moved upwards so he

206

could get a better look at her. Amy watched nervously as she slowly walked back to the entrance to the cave (she no longer thought of it as a tunnel any more) waiting for any movement to come from Kyle. His gaze had definitely shifted again.

She told herself quite firmly that she was just imagining the whole thing, and looked away from Kyle. She had no time to waste contemplating whether a dead body was moving or not, especially when her best friend might be in danger. Then something happened that made Amy temporarily forget Billy. There was no denying she heard it, and it made her flesh crawl.

'Amy...'

The voice hissed her name slowly.

Amy stopped dead. It was Kyle Jacob saying her name.

Holy shit!

'Amy ... Look at me, Amy...'

Amy quickly looked up at the swaying corpse. Not wanting to, but again that little bit of curiosity winning through.

Kyle Jacob's head was indeed moving, even though the rope was so tight around his neck that it was now more like a small waist with a corset on. And his black eyes, full of nothingness, were now firmly fixed on Amy, his pale, purple blotchy skin strangely coming back to life.

'Why are you here, Amy?'

Amy was scared, but tried ignoring the swinging corpse, and kept on telling herself that she was only imaging it all, but she wasn't, and deep down she knew this. The pale swinging corpse, with the black eyes and pale skin, wearing the same old clothes it had been killed in, really was there.

'Answer me, Amy,' the voice hissed again. 'You must answer me. Bad things can happen to people in there, Amy. Your friend, Billy, he has crossed the boundary, and only the dead can walk there, Amy. Must he now become one of them?'

Amy shook her head from side to side and then sent the

207

dangling corpse a piercing look. Surprisingly enough, especially for Amy, she didn't feel at all afraid any more, as if the very idea of something threatening to hurt Billy, living or dead, was enough to make her tap into a hidden strength and bravery she didn't know she had.

'You are dead, Kyle Jacob,' Amy said firmly, still looking at the swinging corpse. 'You are not real, and you must leave this place now.' Her voice was powerful, commanding. 'You are released … go now, I send you on your way.'

Kyle Jacob's eyes widened and the blackness there seemed to spread, dripping down and covering his pale blotchy face, like thick tar, and some of it even started falling down to the ground, next to Amy's beaten-up shoes.

'Tell me why you are here, Amy,' he hissed again, his lips never actually moving when he spoke, just a terrifyingly piercing stare was all he delivered. 'Why have you come here with Billy Cooper? What business have you here? This is my place, my keep, as forever it shall be. You must leave.'

'Our business is our business, spirit,' Amy said, her voice just as authoritative. 'Now leave … I command you.'

'Tell me … Amy, what does he seek inside there? Why has the young one come here to my realm?'

'Kyle Jacob, now hear me,' Amy said, her voice now like thunder, echoing down the valley and over the surrounding landscape. 'You are released from this place. Now go home and leave this place forever, never to come back again.'

The dangling corpse gave Amy a burning look of anger and frustration then very slowly disappeared into the fading day. The noose, that had been around his neck then dropped to the ground, and turned to dust next to Amy's scuffed trainers.

'Rest in peace, Kyle Jacob,' Amy said, finally looking at the ground.

She swallowed hard, not quite understanding where her sudden strength had just come from. It was all down to Billy though. She had to help Billy. Whether she had really seen Kyle Jacob or not was now irrelevant to her. He was gone, for the time being, but Billy was still inside The Tunnel and all alone in there. With the torch in her right hand she ran over to the entrance as fast as her little legs could carry her.

2

Inside The Tunnel, Amy was lost even with the torch on. There was no light at the other end which meant this tunnel had at least one bend. Billy could be anywhere by now.

'Billy!'

Her voice echoed into the darkness.

'Tell me where you are, Billy?'

Amy could hear faint footsteps, they weren't hers because she was not moving any more. She shone the torch ahead and waited. There, a splash of water, someone or something was definitely moving around.

She slowly moved the torchlight over the walls. Some of the black bricks had damp patches and vast green moss all over them. She then moved the torch upwards, highlighting some of the roof. It was about twenty feet up. Weeds had broken through some of the structure, looping around like spaghetti. Water was also dripping down making little tapping sounds as it hit the ground. Further up Amy noticed some of the structure had come away, leaving behind a huge gaping hole. There was rubble directly below so Amy assumed it had collapsed many years ago. Probably one of the reasons why the line had closed, Amy thought. She shouted out Billy's name one more time and waited. There was no reply. She walked on.

Even with the torch Amy's vision was limited. It was just so dark, and what little light she had was not powerful enough to penetrate it. The ground below felt rough, Amy shone the torch down. There was broken glass, rocks and small stones, she had to be careful not to trip or go over onto her ankle. She treaded carefully though, like she was walking over a minefield. A quick look over her shoulder told her that she had walked a fair way in. The light from the archway looked like a portal leading off into another world. She still couldn't see any light at the other end and started thinking that maybe there wasn't an end, or at least one she could escape through. Maybe the other end had been caved in for some reason, sealed off completely. Amy felt even more disorientated the further she walked inside, having no idea of the length or width of it. And to make matters worse her eyes were not adjusting to the darkness like she had hoped they would have by now. She looked back over her shoulder again. The opening was getting smaller still, a mere speck of light now. Suddenly she thought of something horrible that made her want to run back.

Please don't cave in as well, she thought. *Please give us some chance.*

There was no way she would leave Billy in here though. If the entrance did cave in then they would find another way out.

How is Billy even seeing where he is going?

Amy mostly kept the torch aimed at the ground. It really was awkward walking on stones and rocks, grinding together as she stepped onto them.

'Billy!' she shouted again. Her voice echoed, lost in the darkness, but there was still no reply. She kept close to the left side, sometimes catching her arm on the damp cool wall. Amy shone the torch on the wall and could see streams of water dripping down, looking like tears.

The Tunnel felt strange, like she was in some kind of bad dream, Amy half expected the walls to start moving in, splattering her like a bug before she had the chance to escape. It was all very surreal. She and Billy had talked so much about this place over the past couple of months. The horrible stories associated with it, Kyle Jacob's suicide for one, and not forgetting ghosts and monsters that stalked the track at night, living inside here during the days. And now, to be actually standing inside a place that they had only talked about so much in the safety of their homes, talks that often resulted in at least one of them having a sleepless night, really was like a living nightmare for her.

'BILLY!'

Amy heard footsteps and the splashing of water again so stopped. She shone the torch around again, hoping to find Billy. The steps echoed all around her, she wasn't sure whether they were in front or behind, at the sides or even on the roof.

'Is that you, Billy?' Amy shouted.

The footsteps speeded up this time. Amy spun around, shining the torch off in all directions.

'Billy!'

The footsteps continued, so did the sound of dripping water.

The Tunnel felt cooler now, like a huge air conditioner. Amy leaned back against the wall, desperately looking from side to side, the torch her only defence against the looming darkness.

'Billy!'

No reply ...

'Please, Billy, answer me!'

There was nothing again, only the sounds of water dripping from all around her and the occasional sound of the wind howling.

'Billy Cooper!'

The light of the torch made a shield against the wall, slowly moving across it, and it was then that Amy saw him. And it was then that the torch went out. The darkness lunged forward, no light now to keep it at bay. It swallowed Amy completely. She was now gone, lost somewhere in a place that only existed for them.

3

Billy had no choice other than to go inside. He saw the figure standing there just like he had done in his dreams and visions. It was nothing new, except this was no dream or vision, this was now a reality. The ghostly apparition stood in the opening of The Tunnel, enticing him to enter, calling out his name in the wind.

Billy knew Amy had collapsed, and wanted to help, but the pull coming from The Tunnel had made it impossible for him to go any other way other than forwards. A powerful wind had pressed him forwards and towards the opening, whether he wanted to go or not.

The figure standing in front of the darkness looked different from before. Billy only caught a quick glimpse of the man before he disappeared into the shadows, but there was something different this time … something that felt, well, familiar. Leaving Amy outside, he entered, following a ghost that might wish him harm.

The Tunnel felt cold, Billy shuddered as he looked into the darkness. But ahead of him was a light, more of a white glow really, and it was coming from the ghost that had been waiting for him inside this place. He followed the eerie glow into the darkness.

They walked for some time. There was a bend up ahead that the ghost led them both around. It never turned around or spoke, but Billy did. He was starting to feel more like himself now, the trance the spirit had held him in was probably just to make sure he entered The Tunnel alone, but now that grip was releasing, and Billy had questions.

'Who are you?' Billy asked, trying to keep up.

No answer.

'Why did you want me to come here?'

Still no answer still.

Billy got the impression that it didn't matter how many

times he asked questions this other-worldly being was not going to answer any of them until it was ready. They were obviously going to some place deep within the confines of The Tunnel and then maybe the spirit would explain everything. The strange thing was that Billy was always afraid in his dreams. There was an air of tragedy that always felt so close by, the feeling that something was wrong had been overpowering. This was different though. Now inside, Billy didn't feel afraid of the strange being or of The Tunnel like he always assumed he would have been. Perhaps there never really was anything to be frightened of. Maybe Billy had created the monsters and demons all by himself. Nothing is ever what it seems and this was no exception, or maybe the strange being was just leading Billy into a false sense of security? But the thing in front that Billy was following, leading him to a place that had probably not been visited in years, was real, and the more Billy tried to convince himself that none of this was really happening the stronger his belief in it grew. And another thing, Billy was only aware of his own footsteps echoing around the walls, the thing in front was floating. Billy then thought about Amy, the journey, everything they had been through to come this far. Was it all going to be worth while? Billy hoped so, he really did.

A glance over his shoulder told Billy that they had walked a long way through The Tunnel. The entrance was no longer visible, nor was the end; just a void of black nothingness surrounded him.

What am I going to find?

That thought scared Billy, arms reaching out through the darkness, fingers trying to grab at his dirty clothes and pulling him into some place from which he was never going to return. What else was watching him in the darkness? The ghost in front couldn't be the only one that haunted this place. Billy hoped it was. He followed closely.

The glowing figure in front eventually stopped and turned

around to face Billy. Billy stopped, every hair on his body standing up on end like he had just been jolted with electricity. Billy got a better look at the ghost. The pale round face, partially hidden, Billy noticed that first. It was cold looking, like touching it would cause you to shake violently, and eyes that looked lost, like nothing was really behind them. The face was expressionless, purple lips slightly parted but not trying to speak. Billy looked on, not really knowing what to do, and had no files inside his head to tell him what to do when encountering supernatural beings.

Billy would have to look away soon. The glow emitting from the being was beginning to hurt his eyes. The last time Billy had seen this ghost it was dressed in old clothes, now it wore a clean slick black suit, it really did look like a walking corpse, something that had just been buried but decided there was some unfinished business to attend to first so arose from the grave. Billy half expected to see insects crawling all over it, making a nest inside its facial features. The ghost pointed to a door. Was this why it had stopped where it did? But why bring him this far then not allow him to find what he had come for? Billy had to open the door he just had to, but the being was not moving.

The metal door looked old and rusted, only flakes of paint remained, faded with time. Would it even open? Billy reckoned so. It must have been used by the workers on the lines. Maybe it was some kind of storage room or just a place where the workers ate and relaxed in between shifts. But unless Billy got the ghost to move out of the way he was never going to find out who or what was behind the door.

'Why did you bring me here?' Billy asked.

The cold expression of the ghost never changed, lips remained parted and eyes still hiding something.

'Please tell me,' Billy said. 'I have come so far. What do you want with me?'

'Nothing,' the ghost said. 'I ask nothing of you, mortal. What could you possibly have to give?'

The voice was deep and pitiless, sounding as cold as the ghost looked. But the fact that it spoke Billy thought was a good thing. In fact he had been so surprised to hear it speaking he had flinched and stepped backwards so quickly he had almost tripped over some debris on the ground next to him, as if the cold voice of the ghost had shot out and attacked him.

'Why did you speak to me in my dreams then?' Billy asked tentatively. 'Please, tell me. I need to know.'

Billy was well aware that his voice sounded weak and his body was trembling. It was cold inside The Tunnel, but not that cold.

'I am a messenger for the mortal world,' the ghost explained.

'A messenger?'

The being nodded slowly. 'And my message is simple,' it continued. 'But you have to face up to your past first, before I can give it to you.'

Billy was confused, lost. This was bullshit, and to make matters worse, cryptic bullshit.

'I don't understand,' Billy said.

'Demons, Billy Cooper. I cannot let you pass until you release your demons.'

The being then showed Billy what it was talking about. It sent images inside his head making him watch what he never wanted to see ever again.

4

It was a test, it had to be …

The ghost from his dreams, the one that had made him draw The Tunnel was now standing in front of him, but why?

Billy was no longer just watching the images he was part of them, living them. He was no longer inside The Tunnel either. This place was bright, warm and welcoming. Billy looked around as the day slowly moved around him. The trees, fencing, grass, birds singing, cloudless beautiful blue sky with golden sun, Billy had once again stepped back in time to a place when time didn't seem to matter any more. He knew where he was, and knew what was going to happen next, and the painful thing was there was nothing he could do but watch.

'Demons, Billy,' the unfriendly voice spoke again inside his head. 'How can you expect them to move on when you cannot?'

Billy looked around inside this new world, trying to follow the voice. It erupted from the skies like thunder yet he was here all by himself.

'Stop,' Billy screamed up at the heavens. 'I can't see this again.'

'But you must,' the voice erupted again. 'If they are to be forgotten and moved on then so must you, Billy.'

The world suddenly started spinning as if it had been speeded up. Scenery went by in white flashes guiding Billy to where his demons lived.

Billy smelt the freshness of the water before he saw it. The lake glistened underneath the hot sun like a carpet of precious diamonds. Billy waited patiently by the shore, looking at the wooden bridge on his right. There was nothing he could do now but watch. The ghost that wanted him to see this from the other side knew this was the only way, his demons, their demons, could be exorcised.

The water touched Billy's shoes and soaked through to his feet. The car then appeared and tears started streaming down his face. He was forced to watch the most painful moment in his life all over again.

The peace and tranquillity of the summer's day was soon

broken by Billy's screams of anguish and terror. How could this be happening again? The red car appeared on the bridge as it had done almost a year ago now. The car swerved aggressively, smoke pouring out of the tyres as Justin tried regaining control. His efforts would be as hopeless as they had been before.

'Please,' Billy cried out. 'Do something to help us.'

But nothing could be done.

The screeching of rubber grew louder and Billy thought he heard a voice from the past crying out from inside the car, his voice. He watched as Justin wrestled with the car, watching through the eyes of his past self. The side of the bridge appeared, bigger and bigger inside the windshield. Billy looked at Justin, but not just the Billy sitting inside the car. The present day Billy saw it all, he saw Justin flinching then quickly and unselfishly removing his seatbelt and shielding Billy with his body.

'No!' present day Billy protested. 'Don't undo your seatbelt!'

But even though present day Billy was seeing Justin and also seeing past life Billy, neither one of them could actually hear what he was shouting out to them.

'Please!' present day Billy screamed. 'Justin please, I don't want you to die for me!'

The car ploughed through the wooden fence leaving little splinters on the road and floating on the water's surface. It was then that Billy returned to his own body and watched as the car steadily sank to the bottom. He tried to get into the water but that was a boundary he could not pass, even in this world there were rules. He could not interfere with past events.

Billy watched the car vanishing underneath the water with eyes that were now cloudy with tears. This pain was new, like a deep wound almost bleeding him from the inside out.

'Justin,' he shouted out, pulling at his shirt in despair and then falling to his knees. 'Please don't leave me ... JUSTIN!'

His voice echoed out across the lake, birds took flight from the trees. 'Someone please save my brother.'

But Justin had made his choice, and chose to give his life to save Billy's because it was his to give. He chose to save his brother. It was his free will.

As the car disappeared from view Billy was in hysterics, never feeling so useless and powerless in his life. But in the back of his mind he started understanding why he was here again. Then a slow rumbling, sounding like it was coming from the sky, made him take notice. He wiped his eyes and watched. He never understood what saved him that day and why. Billy Cooper then found out.

He saw his own body lying on the shore looking like a shipwrecked survivor. He had seen all he needed to see and now everything was beginning to make sense. Looking back it probably always did. But guilt is a funny thing and had played a big factor in Billy concealing, perhaps not seeing what had always been there right in front of him.

He needed to return now, back to The Tunnel and to find Amy. He had to tell her what he had found out. Jesus Christ, Amy. He had left her all on her own. How long had it been since he had last seen her? Did she even know where he was?

'Please take me back,' Billy said, sniffling and wiping his red puffy eyes. 'I have to find my friend, Amy.'

'You wish to go back?' the voice like thunder asked.

'I do,' Billy said with confidence.

'And with the cross you still bear, you shall return, mortal.'

The daylight slowly faded into a lost and lonely darkness again, soft grass replaced with hard rock. The warmth of the sun replaced with cold air that immediately made Billy shudder. He was back inside The Tunnel again. The strange ghost, with hypnotic glow still stood in front of the metal door.

Billy wanted to enter the doorway, but needed to go back for Amy first. They had come together and whatever he was going to find behind that door he wanted Amy to find it with him. He knew she would be in no danger, if this ghost wanted him dead then he would be dead already. Plus the fact he wanted Amy to see it. This was, after all, a real-life ghost, and would definitely be something to tell their grandchildren about. And the strange thing was he wasn't even afraid any more. Billy Cooper had spent the best part of the last year being afraid. He had lost his brother, his family ripped to shreds like a piece of tissue paper. What was there really left to be afraid of? Billy had forgotten one thing.

5

The Gate Keeper waited by the door, the glow pulsating up the cold damp walls. It was here because of Billy and had been responsible for bringing him. There was a reason why it had guided Billy to this place and that reason lay beyond the metal door. The Gate Keeper looked malevolent but was not. The being simply bridged the gap between both worlds, the one Billy could see and the one he only dreamed existed. It was merely a communication device, a conduit that brought the unseen world and mortal world together. The Gate Keeper could perform this act anywhere. It wasn't just inside The Tunnel. The being existed everywhere, and could appear everywhere. There was nothing magical about The Tunnel, there never was, it just so happened something of significance had happened there, and Billy was meant to discover it.

The Gate Keeper would not let Billy pass until he had cleansed himself. To do this he would have to exorcise all of his demons. Billy's demon was guilt about Justin. Nothing came without a price, and even though this strange new being Billy was seeing was powerful, it still had others to answer to. Billy would not be able to enter the doorway until he was cleansed. Those were the rules, and they could not be broken. The Gate Keeper knew all about Billy, and by playing back his fears he realised the boy was still not clear of guilt. Guilt his father had placed solely on his shoulders. But to move on, like Billy only hoped his family could, he would first have to forgive himself. Then the hard work could begin, and the cleansing too, for his family.

The Gate Keeper had made a deal, bring Billy here and allow him to find what had been left behind. But for that to happen, Billy would first have to give up something he had been clinging to. The Gate Keeper knew too many rules had been broken for this mortal already, so something would have to be passed back. It was all a question of keeping the balance between the worlds.

'You are not going to let me pass, are you?' Billy asked, sniffling, and wiping his eyes.

The Gate Keeper did not speak, didn't have to. But still Billy understood very clearly the answer given.

'Why allow me to come this far, why show me what you have shown me only to stop me here?'

'I cannot help you any more,' the Gate Keeper spoke in the same low level tone that made Billy flinch.

'Help me? How have you helped me?'

'You have been helped in many ways, Billy Cooper,' the Gate Keeper said. 'The rules can no longer be swayed for you.'

Billy, even surprising himself, suddenly felt rage boiling up inside his stomach, beginning to erupt like a volcano.

'This is bullshit!' Billy shouted looking for some kind of reaction. 'How have you helped me? My life is a mess. My brother is dead, my parents don't know I exist. The only person I have is Amy. She has helped me, not you.'

'Your memory is as short as your tongue,' the Gate Keeper said sharply.

'Bullshit!' Billy shouted again. 'That's what this is. You –'

'BILLY COOPER!' the Gate Keeper bellowed, stopping

220

him before he could finish. Billy suddenly felt his legs turning to jelly, and any confidence he was amounting against this thing slipped through his fingers like sand on a windswept beach.

The Gate Keeper moved forwards, not by walking but floating. It entered Billy's mind, again flooding it with images. Billy closed his eyes, but there was no escaping what he was about to see.

He was back by the side of the busy road again. Amy had left earlier on and Billy was about to perform the final act. It wasn't something he had planned or even thought about doing until today. Billy Cooper used to love life, and the thought of suicide was as far off in his mind as old age would be to a child. But circumstances change, people change and Billy Cooper was being played and guided by his fear and guilt. He just wanted it all to be over, and to stop constantly being reminded of how he had failed his brother and allowed him to die every time he looked his father in the eye. He felt like his parents both hated him, and blamed him for Justin's death. This was the only way out he could see, and the only way he could earn his parent's forgiveness. A life for a life, right, isn't that how it should be? Yes, The Tunnel no longer seemed that important.

Billy watched on, now feeling everything he had felt back then. He heard the cars, smelt the fumes from the exhausts. It was the same. He waited for a suitable gap in the traffic. This was it, the final jump, then it would all be over. His parents would be glad he was dead, and he would be glad not to feel anymore.

Billy could see the headlights of the car as he stepped out in front of it. He wasn't thinking about the driver in that moment, he wasn't even thinking about Amy, he wasn't thinking about anything. But as he stepped off the pavement and into the path of the oncoming saloon that would have had no chance in hell of stopping in time, Billy saw it. The figure was standing on the opposite side of the road, watching him. Billy heard the car tyres screeching as he looked up at the figure that he had seen so many times before, but only in dreams and visions. That had been his first assumption, that what he was experiencing was a delayed vision, that maybe he was just day-dreaming again?

Billy Cooper looked on, still hearing the car tyres gripping against the Tarmac and a horn blasting for him to move out of the way. He didn't even turn to look at the car that was about to hit him, he was too transfixed with the ghostly apparition on the other side of the road. There was a glow around it, just off the surface of its clothes. The being slowly shook its head, as if displaying total disgust at what Billy was doing, and then vanished as quickly as it had appeared.

It was then that Billy turned to face the oncoming car that was about to seal his fate. The headlamps looked like huge eyes blazing at him in the fading light. Billy closed his eyes hoping it wasn't going to hurt too much.

Billy had only fainted once before in his life. It was when he was ten years old and having the TB jab. He'd always assumed that he didn't have any qualms as far as needles went, but he had been wrong. As soon as the nurse raised the needle, and aimed it towards Billy's left arm it was good night Vienna. His head felt light, like there had been nothing inside it but cotton wool. Then his legs turned to rubber, it really was the strangest of sensations. It was like his body was suddenly crashing, like a computer would, every-thing firing up in the wrong sequence. But the oddest sensation he remembered was the feeling of floating. It was like he was being lifted off the floor and floating upwards towards the clouds. That was the feeling Billy felt again when he closed his eyes, waiting for the car to destroy his little body that was yet to experience so much. The feeling of floating was as real as the smell of burning rubber and fumes in the night air. He was somewhere in the darkness, perhaps between worlds, but was safe. And when he opened his eyes again Billy Cooper had been standing in front of his front door like nothing had ever happened. The memory of what he tried to do was still as fresh in his mind as a summer flower, but the strange circumstances of how he had survived made him question so much more. Billy Cooper had been given another chance, and it hadn't been the first.

The Gate Keeper floated away.

'Now you understand,' the Gate Keeper said, still moving backwards towards the metal door. 'You have more people on your side than you think, Billy Cooper.'

'Why?' Billy asked, not being able to look away from the strange being in front of him.

'Why?' The Gate Keeper repeated, sounding like it was confused by Billy's question. 'Why save a mortal who did not wish to be saved?'

Billy thought about that question. Was that true? Did he really want to die? The answer was yes. But if he had then everything would have been lost. He would have been lost, his family would have been lost, and Justin's sacrifice would have all been for nothing. That's what this was really all about. Justin had given his life for Billy. It was his choice to make and he made it without hesitation. Billy was special, Justin had known that, and one day Billy would understand it too.

'Yes,' Billy said, not quite believing the answer slipped off his tongue so easily.

The Gate Keeper deliberated. 'The dream, the visions, everything led you to this place, Billy Cooper. Justin has a message for you ... That is why I spared you. And your brother's sacrifice would have been all for nothing if I had allowed it to pass. So now you understand?'

'Yes,' Billy said softly, suddenly seeing the bigger picture here.

Hearing Justin's name, hearing that he had a message from beyond the grave stopped Billy dead. He needed time to process this. The question of whether this was all some fucked up day-dream had now passed. This was really happening and the thought that Justin was behind it all made Billy want to cry. It was all down to Justin then. The Gate Keeper, a conduit between worlds, had a message from his hero.

He wanted his brother back more than anything now. There was so much he never got to say to Justin. Billy never thought people got second chances like this.

'My brother is here?' Billy asked hoarsely, trying to fight back his tears, and ignore the lump forming in the back of his throat.

'Your worlds will always be linked,' the Gate Keeper said. 'And now that you understand, and now that you see what was never your cross to bear, you must hear the message Justin left for you.'

The Gate Keeper stepped away from the door. The way was now clear, but Billy had not noticed. He had been too busy thinking about Justin, and what the Gate Keeper had told him. He wiped his eyes.

'My brother was here?' Billy asked. 'He had been to this place?'

It was then that Billy heard Amy calling out his name. She was close and Billy ran to her.

Billy could see Amy's torch bouncing around The Tunnel like a luminous ball. He ran to her, hearing her calling out his name, echoing down the huge tunnel. When he finally reached her, the light went out.

6

Billy had so much he wanted to tell Amy about, but he didn't know where to begin. It was one of those situations where he had to steady himself, and to think before he spoke otherwise he would have talked so quickly and mumbled and Amy wouldn't have understood a word he said.

'Come on,' Billy said, holding Amy's hand and leading her through the darkness. They stayed close to the wall, and Billy was hoping that he would see that all too familiar glow soon, he would then know where the door was.

'Billy, wait,' Amy said, finding his enthusiasm a little overwhelming. 'What have you been doing all this time?'

Billy stopped and turned to Amy. He could just make out the outline of her eyes. 'With the Gate Keeper,' Billy said in a casual like tone that suggested everybody had heard of the Gate Keeper before. 'Now let's go.'

'How do we know this Gate Keeper is on our side?'

'I don't know,' Billy said. 'He just is.'

'Billy … I saw Kyle Jacob outside, he spoke to me.'

'Where?' Billy asked, suddenly interested.

'Swinging from the tree he hung himself from some twenty years ago.'

'He spoke to you?'

'Yes.'

It was so dark that Billy and Amy felt like they were having a conversation with each other with their eyes closed.

'I'm sorry, Amy,' Billy said. 'I didn't mean to leave you on your own. But I guess we have both seen a ghost now.'

Amy wasn't too worried about that. She had handled that swinging corpse without too much bother, but what she did find a little weird was that Billy never even questioned her on having a conversation with a boy who had killed himself so many years ago. He passed it off as simply as one does when told it might rain tomorrow.

'Are you ready?'

Amy didn't answer straight away. The Gate Keeper, she didn't like the sound of that. Was it keeping something in or out? Amy wondered.

'Billy,' Amy said in her most untrusting tone, 'I believe you saw this ghost, I really do. But why should we trust it? I mean, what is a Gate Keeper anyway?'

'Simple,' Billy said. 'Justin sent him.'

'Pardon?'

'Justin, Amy,' Billy said. 'The Gate Keeper is a messenger between worlds. Justin sent him to me because he has a message for me.'

'Why didn't Justin come himself?' Amy asked, sounding suspicious.

'I don't think it works like that,' Billy said. 'The Gate Keeper has to know you are worthy of the message first.'

'I don't understand,' Amy said.

'You will,' Billy said confidently. 'Come on.'

They made their way through The Tunnel, staying as close to the right wall as they could. The bricks felt cool against their skin. Billy slid his free hand across the bricks, feeling for the door. He tripped a couple of times, despite the torch, so did Amy, but they were almost there. There was no glow further down The Tunnel. The Gate Keeper had gone, for the time being, but would be back.

'Wait,' Billy said.

Amy stopped, still holding his hand.

The blind leading the blind, she thought.

Billy slid his hand over a surface that was too smooth to be mortar. He knocked on it, like he would have on a neighbour's door.

Metal!

'This is it,' Billy said. 'We are here.'

'Where's The Gate Keeper?' Amy asked, shining the torch on the door.

Billy didn't answer her question, he didn't care. The only thing that concerned him now was getting behind that door. And by the looks of things that was going to be yet another challenge in a short life that so far had been full of them. And it was then that the torchlight faded, but Billy's desire to get beyond the door remained.

17

Leaving Behind

1

Justin had a message from beyond the grave, that much Billy now knew. He also knew that Justin had used the Gate Keeper to summon him here so he could pass on that message, which told Billy another thing too. If he could only find what Justin had for him here inside The Tunnel, then Justin must have been here before, but why? Billy could only speculate.

'What if it won't open?' Billy asked.

'You won't know until you try,' Amy replied.

'I guess not,' Billy said, still with his hand on the cold catch.

It was one of those old locking mechanisms where a bolt had to be pulled down to release the catch. It all rested on this then. In the end everything came down to a rusty old door catch. The visions, the dreams that had made Billy cry sometimes, the long walk that had been anything but easy, everything rested on this rusted brown door. Amy was right however, there was no use assuming the door wouldn't open, but still Billy thought it wouldn't.

'Billy!' Amy said; her voice full of authority, strong again, like it had been when she had spoken to Kyle Jacob.

Even in the darkness, Billy's vacillation was clear, and Amy understood his reluctance.

'What am I going to find?' Billy asked, turning his head slightly.

Suddenly Billy heard the words muttered by the old man he had met back on the track on their first day. They were so coherent it was like he was standing alongside Billy speaking them.

Whatever you take in with you.

'I don't know, Billy,' Amy said, 'but whatever it is we will find it together.'

Amy's words warmed Billy's heart, and in a place that was so dark and damp provided him with a little piece of light that he so needed.

'Go on, Billy,' Amy said. 'You can do it.'

Billy nodded then moved the door catch down. At first it was a little reluctant to move. It strained, making a grinding sound. Eventually the catch squeaked and then released, and they both heard a rusty clicking sound. The door then opened a little, making a whining sound.

The door squeaked open, grating against the rough ground as it went. It was quite heavy, making Billy's arm muscles ache. He held both hands around the edges of the door, straining all the way until the door stopped, resting against the side wall.

Billy could see nothing as he peered into a room that seemed to be a void of eternal darkness. It was dusty though, and he had to fight off a sneeze. Amy walked forwards and stood next to him.

'Another room,' Amy observed.

'Or a large pit,' Billy suggested, hoping that his eyes would adjust to this new found darkness and an outline, anything, would be shown just to give him some idea of what he was about to walk into. Billy had visions of stepping in and suddenly falling hundreds of feet down into some kind of lost chasm. It was a terrifying idea and no way for a hero to meet his end.

'I can't see a thing,' Amy said holding onto Billy's arm, peering into the open door. This was frustrating for them both, because they were once again so near yet so far away from their goal, and there was just no way they could both enter this new room without light.

'Try the torch again,' Billy suggested.

Amy let go of Billy's arm and took the silver micro light out of her pocket. She twisted the end of it but nothing happened.

'It's still not working,' Amy said disappointedly.

'Here,' Billy said, 'let me try.'

'Billy Cooper,' Amy said sternly. 'If it doesn't work for me then why do you think it will for you?'

It was a fair question. Billy's father had once said the same thing to him when the television remote had stopped working. And indeed it hadn't worked for him either when Billy had handed it to him. But the problem was they didn't have any spare batteries out here.

'Just let me see,' Billy said, trying to feel for Amy's hand.

It was probably a good thing that Billy couldn't entirely see Amy's face. She handed him the torch, reluctantly.

Billy fiddled with the end of the torch, turning it this way and that whilst Amy looked on wearing an 'I told you so, Billy Cooper,' look across her face.

Amy was just about to tell Billy to give her the torch back so she could try when a couple of knocks against his left leg brought the torch back to life.

'Oh,' Amy said, looking surprised.

Billy held the torch up to his face so Amy could see the huge grin he was sporting. She wanted to punch him or at least stick the torch where it would never shine again. After Billy's mirth had passed it was time to get serious again.

It was great to have light again. It had crossed Billy's mind why the Gate Keeper had suddenly departed, and why it had allowed him access to the door. But he reckoned he knew the answer to the latter. Nothing in life comes without a price, and Billy knew of the sacrifices made for him. The day of

Billy's asthma attack, Justin saved his life, twice. The last time he sacrificed his own in the process. But Billy still held on. That dream he'd had about Justin dying. If only Justin had listened to him and not gone back into the car simply dismissing the warning. Sure, Billy had only really thought of it as a nightmare too, but there was always an element of doubt surrounding that notion, thus the reason for telling Justin about it. But what Billy found out from the Gate Keeper was that he should never have been in that car with Justin the day of the crash. The asthma attack which Billy had suffered, which made Justin take him back to the house, had been a spontaneous event, and could have happened anytime. It had just been Justin's time, but not Billy's. And the harsh fact is just that. Justin died at eighteen, so how can that have been his time? Billy didn't know and would never want to. But if the experience of coming to The Tunnel, and meeting the Gate Keeper had taught him anything then that would be there is a far bigger world beyond the one he could see, with forces inside it that pull our strings like we are puppets. Maybe the answers are not that important as the journey taken to strive for them. It wasn't what he wanted to accept, but for the time being it would have to suffice. And most importantly, Billy Cooper finally accepted that he had not been responsible for Justin's death.

Billy's rescue from the water on that day was because it simply had not been his time to die. The force that saved him was the reason behind his dream of Justin dying too. Hence, the Gate Keeper telling Billy that too many rules had already been broken for him. Billy understood everything now, but Amy didn't. He would tell her when the time was right. After all, this all affected her too. And if he was right, then it had been the Gate Keeper that had pulled him out of the water that day.

'Ready then?' Billy asked.

'Let's go.'

They entered the room, tentatively looking around, both hoping not to fall down a gaping hole to an almost certain death.

2

'Wait!'

Amy did so.

There was an urgency within Billy's voice that made Amy not even question him.

Billy slowly shone the torch, both of them watching the light beam pointing out the way. After walking roughly ten paces they turned a corner. The damp dusty air made Billy want to sneeze again. He brushed passed something as well, maybe a cobweb. He rubbed his free hand frantically through his hair, cleaning it out. They waited at the corner – Billy moved the torch around slowly.

'Stairs,' Amy said.

Concrete stairs led down to another section of the room. The corridor they were standing in was quite narrow, only about seven, maybe eight feet, and the stairs looked steep, leading down to some place deeper and darker beneath the ground. The air was cool, even cooler than it had felt inside The Tunnel. Billy finally sneezed.

'Do we go down?'

Billy looked at Amy. He didn't know. He wanted to, but something in the back of his mind was telling him to tread with caution here.

'Billy?'

'OK,' Billy said, reaching to Amy. 'Hold my hand and watch your footing, the steps could be slippy.'

Billy led the way, keeping the torch aimed down on every step. The steps were quite narrow, so it would be very easy to miss one and fall down to almost certain death. They moved slowly though, and Billy counted each step inside his head.

Billy had counted forty steps already, each one echoing, and they had still not reached the bottom yet. The micro light was dimming a little. Billy prayed that it would last until they reached the bottom.

Sixty now and still they carried on down.

'How far down are we going?' Amy asked.

'I wish I knew,' Billy said.

He felt Amy's grip tighten. Maybe she nearly slipped, or maybe she had reached her limit of bravery. Billy felt strong though, and was not going to stop until he reached the bottom. But in the back of his mind a little voice kept on telling him that this was a strange place to receive a message.

'There,' Billy said, 'I think I can see the bottom.'

The light from the torch made a dim shield against the ground below, getting bigger as Billy and Amy continued down the steep steps nearing the bottom.

Eighty steps, Billy reckoned. They were now at the bottom.

Billy shone the torch around, both of them feeling totally disorientated, and having no idea about the size of the room they had entered. The idea that Justin had left a message down here for Billy to find was starting to feel a little ridiculous to both of them. It was starting to feel like a trap. When did Justin come to The Tunnel anyway? Billy didn't recall him ever saying anything about it to him. And surely he would have.

'Where are we?' Amy asked, her voice echoing around the cold room.

Billy shone the torch upwards. The roof was high, maybe eighty feet. 'Underneath the tunnel.'

'I know that,' Amy said. 'But what do you think this room was used for?'

That was a good question.

Torture, murder, sacrifice, you know all the wholesome human activities ...

'Storage, I'm guessing,' Billy said. 'Maybe even a place where the railway workers used to eat and shit. Or even a bomb shelter?'

Amy frowned. 'And Justin was here?'

'I think so,' Billy said. 'We just have to find what he left for me.'

'In here?'

It was certainly going to be a challenge. The torchlight was forever growing dimmer and they had no spare batteries.

'We have to,' Billy said. 'Justin wants me to have whatever it is. So I can't leave until I find it.'

'I know,' Amy said understandingly.

In that moment Amy suddenly saw something in Billy she had not seen before. He was no longer a twelve year old boy who used to spend hours telling her about how shit his life was. He was no longer the same little boy who would come around her house after school and sometimes spend the night there on her bedroom floor because the thought of going home to a house that was as silent as a cemetery at night was too much for him to handle. He was no longer the same little boy who would not cry in front of her because he had told himself that is not what boys do. Whatever happened next, and whatever he would find, Amy reckoned Billy had found out a lot more about himself than The Tunnel could ever have taught him. Amy was witnessing the man Billy was to become, and she liked what she was seeing.

'We'll find it Billy,' Amy said.

Billy held her hand tightly. 'I know.'

3

The torchlight grew weaker still, now barely making any impact in the darkness.

'It's not going to last much longer,' Billy said, sounding despondent.

Amy realised something too, something so obvious she couldn't believe she or Billy hadn't thought of it sooner.

'The walls,' Amy said enthusiastically.

'What about them?' Billy's voice crept back from somewhere within the darkness. 'They're not closing in around us are they?'

'You're missing the point,' Amy said. 'This is a room, right? And used by people that used to work here?'

'Well, yeah,' Billy said, sounding like Amy was pointing out something so blatantly obvious it was hardly worthwhile speaking out aloud.

'So they must have needed light down here,' Amy said.

Bingo!

Billy moved the torch slowly over the brick walls trying to find anything that might resemble a light switch.

'There has to be one,' Amy said confidently.

Billy hoped she was right because the torch batteries were quickly running out of juice. And he didn't particularly want to be left down here with no light. But were they really going to find a light down here? Amy did have a point though. The workers would have needed light in here, but The Tunnel had been closed for such a long time now, and that probably meant the juice had been turned off too.

'Wait!' Amy said. 'Quick, go back.'

Something on the wall caught her eye.

Slowly, Billy moved the torchlight back along the black damp wall. He then saw what Amy had noticed. There was a small white box on the far wall resembling a light switch.

'There!' Billy said.

Amy followed Billy over to the wall.

It was definitely a switch of some sort. The white plastic casing was cracked with a jagged line running down the centre. It was heavily stained too, like many dirty fingers had once used it on a regular basis. They both stood around the little white box on the wall.

'Are you going to press it then?'

It would have seemed an easy thing to do. Amy's question was almost implied. But still, Billy hesitated, keeping the ever fading light from the torch over the old switch.

'It could be a trap,' Billy said.

He had only meant to think that, and not actually say it out loud.

Billy was having visions of some action adventure movie currently running through his head. The kind of ones where the hero of the epic is about to reach the end of his quest, to find the hidden treasure, only then to have everything jeopardised by a hidden trap. Maybe a secretly hidden pit with fake covering with spikes at the bottom. Or even a light switch on the wall, that looked harmless enough until pressed.

'It's just a light switch, Billy,' Amy said, as if she was reading his mind again.

'How do you do that?' Billy asked, pointing the light at Amy.

'Do what?'

'Know what I'm thinking.'

Amy giggled then smiled so widely Billy expected the dark room to suddenly light up.

'You're easy to read,' Amy noted. 'You always have been, Billy Cooper.'

'Only to you,' Billy said.

There was then a silence. All that could be heard was the faint dripping sound of water against rock somewhere up above. In that moment Billy realised how well Amy knew him, and vice-versa. They once again felt like the only two people in the world, and in an isolated room like the one they were in, it did seem very plausible that they were. And seeing the partially lit look on Billy's face, Amy knew it was going to be difficult. She hadn't told him yet that she would

235

be leaving soon. Her family were moving away from Harborough, it was her dad's job again. She had known for some time now, but with all that was happening with Billy she couldn't bring herself to tell him. He'd lost enough people recently, and even though they could stay in touch it would never be the same. But people sometimes have to move on, Amy knew this. She also knew she would never forget Billy, and the time they shared, and only hoped everything would work out OK for him before she left.

'What?' Billy asked.

'Nothing,' Amy said, swallowing uneasily. 'Are you going to press the switch or not, Billy Cooper?'

Billy smiled gently, his young face now looking tired and strained, and in need of a good wash, blue eyes blazing in the darkness, full of wonder and hope. There were black marks on his cheeks, making him look like he was a soldier wearing camouflage rather than a twelve year old boy.

'Let there be light,' Billy said.

He pressed the switch.

4

Billy and Amy both assumed they would have been relieved by the light. The fact that the switch did anything at all was a bonus, but for three high-powered lights to come back to life and provide enough light for a prison on high alert during a break-out was not quite what they had expected, and hurt their eyes. Billy turned the torch off and looked around. The walls were now a greyish colour, concrete that was so rugged it looked like huge ugly wrinkles had appeared everywhere. The ground was wet, little puddles of water had formed in various places, looking like small paddling pools. It suddenly brought back memories for Billy of the dip he'd had with the Legend.

Overheard there was a network of metal piping leading off in all directions. Billy assumed they were water pipes. There were also four wooden beams running across between the copper pipes. The room was about thirty feet in length by fifteen wide. Next to the left wall was an old metal sink that looked all rusty. The tap was still dripping. There was also a large black storage cabinet next to the sink, the doors were closed and Billy reckoned they would be locked too. There were cobwebs hanging down from the ceiling, some of them looking rather large. Billy didn't mind spiders in general, but didn't fancy meeting the mean motherfucker that weaved those.

'This looks like a mine,' Amy said.

Billy walked a few paces forwards, constantly looking around for Justin's message. He wasn't expecting to read 'Hi Billy Boy,' spray-painted on the walls or anything but was hoping something would jump out at him. But there was nothing.

'I don't understand,' Billy said casually, walking around. 'There's nothing down here, Amy. All this way to find nothing.'

'Don't say that, Billy,' Amy said. 'We haven't even looked around yet. Let's at least have a look around before we give up.'

'There's nothing here, Amy,' Billy snapped.

'But the Gate Keeper said –'

'I know what he said,' Billy interrupted. 'I was with him. But maybe he didn't think I deserved to see what Justin left for me.'

'Don't say that,' Amy said. 'How can you even think that way, Billy Cooper?'

Billy couldn't speak any more. That lump that had felt like a tennis ball was now beginning to return to his throat again. Everything had been for this empty room. And it wasn't just the message either. Billy secretly hoped that maybe he would have found Justin down here too. He felt like his world was suddenly crashing down all around him again, like a house of cards, and once again there was no sheltering from it, his own personal storm of pain and sorrow.

Billy sat down and leaned back against the cold rock wall. It felt damp and rough on his back, but he didn't care. He brought his knees up and rested his arms on top of them.

Amy watched Billy, thinking how lost and lonely he looked again. She wanted to find some words to offer him as comfort but sometimes words are not enough. She walked over to Billy, removed her back pack and sat down next to him.

'I'm sorry, Billy,' she said gently.

'Why, Amy?' Billy asked, turning to her. 'Why have me come this far and only to find nothing?'

A single tear rolled down Billy's dirty right cheek, leaving behind a clean line as it went. 'I thought my brother was going to be here,' Billy continued. 'I thought I was going to see him again.'

Billy was well aware that he was crying but no longer cared. The files he kept inside his head on such matters could burn as far as he was concerned. It was like everything had finally caught up with him, showing him once again that life hurts and can be full of disappointment, bite you on the ass when you least expected it. And what made it worse was that Billy accepted that Justin was dead but to have his dreams destroyed like an eggshell under foot was too much. He couldn't handle that. Billy needed his dreams, what little boy doesn't? And to have those dreams lying around the ground in tatters inside a place that had tormented him for so long was the hardest boot in the gut ever.

'I just wanted to see my brother again,' Billy said. 'Is that really asking too much?'

Billy knew the answer, really.

More pearl drops began running down Billy's mucky face, each one reflecting the light back like small mirrors. Amy put her arms around him, this time she had no words.

5

The pipes overhead began knocking. Amy looked up, but Billy remained looking at the ground, seeing faces in the concrete. Everything felt like one big façade to him now. But in that moment of self-pity he suddenly remembered something, and it was about Justin. And strangely enough the memory was from the happiest, but most tragic day of his life.

It was then that Billy also remembered he had lost his brother's watch. The one he had given him not twenty minutes before he died, and that watch was what made him remember something else that Justin had lost.

'The watch!'

The sudden urgency in Billy's voice made Amy flinch and remove her arms from around his cold shoulders.

'The one you lost?' Amy asked.

Billy nodded slowly, his teary eyes widening as he gazed at Amy in wonder.

'We can find it on the way back,' Amy said reassuringly, even though she reckoned they wouldn't. 'You lost it on the first night, near the stone camp, right?'

The stone camp?

God, that all felt like such a long time ago now. What day was it now anyway? Billy couldn't remember and that scared him. After thinking long and hard about it he decided it had to be Monday, late Monday afternoon perhaps.

'What, Billy?' Amy said, still looking a little puzzled.

'The message,' Billy said so quietly Amy only just heard him. 'It has been here for a long time now. Justin was here, Amy. This must have been one of the last places he went before he died.'

And he lost what he really wanted to give me down here.

'Why would he come here, Billy?'

It was a good question that Billy didn't really know the

answer to. But how could he? The truth was Justin was leaving town, and he too, like Billy, had heard the stories about The Tunnel. One of the benefits of living in a small town was that everyone mostly knew the same shit. Justin had come out of curiosity, and it had been as simple as that. But unlike Billy, he had found nothing. No Legend of The Track, no old man with a shotgun, and certainly no corpse swinging from a tree. The Tunnel was just that to Justin. There had been a room he found though, and it was inside there that he had lost his most personal item. Justin had failed to find the light switch that Amy had, and it was in the darkness that Justin had left it behind, and there it remained until now. He never heard it fall out of the small opening in his bag. The truth was Justin had left in a hurry. He had found nothing yet had seen everything. Justin wanted Billy to have it, and even in death he could not forget. It was meant for Billy, and Billy's it would be.

Billy got up quickly as if he were suddenly jolted with electricity. He started walking forwards to where some old wooden chairs were stacked, most with enough surface dust that it was possible to write something in. Amy watched Billy for a few seconds then got up too. She could see something underneath one of the chairs.

6

There was a steel grate on the ground, a drain. It appeared to be loose. Billy was moving some of the old chairs out of the way. Three, maybe four of the heavy wooden chairs were already lying in a heap on the ground next to the grate. They had been knocked over by something.

Amy stood over the grate and tapped her right foot against it. It was definitely loose. It was too dark to see what was down there, so as Billy carried on looking around the chairs to try

240

to find the item Justin had lost, Amy realised she needed the torch again. She didn't need to ask Billy for it though. The torch was next to the wall where Billy had been sitting. Amy went over and got it.

On her return Billy was still searching around the chairs, determined to find what he had come for, but Amy already had. She switched on the micro light and shone it down the steel grate. There was something down there all right.

It was a drain. Roughly five feet down with dirty water at the bottom. However, just beneath the grate, towards the side, was a narrow rock ledge that the item was resting on. Amy shone the torch on it then turned back towards Billy.

Billy hadn't heard Amy the first time she called out his name. He had given up on the chairs and was now looking around the storage unit again.

'Billy!'

He heard that time.

He turned and looked at Amy. At first he didn't know what to think. Even though Amy was his best friend he didn't always know what she was thinking just by looking at her. There was urgency in her voice though, that much was clear.

Billy rushed over.

'What is it?'

Amy motioned for Billy to look down the drain. Billy did so.

At first he saw what Amy had, water that looked like someone had taken a dump in it, and smelt that way too. But he then looked a little harder and saw it.

Billy immediately knew what it was, and gasped, almost falling down the hole too. How it had not tumbled all the way down into the shit-infested water below was almost unfathomable to Billy.

'Do you know what it is?' Amy asked.

Billy nodded then said, 'Yes … I know what it is, Amy…'

It was what Justin had wanted to give me instead of the watch.

241

And that was that then. The reason for Billy being drawn to The Tunnel, well not quite, there was something else, but for the time being he just wanted to hold the item that had been missing for so long now. His parents knew of it, and couldn't understand where it had been for all of this time either. They had searched high and low for it for weeks after Justin's death. It was just another piece belonging to their son that they wanted to keep close to them. Sometimes memories, old pictures, songs that have special meanings are not always enough. Sometimes people need to hold onto that which has substance. Something more personal that is not just a random memory that becomes distant as the shores of time can. This was Justin's legacy in a way, and Billy had found it. It was meant for him to find.

Billy tried lifting the grate. It was stubborn at first but eventually came up with a scraping sound that made him flinch again. There was now nothing standing in his way. He went down on his knees and slowly reached down. Amy left the light where it was. If Billy knocked it, even a little, it would fall into the water below and then be lost forever. He reached and touched it. It was now his, had to be. But then something strange happened. Sounds and flashing images suddenly appeared inside Billy's head. It was like trying to watch and listen to a movie that was being speeded up. None of the sounds or images made any sense at first. Dancing white lights and distorted sounds overwhelmed his senses.

'Billy!' Amy said.

Billy did not hear Amy. His eyes flickered from side to side, like a candle in the wind, as the images still played on inside his head, making him look like he was having some sort of seizure. The images then slowed down and started sliding together like a jigsaw puzzle. Billy could see the images properly now. He watched on whilst Amy continued to call out his name. He went back in time again. This he had to see.

Rewind <<

A red car appeared, sparkling in the sun, driven by a strong-looking and handsome young man. Justin looked ahead and saw it, he had arrived at last.

18

The Farther Side

Park

The car parked on the dirt road, sending up a cloud of dust into the warm still air. The day was humid and already his armpits were damp and sticky. He wiped his brow then got out of his car. He was leaving for college soon, so had to do this before then. Like most people he had been curious about this place for quite some time now, but unlike most he'd done something about it.

Most had heard the stories, God only knew he had. His being here was really more of a dare then anything. And to think that John Harris had said that he wouldn't have had the balls to go, ha, Justin never liked that asshole anyway. Too full of himself, and the type of guy that you couldn't bear to be in the same room as for more than thirty seconds.

Justin was relieved that he had driven to The Tunnel. If he had taken his bike, or God forbid, walked, then he would have entered the end Kyle Jacob had hung himself. That was the one story that everyone believed in, especially Justin. Always a bit of an outsider, apparently. But looks can be deceiving, just like The Tunnel for instance. As most things though the truth is far less interesting than the legend. Kyle Jacob had been an acute depressive shortly before he had committed suicide. His death had been a kind of declaration

Justin had thought and a big fuck you to all those people at school that never bothered to learn his name or even look him in the eye, and to the mother he had never seen but longed for day and night. Nobody would forget his name in death though, certainly not the driver of the train.

Kyle had never told anyone about his cancer either, not even his crazy old man who had shot himself two days later. Living all alone in a small run-down shack next to the track, no-one had even found his body until two weeks later. It was a woman walking her dog that had made the discovery. Ricky, her border collie always did have a nose for trouble. Before he killed himself, the old man must have cut his dog's head off. When Mary Taylor found him, Royal it had said on his collar, the poor bastard had been headless, much the same as William Jacob had been. Legend had it that William Jacob's ghost now haunted the track too, apparently holding the same shotgun he had blasted himself with and wearing the same dirty overalls he had been found in. Apparently he also wore a brown hat to hide the gaping hole the shotgun blast had left behind.

Justin looked down at the track that led towards the cool tunnel. He grabbed his backpack and began walking over to where it was always dark no matter what time. It was time to put the legend to rest.

Walking

The Tunnel soon came into view. It wasn't as far as he first thought. He knew his little brother, Billy, would have wanted to come if he'd asked him. But this was something he had to do alone. One day Billy would know what he found though. Hell the little toe-rag might even come himself one day. It would certainly make a good story for him to write. Justin knew that Billy was a keen writer, even though he hadn't even turned twelve yet the boy showed tremendous insight for one so young. Justin was allowed to read one of Billy's stories the other day. It was called 'Grasshoppers'. In short Justin loved it. It was basically the story of raging war between grasshoppers and spiders, the latter being the evil of the narrative who were trying to invade the grasshopper HQ. Kind of dumb really, but Justin was impressed with the narrative and prose. In actual fact Justin had only finished reading that story last night.

The darkness grew nearer and nearer. Justin felt a soft cool breeze coming out from The Tunnel. He didn't really know what he was looking for once inside, and perhaps the reason for his coming was not to find anything. And at the very least he could tell John Harris to suck-cock the next time he made up some more bullshit story about this place and Justin having no spine for not daring to go.

If Justin's memory served him correct, then it was John who had told him the stories about The Tunnel in the first place, and about the Jacob family. It was a classic case of the ripple effect. But nonetheless, he carried on walking, occasionally looking around for the ghost of an old man holding a shotgun and wearing a brown hat, who was also supposedly very hard to understand.

0

He reached The Tunnel and gave it the once-over before going inside.

Shit! No torch.

He would have to go in blind.

Justin had been hoping The Tunnel was going to be straight, at least then he would have some goal to aim for. But this was darker than his worst nightmare. It was now decision time. Should he go in and see if there was any truth

246

to the stories or go home with his tail between his legs? Justin made his decision.

Forward >>

'He liked my story...'

Amy looked on biting her lower lip without even being aware that she was doing so.

Billy was still in some kind of trance here, bridging a gap between his world and the one that had passed. He had spoken Justin's name twice now. The item had not fallen yet, and Amy was half-tempted to push Billy out of the way and reach down for it herself. She knew that would be a mistake though, because if Billy even had a finger on it then any sudden movement would send it tumbling down into the shit pit below.

'Don't go in... Just don't go in...'

Billy was linked to Justin now. He was amazed to find that Justin had felt all the same anxieties he had felt when entering The Tunnel. Those same anxieties had somehow made Billy call out, the ones he had been feeling whilst stepping into the unknown. The images played on. Justin had entered The Tunnel, and whatever his reasons for going had really been, Billy reckoned they were not that different from his own. Sometimes a place simply being there can be reason enough. And sometimes the only way people can grow and move on is by confronting their fears. Justin was normally brave, pleasantly cheeky and fun-loving, but he was afraid of The Tunnel. The legend had done its job, and stories are not just stories when people really believe them, are they?

Amy maintained the torch where it was, the item was close to the edge and Billy's right hand was pressing on it. If he moved his hand any, it would fall.

'The door … He found the door … how?'

'Billy please,' Amy said, 'you have to hear my voice. You are dreaming.'

And he was, but there was a reason why he was seeing what he was. Billy was now blind, only seeing what Justin had been seeing and feeling what Justin had been feeling over a year ago now.

Rewind II <<

The harsh rock seemed never-ending so to feel the cool metal exterior was unexpected and almost welcoming.

Justin stopped.

It was a door, had to be. He moved his hand over it feeling flakes of paint coming off. The sweat that had overcome him not ten minutes ago had now been replaced by goose pimples accompanied with the desire to run back outside again.

He found a handle and pressed it. There was a worn clicking sound, like metal rubbing against metal. The door opened slowly, whining on old rusty hinges that had not been used in such a long time.

'There are no ghosts,' Justin muttered as he pushed the door open as far as it would go. But Kyle Jacob, Justin could picture him in his head. Not that he'd ever seen the swinging corpse that had later been hit by a speeding train. The notion of what had happened and the tragic circumstances surrounding it were enough though.

'Stories… they are nothing but stories…' He reminded himself.

Do you really believe that, Justin?

Billy looked on through the eyes of his dead brother, he knew the staircase was coming up but reckoned that Justin didn't. There was nothing he could do to help him. After all, what was happening had already happened, history could not be rewritten, only re-lived.

Justin used the cool left wall as his guide, and as rough as it felt against his hands it was better than nothing. He now felt pretty stupid. What the hell was he doing here anyway?

But wait…

Justin stopped.

He had been about to put his foot down when it had been greeted with nothingness. He slowly bent down and felt around with his hands.

'Holy shit, stairs.'

The darkness was unkind. His eyes had not adjusted at all and he might as well have walked into The Tunnel with them closed for all the use they offered him. He slowly got back to his feet and carefully descended the stairs. This was the first and last time he would come to The Tunnel so he might as well go down. Justin knew this would make a good entry, maybe even a great story one day. Hell, maybe Billy could even write about it.

Lost Then Found Again

Justin made it down to the bottom, and if it was even possible it looked even darker. He had absolutely no idea where he was but as long as he didn't venture too far away from the staircase then he thought he should be able to find his way back out all right. But once again that little bit of curiosity that seemed programmed into the Cooper family genes, wanted him to go that little bit further.

Splash …

He stepped into a puddle. The air felt cooler down here. How far down was he anyway? Justin found a wall again and used it as his guide. He was blind in this place.

There was a dripping sound. He felt something wet

touching his shoulder. He spun around quickly, not really knowing why because there was nothing to see down here. Justin carried on walking.

It was close, Billy knew it, but Justin didn't. The voice in the back of his head was telling him it was time to leave, however the other voice, Mr Curiosity, spoke the loudest. A knocking sound brought Justin to a stop again. He looked into the darkness waiting for something, anything to jump out. He was then aware of another sound, a thumping like the beating of a drum. It was his heart.

Knock…

It really was time to leave now.

Mr Curiosity denied him again.

Knock … knock.

'Hello?' His voice echoed but was soon buried in the darkness, going nowhere.

Billy felt Justin's fear creeping over him like a rapid cold fever. But Billy thought Justin showed more bravery then he ever did, what with coming down here alone in the first place and without a torch.

Justin shivered, like a cold hand had suddenly touched his shoulder. Then the knocking sound started up again, but this time it was all around him. Justin spun around again looking like he was doing some sort of funky 70s disco dance.

'Careful,' Billy shouted, reaching through time and space. 'It is only the pipes you can hear.'

Fall v

Justin tripped and fell into something.

The knocking sound was enough to impede his curiosity. He quickly started running back. Pretty stupid really but he didn't care. He had come to The Tunnel, probably not seen, but definitely heard enough. Justin lost his footing again. A hole or drain maybe. He then knocked into something, sending whatever it was crashing down. It was in that moment that he lost it. As one of the chairs landed on his back, knocking his pack sideways, it fell out and landed somewhere in the lost darkness. If the backpack had been zipped fully it wouldn't have fallen. Justin didn't hear it fall. But Billy did. He saw it too.

All Justin heard was the pandemonium going on around him, and the knocking sound coming from above, that made him think that the roof was going to cave in. Enough was enough. His stomach suddenly tightened, and the need to get the hell out of there now beat out everything else inside of him. He knocked into some of the fallen chairs as he went, hurting his shins and swearing.

The wall, he found the wall again. Sliding both hands along it until he felt his way out. It seemed forever before he found the staircase.

Climb ^

Up he went, displaying the same caution he had done on the way down. That knocking sound, holy shit, thinking that the cave was still going to collapse all around him he had nearly shit himself the last time he'd heard it. But knowing that he would soon be back at the top again filled his body with the same elation as a man watching his girlfriend undressing for the first time. Up and up he went, almost crawling on all fours. The top was close, it had to be.

Justin hurried to the door, never looking back. He then had a horrible thought that made him suddenly panic. What if the door didn't open again? Jesus! He hadn't even brought his mobile phone. He reached the door, hoping against all hope that it would open.

It did.

Justin was met by the same cool darkness again, but didn't care. He knew that he would soon see the opening and then it was only about seventy metres back to his car from there. So applying the same wall technique he had used on the way in, Justin groped his way out of the cave. Billy carried on watching through his eyes. Then something happened. It was the same experience of two separate times coming back together like he'd had back on the track. They were joined, mind, body and soul as Billy finally touched what he had come for. And Billy and Justin were once again brought back together, joined through two separate places in time. The past and present intertwined to give them both that one last moment – that one last memory to take away with them. And it happened when Billy touched the journal.

Forward >> Rewind << Pause ||

Amy panicked when she saw Billy's arms emerging from the hole. She hadn't heard a splashing sound so assumed it would be in Billy's hand. But Billy was still wearing the same dazed expression. His eyes were not still any more, they were set in wonder, flickering wildly. Then Amy saw him too.

When Billy stood up he was holding Justin's journal in both hands like one would a prayer book. He was however, only holding one end of it. Justin had the other. Amy stepped forward slowly as Justin looked at her and smiled. He was wearing the same blue jeans and blue top he had on the day he died, and looked just as handsome.

Justin looked at Billy; he was back in his own time zone again.

'Justin,' Billy said slowly, looking up in awe of him.

Justin smiled gently. 'W'cha, Billy Boy. You finally found it then?'

Billy looked on in amazement at the hero he had lost but

somehow found again. He knew it was only temporary though.

Billy looked down at the journal.

Justin let go of it, finally giving to him what he had always wanted to. 'I wanted you to have this, Billy,' he said proudly. 'Most of it is my feelings from certain times of my life but there are things in there that I think will help you in the course of yours.'

Billy smiled but all he really wanted to do was hug his brother. Would that even be possible? God, it had been so long.

'Thank you,' Billy said, a tear rolled down his dirty cheek, making another clean line as it went.

Billy realised what Justin was giving to him here was the most personal item that any person could give to another. It was a part of him, his innermost thoughts and feelings.

'I know things have been tough on you, little brother,' Justin said. 'But I promise you this they will change when you go back. Your coming here has changed many things Billy, things that you will not yet know about.'

'What things?'

Justin smiled.

'You will see, Billy,' he said softly. 'I promise.' He then looked over at Amy. 'So you're Amy? Billy has told me all about you.'

Amy smiled, perhaps a little embarrassed, and then nodded, thinking how alike they both looked.

'Thank you for looking after my little brother.'

'Can you stay?'

Justin looked back at Billy. 'No, Billy. I'm afraid that I can't.'

Billy sniffled then wiped his eyes. 'Why not?' He asked hopelessly.

It was a question that was so easy, but also at the same time impossible to answer.

'Please stay,' Billy said. 'I don't want you to leave again. I want things to go back to the way they used to be.'

'They can't, Billy,' Justin said gently, 'not everything anyway.'

'I know you died,' Billy said, 'but you are here now so can't they send you back? Can't you come home again and live with us?'

Billy's insides felt like they were being twisted by someone's hand. It hurt more this time then it had when Justin had died before because Billy now knew he was going to have to lose him for a second time, and feel all that same pain all over again.

Amy looked on, feeling every emotion that Billy was in that moment, her eyes shining.

'I wish I could,' Justin said. 'But it's not possible, Billy. You have found what I wanted you to have and now I must return.'

'To where?'

'To the other world that exists beyond this one.'

Billy wiped his eyes again then looked down at the journal. Justin's name was written on the front cover, followed by the word 'Started' then a date of '1998.'

'It is unfinished, Billy,' Justin said. 'You can finish it for me.' He smiled.

'I will,' Billy said proudly, looking back at Justin who was now slowly fading out. 'I promise.'

Justin smiled then ruffled up Billy's hair again like he used to. Billy smiled then lowered his head. It was a simple gesture but one he had missed so much.

'It will be all right, little, bro,' Justin promised.

Billy never asked Justin about what he was referring to but guessed it was their parents he was talking about.

'A lot will change, Billy, when you go back home, but some things will also remain the same.'

'I know,' Billy said, wiping his eyes.

'I love you, Billy.'

In that moment, Billy dropped the journal then rushed over to his brother and wrapped his arms tightly around him before he had the chance to disappear. It was something that he had wanted to do the first time he saw Justin again but didn't know whether he could actually do so or not. He got his answer, and it was the one that he had wanted. Justin held Billy too.

'It's going to be OK, Billy,' Justin said, holding his little brother like he once did in his world. 'I will always be with you, no matter what.'

Billy buried his face into Justin's chest, before he eventually disappeared as quickly as he had appeared.

Billy felt his arms loosen and then opened his eyes. The room still felt different but Justin was now gone

'Come back!' Billy shouted out, looking around. 'Please, Justin ... Come back.'

He heard the shuffling of feet.

Billy turned quickly and saw Amy. She had now seen him in every way possible, even at his lowest and most fragile.

Amy smiled softly, perhaps not knowing what to say.

Billy looked down at the cold grey ground and saw the journal lying there. The red cover was open. He walked over, picked the journal up then closed the cover. There would be plenty of time to read it later.

The dream was now over so Billy walked over to Amy, keeping a tight hold on the journal. And even though he had finally found what he'd come for, he still didn't feel like going home.

He looked down at the journal again and said softly, 'Goodbye Justin.'

| Soldiers |

It was now dark outside.

The moon was full and highlighting the track and tunnel entrance. The night was peaceful with only a soft breeze

255

occasionally blowing, rustling the leaves of the trees. Strange shadows moved, stretching out across the path. Billy looked on, holding the journal tight in his right hand. He looked up at the moon, the left side of his face glowing. Amy was still asleep inside the storage room. Billy reckoned she would be safe enough. There was nothing left to be afraid of any more. He was thinking about Justin, trying to make sense of everything. It hurt to let go again, but what else could he have done? At least he had the chance to say goodbye to him, and that was more than some people get. Seeing Justin again made Billy realise just how much he had missed him, and now that he had the journal he knew Justin would always be with him, and that was reassuring. Still looking up at the moon, Billy wondered where Justin was right now. A star twinkled down at him, looking like a jewel in the night sky, telling Billy that he was not far away.

Amy awoke. It was actually the knocking of the pipes above that made her open her eyes. She had been dreaming. It had been a nice dream for once. She was home again with her parents. That's where she wanted to be right now. Amy was split in two though, because one part of her wanted to be home right now, and the other wanted her to be here with Billy. The latter would win, it always did. But Amy still hadn't told Billy that she was leaving town. She forgot about that for the time being. It wasn't for a while anyway. She had time.

Amy sleepily looked around for Billy then went up the stairs. She didn't want to be alone right now.

Billy was standing against the archway when Amy saw him. He heard Amy's footsteps but did not turn around.

'So this is where you have been hiding,' Amy said.

Billy smiled and carried on looking up at the moon. A cloud, looking like black smoke was partially hiding it.

'Are you all right, Billy?' Amy asked.

'Yeah,' Billy said still looking up towards the heavens. 'I just wanted to see the stars again tonight.'

'They're beautiful,' Amy noted, looking up. She looked back at Billy. He looked like he had the weight of the world on his shoulders again. 'So tomorrow we go home.'

Home?

Home seemed a thousand miles away to Billy in that moment. Did he even have a home any more? But Justin did say things would have changed when he returned. How, he didn't know, but Justin did not lie. The problem was Billy didn't feel like going home tomorrow. This was his time, his place, and the thought of going back home tomorrow was inconceivable, like short-changing yourself out of money or love.

'I guess we do,' Billy said.

'You found it, Billy,' Amy said. 'You found what you came for.'

Billy smiled and looked down at the journal.

'Have you read any yet?'

'No,' Billy said. 'But I will …'

Billy sat down, leaning against the archway and putting the journal in his lap. Amy sat down next to him.

'Thanks, Amy,' Billy said, turning to her.

'For what?' Amy asked.

'For coming here with me and for not going home the other day because I don't think I could have done it without you, even if you did slow me down a little.'

Amy smiled then playfully nudged Billy in the arm with her right elbow. 'Why thank you, Billy Cooper.'

'You're welcome, Amy Johnston.'

Amy leaned in against Billy as they both carried on looking up at the moon and the wind blew softly against their faces.

- Sleep -

As they slept together, the Gate Keeper looked on. The job was now done, almost anyway. There was one further matter

257

that needed attending to, but this could wait until another time. Right now Billy and Amy were where they needed to be. The world shifted and the Gate Keeper returned, and what needed to pass would soon enough.

19

Departure

1

Billy awoke early Tuesday morning to the charming sounds of singing birds. He had gone well before Amy had opened her sleepy eyes. She felt the sun beating down on her face. The day was already warm and it was still only early.

'Billy,' Amy called out looking around.

Billy's red cardigan was still lying on the ground next to her so he couldn't have gone far, she hoped.

Amy had been having the same dream about going home prior to waking. Her parents were calling out her name, waiting for her to come back. It saddened Amy to think that she was upsetting her parents. They had now been gone for three full days. There was bound to be panic setting in by now. Amy knew it was now time to return.

She got up slowly and looked around. The air coming out from The Tunnel felt refreshing, like air conditioning, and that was far better than the sticky humidity the day offered. Amy retreated into the opening. Billy would find her, he always did. She then thought that maybe Billy had gone, not home, but to try to find the watch he had lost. But that was crazy. He had lost the watch on the first night, next to the stone camp, and that was miles away.

'Billy.'

There was still no answer. She leaned against the cool wall, folding her arms.

'Billy Cooper!' Amy shouted.

'Yes,' a voice spoke echoing out from The Tunnel.

Amy turned, seeing Billy appearing out of the darkness. It had looked like some kind of magic trick how quickly he appeared in front of her.

'Where have you been, Billy Cooper?' Amy asked, placing her hands on her hips. She then noticed Billy was not holding the journal. 'Where is the book?'

'It's safe,' Billy said, now standing next to her. 'I left it on the table in the storage room.'

'Well, what for?'

'I was going to make an entry,' Billy explained, 'then realised I didn't have a pen.'

Amy smiled, letting out one of her trademark giggles.

'You didn't get scared by yourself, did you?'

'Don't be stupid,' Amy said, with a straight face. 'I just wasn't sure where you were.'

Billy leaned up against the archway wall. The air felt cool over his arms and face.

'I realised something when I woke up this morning,' Billy said.

Amy noticed his face suddenly looking all grown-up again. He didn't look or sound like a twelve year old any more.

'What is it?'

'It's the anniversary of Justin's death today,' Billy said, turning to Amy. His voice was strained, like all the energy in it had suddenly diminished. 'I can't believe I almost forgot it.'

'But you didn't,' Amy said softly. 'And no matter what, Billy, Justin will always be with you. He told you so.'

Billy smiled and nodded his head. He liked the idea of that. But deep down he knew he would never see Justin again, at least not in this world. And even though he was only twelve, he realised seeing Justin again last night, seeing the person he aspired to be like who had died so tragically, was more than most people got. The best part about it was he knew Amy was right, Justin would always be with him, and now he had the journal they could write history together and that made Billy smile inside, restoring a hope within that had been absent for the best part of a year now. Billy started believing again, that maybe he did have a future, and once again home didn't feel so far away.

The mystery that had been The Tunnel was now uncovered. Billy had been afraid of this place even in his dreams. But now a sense of liberation had overcome him. He was free again and had played his part in the larger scheme of things. But there was one question remaining. He figured that could wait, because right now Billy Cooper had a plan. He had a legacy of his own to leave behind.

'What?' Amy asked.

'Come on,' Billy said, taking Amy by the hand.

'Where to?'

'You'll see,' Billy said beaming. 'I have a plan ...'

They both disappeared back inside The Tunnel, no longer scared of the cold darkness.

They found the door surprisingly easy, considering Billy had left the torch inside the storage room.

'Don't forget about the stairs,' Billy said, still holding Amy's hand and leading the way.

'I won't,' Amy said, trying not to trip over Billy's clumsy feet.

They walked down the stairs, the light from the room still visible, painting the floor in a yellow glow.

Amy didn't understand Billy's sudden enthusiasm to go back down to the storage room, because it didn't look any different from last night. She was half expecting Billy to have discovered and shown her a new room or something or maybe a trapdoor full of treasure. Their bags were still on the floor next to the wall and the only difference Amy noticed was that one of the lights was now fading.

'Right,' Billy said, still sounding enthusiastic. 'This is where we leave it.'

'Leave what?'

Billy heard Amy's question but his mind was so jam-packed at that moment he didn't answer. He walked over to the table against the left wall. He then turned back towards Amy.

'Now,' Billy said, 'I know you always come prepared, Amy.'

'Really?' Amy said, suspiciously. She had no idea where Billy was going with this. He used to be so easy to read.

'Oh yes,' Billy said. 'And I am willing to bet that you brought some paper and something to write with.'

'Is that right, Billy Cooper?' Amy asked, folding her arms. 'Well did you?'

Amy didn't like the way Billy had all of a sudden become so insightful. 'Perhaps ...'

'So have you got paper and a pencil?'

'No!' Amy said, watching Billy's enthusiasm suddenly disappearing like a shooting star across the night sky. 'I have some paper and a pen.'

They both shared a smile then Amy walked over to her backpack and took out the A4 notepad along with her pen. She also brought out the water and packet of biscuits. She couldn't remember the last time they had eaten.

'Later!' Billy said, after Amy offered him the biscuits and water.

Billy was waiting by the table when Amy walked over with the notepad and pen.

'So what do you want these for?'

Billy smiled then told her.

2

It must have been 3am last night when Billy awoke. Amy was asleep next to him, all curled up like a cat in front of a fire.

The night was still clear and the moon looked like a saucer of milk in the sky. The air was biting so Billy moved Amy's jacket up over her then stood up. Seeing Justin again yesterday had left him feeling empty inside. But Billy wouldn't have changed it, he saw his brother again and that had been a miracle. There was a familiar feeling surging through his body now that was preventing him from sleeping, and that was sadness.

He had wanted to see Justin again so much and didn't feel like he made the most out of the opportunity. After Justin had died Billy used to talk to him at night times. Not out loud, just inside his head. But he still remembered the conversations being riveting, really edgy shit that two guys could only chew the fat over. Better still, he had told Justin how much he missed him and prayed to God that he would get the chance to see him again. He spoke to Justin about mum and dad, about how the lines of communication between the three of them had been destroyed by some emotional bomb left by his passing. He had told Justin about how shitty his life felt at that time. But then a light came along, only small, but it had come just the same.

'Amy,' he had told Justin, 'she is my new best friend.'

And last night Billy realised Justin must have heard him talking because he remembered, despite how poignant he had felt at that time, Justin had looked at Amy and spoken her name.

'He did hear me,' Billy said, looking up at the night sky and counting the stars. He reckoned there was a new one up there tonight, and it dazzled brighter than any other. He smiled.

It seemed that God had answered his prayers, he had actually answered him. But Billy knew everything comes with a price, the Gate Keeper had shown him that, and maybe that was a life lesson everyone has to learn so Billy Cooper was way ahead of the field on that score. Justin had saved Billy, given his own life for him, and Billy had been left behind with a family that couldn't understand that magnificent gesture of love. He had tried to take his own life but then Justin's sacrifice would have all been for nothing. Billy had to live on; there was a family that needed him, and vice-versa. Justin knew that, so too did the Gate Keeper, but there was also something else.

It was in the moonlight that Billy had made his mind up. As far as he was concerned The Tunnel, this place, belonged to him and Amy. This was their time, their chance for an adventure, and Billy Cooper wanted to leave a mark. He left Amy sleeping peacefully and disappeared back up the track, he remembered seeing something next to an old wooden gate not far from here, when their journey to reach The Tunnel had almost been at an end. He went to get it.

Into the cold lonely night Billy went, talking to Justin in his head. He told him what he wished he had said when he'd been alive. He told him what he wished he'd said last night after seeing him again. He said the words over and over again all the time looking up at that one star that seemed to be dazzling brighter than any other in the sky.

3

'And you understand then?' The Gate Keeper asked.

Billy frowned, but understood the complexities of what had just been explained to him.

'Then you can pass.'

Billy knew really, it had been no surprise, but what was he going to tell Amy? Did she even have any idea?

Holy shit, Billy had thought. *How can I tell her this?*

Everything has a price; that seemed to be his motto of late, but how true it was. The Gate Keeper had fulfilled his part now the rest was up to Billy. It hurt him to think about it too much because this didn't only affect Billy any more. Amy was now part of his life too, the biggest.

Last night Billy had thought about a lot. He no longer felt like that scared little kid who three days ago had set off on a journey of unknown dangers and self-discovery. There was no doubting that life had been tough, almost impossible to live at times, but Billy had come through, and had no doubt that Amy had played a huge part in that. It was like they had both realised at the outset of their journey. This was their time ... and their chance to make history *together.*

Billy stopped digressing for the moment and then tore the A4 sheet and handed Amy half.

'Here.'

'Why don't we use a sheet each?' Amy asked as Billy handed her the torn half.

'It looks better this way,' Billy said. 'Now you go first.'

'To do what?' Amy was holding her pen in one hand and the paper in the other. She suddenly felt like she was back at school again.

Billy smiled.

'History,' he said. 'Before we leave, Billy Cooper and Amy Johnston are going to make history together.'

Amy frowned, whether it was hearing Billy referring to himself in the third person or because he was starting to look a little crazy didn't matter. She now knew what he wanted to do, and she kind of liked it.

'A time capsule.'

4

Where to start?

They both wrote like they were sitting an exam, not talking or even looking up apart from when passing the pen to one another. Amy found the whole thing quite amusing really, besides from how seriously Billy was taking the exercise, the silence of the room reminded her of test conditions at school. Billy wrote something then passed the pen to Amy, the whole process going back and forth for quite some time.

It was on Billy's turn when things slowed down. He held the pen in his right hand, looking down at the paper with intense concentration. Amy could see creases in his forehead looking like tiny valleys. His blue eyes focused hard on the nearly-filled piece of paper, trying to find that little extra inspiration. It was not coming. There was nothing left to write. Billy put the pen down and started reading over what he'd written.

'Are you finished?' Amy asked.

Billy turned to her, the creases disappearing from his brow. 'Yeah, I think so. And you?'

Amy answered his question by picking the pen back up. She quickly started writing again covering up the page like she thought Billy was going to start copying her. The scraping sound of the pen stopped and Amy looked back at Billy.

'There,' Amy said, putting the pen down. 'All done.'

Billy folded his sheet of paper and watched as Amy did the same. He then picked up the glass jar he had found earlier next to the crooked gate, putting it on the table.

'So this is what we leave behind?' Amy said, putting her folded piece of paper into the glass jar.

'Yes,' Billy said after putting his piece of paper in too. 'And who knows, maybe some day somebody will even find it.'

'And know that we were the last two people to come here,' Amy said, glowing.

Billy smiled. He didn't believe that, couldn't, but it was a nice thought anyway. 'Now we need to find somewhere to put it.'

They both looked around but there was really only one place. The jar was made of thick glass so was quite heavy, it would sit sturdily enough. It was the perfect place to leave it. Now there was nothing else keeping them in The Tunnel.

266

They both sat down against the wall and had something to eat. After that they would pack up and leave. It was now time to go home. The only problem with that being Billy didn't feel like going back any more, despite what Justin had said to him.

They grabbed their bags and headed for the stairs. Billy looked back at where he had left the glass jar on the spot where he had seen Justin. The room seemed to spin for a couple of seconds.

'Are you ready, Billy?' Amy asked.

'Yeah,' Billy said. 'When you are at the top I will turn off the lights.'

'What about you?'

'I'll be all right,' Billy said. 'I'll be right behind you.'

As he listened to Amy's steps echoing up the stairs Billy once again looked around the room. It was still, peaceful, and had told its own story. Billy almost felt saddened to be leaving because he knew he would never be back. This was, after all, their time and their place, and that would never be again. They would only ever be this age once, and to be able to look at The Tunnel with the wonder that such an age only brings.

'Are you coming, Billy?' Amy shouted back down.

'Yes,' Billy shouted up, and then flicked the light switch off.

It didn't take them long to get out of The Tunnel, and each step outside took them further and further away. Billy continually glanced over his shoulder, the dark opening of The Tunnel still looked like a mouth to him, but less scary, getting smaller.

Amy didn't look back, but she was aware that Billy did, and not just the once either. She wanted to go home now, and wanted to be with her family, but she also wanted to stay with Billy. It was hard for both of them because they knew once they arrived back to an all too familiar reality things would never be the same again. How could they?

They walked on, Billy still peering over his shoulder. Once around the bend ahead, the only bend, The Tunnel would no longer be visible. Billy thought back to a time when he was five. The memory clicked in his head like a coin going inside a slot machine.

When Justin had been alive they used to holiday along the East Coast. Billy's parents had bought a caravan there shortly after getting married. The caravan was on a nice spot not far away from the beach. The humidity of the day made it easy for Billy to imagine the sand between his toes, the smell of the sea air, and the sounds of the waves crashing. He loved going to that caravan. He and Justin had some great times there. There had been arguments too, but that didn't matter, what brothers didn't argue? The memories were still magical though, of which Billy would gladly re-live again.

The hardest part about the holidays was leaving. Billy remembered the long stretch of road that led down to where their caravan was. Caravan sites ran all the way along the road, as well as shops and arcades. Leaving, Billy always used to stare out of the back window of the car, watching as the caravan got further and further away in the distance until it was only a speck. By that point Billy would feel deflated, with only the memories of the holiday preventing him from breaking down in tears. That was the same way he felt right now. The Tunnel was now only a speck and a place for some strange reason that he didn't want to leave. But he had to think about Amy. She wanted to go home. He could ask no more of her, she had done so much for him already.

Before going around the only bend Billy had one final look back over his shoulder. He then stopped. Amy stopped too. She looked at Billy, wondering what was wrong.

'What is it?'

Billy shook his head. He didn't want to go home yet. Something was still calling out for him to stay put.

5

Ten miles, as the crow flies, the distance between Billy and a family he was not yet ready to see.

The only thing Billy had missed from home was his bed, and possibly the toilet. The deathly silence at meal times and that feeling of never quite being good enough were not missed. Plus the fact Billy's last contact with his father was something that still frightened him, and the horrifying realisation was Billy felt afraid of going home, and facing his father again. What could there possibly be left to say anyway? It would have to be a bloody good apology. His face still felt tender even though the bruise had started to fade into a yellowy colour now. Billy rubbed his fingers over his left cheek. He didn't hate his father but wasn't sure he loved him either. How could he love a man that treated him so cruelly, deciding to place the blame for losing a son squarely on Billy's shoulders? Billy suddenly started feeling angry. In actual fact he couldn't ever remember feeling so angry before. But it wasn't just anger. He also felt disappointment. Disappointment towards a man who had never once said sorry or asked how he was feeling. And right now if he had the choice between going home and staying inside The Tunnel, staying here would win out every time.

'I understand why you are afraid,' Amy said. 'But it is time to go home now, Billy.'

As if reading his mind, Amy had once again told the truth.

'I'm not ready to go home yet,' Billy said, his voice sounding like that of a defiant child.

'Well, I am not leaving you here alone, Billy Cooper,' Amy said. 'So I guess we have a problem, don't we?'

'I can't go home, Amy,' Billy said, almost pleading with her not to force him to. 'There's so much shit waiting for me back there.'

'But think about what Justin said to you,' Amy said. 'He

269

would not have said those things to you unless home was going to get better for you.'

Billy had thought about that, but sometimes wanting things to change, wanting to believe in a family that had acted like strangers towards one another for the best part of a year, that somehow they could miraculously go back to being like the Waltons was too far for Billy to reach right now. He loved Justin, and believed in Justin, but he just couldn't face the man that hurt him more with one single blow than he ever could have for a year's worth of silence and solitude. Billy concluded that there was nothing waiting for him back home and he wasn't going to go back.

'If I go back home, Amy,' Billy said softy, 'this has all been for nothing.'

'I don't understand, Billy,' Amy said. 'Whatever happens we shall always have what we shared here. Nothing can take that away from us. Do you understand that?'

'No!' Billy said, raising his voice a little. 'You don't get it, Amy. Right now this is our place, and our time. We can do what we want here with no parents complicating matters. If we leave this place then all that changes. I go back to being the lonely kid at school who no-one likes and talks to, except for you. I go back to sitting at the table with my parents, asking myself over and over again how I can make them love me, and why they choose to treat me like shit.' Billy wiped his eyes.

Amy could do nothing but watch and listen. She knew Billy had to get this off his chest, and he had to do it right now.

'Sometimes I lie awake at night just because I know that if I fall asleep I will dream about Justin and this place. The hardest part is always waking up again because then the pain comes back. Justin is dead again and the sounds of my parents arguing in the other room drives me insane.'

'Billy.'

'I can't go back, Amy,' Billy said. His face was angry, tears running down his cheeks at the same time, falling and making little wet spots on the track. The warmth of the sun dried them out but fresh ones soon fell. 'I'm sorry, Amy, but I just can't go back.'

'Billy,' Amy said, taking a couple of steps closer to him. 'It's OK to be scared, it is. I'm afraid of going back home too because you are right Billy, this is our time. But when we get back home things are going to change, Billy. Not everything will be great at first, but I promise you, they will get better.'

There was a slight pause, where Billy looked like he was thinking long and hard about what Amy had just said.

'Our time?' Billy said, wiping his eyes and forcing a smile.

'Yes,' Amy said. 'And it always will be, Billy. This place will always belong to us.'

They hugged.

Our time … this place belongs to Amy and Billy …

'Our place.'

And it did.

The time capsule that they had left behind contained a little part of both of them that would always be inside The Tunnel, waiting to be found.

They separated. Billy wiped his eyes again and then looked at Amy. She smiled, her hazelnut eyes burning holes through him.

'It is going to be OK, Billy Cooper,' Amy said understandingly.

Billy smiled. But Amy had just lied to Billy, the first time she ever did. Billy wiped his face then looked back at The Tunnel for one last time. They then carried on walking along the path. They knew the track, and this time it led the way home, and at the other end something else was waiting for Billy that he was now afraid of.

20

The End of the Line

1

Ten miles … Mid-day … Tuesday …

They had already reached the part of the track where the Legend had met its ugly end. Billy kept his eyes fixed on the water again as they approached. It gleamed like a sheet of glass. Everything was now happening in reverse. The same obstacles in their path, only now overcome in a different order. They stopped near the wooden platform and ate. The supplies were low, but that didn't matter. If they walked quickly, not stopping like they did on the way, then the journey back would be considerably quicker than the journey going. There would be no Legend to contend with. There would hopefully be no old man wearing a hat and pointing a shotgun. But there was one thing that may postpone their journey. Justin's watch, Billy was not going home without it. It was the first night when he had lost it, inside the forest next to the stone camp, so back in the forest he would have to go.

The hours passed by quickly, even though the sticky humidity did not let up. Billy and Amy maintained a steady conversation, talking about everything and nothing; and talking helped Billy forget about going home and facing his parents. Billy's ankle began to throb again but it wasn't bad enough to cause him to want to take a rest. He was sweating, and the new top he had put on a few days ago now felt unclean against his skin. But still they marched on underneath the clear blue sky with only a faint soft breeze offering any comfort.

They stopped another two times that afternoon before reaching the stone camp. Once to eat and take a toilet break, and the other when Billy noticed the old man's house again. This time the old man did not jump out from his hiding place brandishing a shotgun. There was no smoke bellowing out from the chimney like before either. Billy walked up the small grass verge and peered down at the house. The crooked door was closed and a wooden beam was nailed against it and the side of the house. And it wasn't just the door. All the windows were boarded up too. Even though the place needed a hell of a lot of work doing to it the last time he had seen it, Billy was almost certain that the windows had not been boarded up. The place had looked dilapidated, there was no denying that, but now it didn't look lived in, and perhaps hadn't been for some time now.

'That's strange,' Billy said. 'Come and look at this, Amy.'

Amy walked up the grass verge joining Billy.

'Why would he board up his house?'

'I don't know,' Amy said, but having her suspicions just the same.

'I was here, like three days ago,' Billy said, confused.

Maybe Amy had heard one of the stories concerning the track that Billy hadn't. That was why she had been wary of the old man in the first place. And the same story that Justin had heard about William Jacob, Kyle's father – the story about the old man who had killed himself and his dog, after his son had hung himself in front of The Tunnel, and now roamed the track with his gun and makeshift cowboy hat, haunting it.

'Maybe he moved,' Amy said.

273

'Moved? Where to?' Billy asked. 'I don't think he had anywhere else to go.'

'Well who knows then,' Amy said, feeling a sudden impulse to flee this place. 'But I think we should go now, Billy.'

Billy nodded, still looking around the house. He couldn't see the dog either.

'Just one of the many secrets the track has,' Billy said quietly.

Amy nodded her head in agreement. 'I guess so,' she said, not sounding like she particularly cared one way or the other.

Billy and Amy shared a quiet moment before walking back down the grass verge, perhaps once again going over in their minds all the strange things they had witnessed since setting off last Friday night, when the thought of adventure had been as fresh as morning dew. They both smiled at one another, as if to let the other know that they really had seen what they had seen, but perhaps more importantly that they had faced The Tunnel and won. Victory was theirs, and it felt good.

Billy looked back over his shoulder once. There was still no smoke coming from the chimney. And there never had been in the first place. The house had been empty for years.

2

It was now five hours since they had departed The Tunnel. They were making good time. The pace was quick, and Billy hoped that they would reach the stone camp before nightfall. He knew his chances of finding the watch in the darkness would be all but zero. The closer he got to home the more he thought about what he would say to his parents. They had left Friday night, and it was now Tuesday. He wondered if his parents would have even noticed he was missing. But it wasn't just his parents he had to worry about.

There was also Amy's. Billy hoped she was not going to be in too much trouble because of him. Maybe he could go back to Amy's house first to help explain everything to her parents. That way he could delay going home that little bit longer. Anything that could stall his return would do really. And maybe after going back to Amy's he could go for a walk. Market Harborough was quite the place to be at night time. Yes, there was plenty to see. The church, library, local shops … Who was he kidding here? Billy knew that wouldn't work. The quicker he confronted his parents the better. The way he was thinking he would never go back home. But then he did think about one place he could go after taking Amy home.

'Penny for them,' Amy suggested.

'What?' Billy asked quickly.

'Your thoughts, a penny for them.'

Billy smiled. 'Sorry, I was just thinking about home again.'

'I thought so,' Amy said. 'Anything you want to run by me?'

'No,' Billy said. 'Not yet. But thanks for asking.'

Billy tried not thinking about home again for the time being, or what he was going to say to his parents, especially his dad. But he couldn't help wondering if anything would be different when he was back home. What would his father say to him? What would his excuses be for knocking Billy to the floor? Billy's mind raced on, like a speeding car around a track, the first encounter with his mum, that should be one to remember. As far as Billy was concerned she always followed suit with his father, but she never hit him, and Billy took some comfort from that. His father though, what was he going to do when his father stood in front of him and said sorry? Billy didn't know.

Justin said they would get better, Billy was dubious, and for the first time ever found himself doubting his brother, but maybe just maybe … Was it the thought of him not coming back that had tilted the scales, or was it something else? Did his parents still think he was even alive? Was he going to return home to the sound of police sirens or find his photograph pinned to every telegraph pole in town, *Have you seen this boy?* Would he be in the local newspapers, holy shit, what if he'd even made the front cover? A little part of Billy liked that idea, a little ...

Billy noticed Amy looking at him every so often like she was trying to read what he was thinking. Billy had no doubt that she did.

Another hour passed, and their journey was now drawing to an end. Billy and Amy didn't talk so much in the latter stage, and maybe it finally dawned on them that their time was coming to an end. And Amy realised she was going to have to tell Billy about her family moving. The 'For Sale' sign had been up outside her house for ages now so Billy must have seen it at some point. Amy reckoned he had just chosen to ignore it, knowing their time together was drawing to an end, trying to hold onto something that was slipping through his fingers like water. And it broke her heart to think that.

3

It was almost dusk when they reached the stone camp. They had stopped an hour ago to finish off what was left of the food and drink. If Billy needed a reason to go back home then at least he now had one. Hunger would always win out in the end. But Billy had been known to be stubborn, even with the insatiable need for food and drink he would not go home until he felt ready, and ready was a word he did not like to use at the moment. Billy Cooper was going to find Justin's golden watch, walk Amy home, and then consider his options. At the moment he was hoping he would come up with something before then because right now he had jack shit.

'Home sweet home,' Amy said.

The sound of her voice made Billy smile, soothed his soul like a sonnet. He then stopped smiling because if they had reached the stone camp then that also meant they were less than mile away from home, the end of the line. But there was now another problem.

'Does the torch still work?' Billy asked.

'I sure hope so,' Amy said, putting her backpack down on the track. She knelt down and rummaged around inside it before finally bringing out the silver micro light again.

Click…

The beam was weak, and what had once been Billy's shield, protecting them from the hideous horrors that only seemed to be known at night, was now just a dim light that hardly made its presence known at all.

'Sorry,' Amy said. 'I didn't think there was much life left in it.'

'It's better than nothing,' Billy said, sounding quite positive.

'Agreed,' Amy said, nodding, and then turned the micro light off.

Once they were next to the stone camp Billy reckoned he would remember the path he had taken into the forest, and hopefully find the small pond, then the prize, Justin's watch.

'Billy,' Amy said, stopping him as he made his way over to the embankment. Amy wanted to tell Billy, she really did, but the look on his face told her that it was not the right time. It could wait … But maybe there is never a right time for hurting someone you love.

'What is it?' Billy asked.

I'm moving, Billy, out of Harborough … My dad has got another … I leave…

Amy couldn't do it, the words stayed put, floating around inside her head only for her to listen to.

'Don't slip, like last time …'

Billy smiled. 'I won't.'

Billy knew that wasn't what Amy had wanted to say, and Amy knew that Billy knew that too.

They went down the embankment.

Billy did not slip.

4

Amy handed the torch to Billy and he did not switch it on until they entered the forest. The stone camp looked no different, and it felt strange being back again. It was almost like the shelter had been waiting for their return. The forest was as dense as Billy had remembered, tree branches entwining, blocking out the night sky.

A noise, an owl maybe, Billy hoped.

A twig snapping, Billy hoped caused by him or Amy. The torch beam diminished quickly, there wasn't going to be much time.

On the first night there had been sufficient space between the trees for the light of the moon to penetrate deep into the forest. It was almost like that gap had been deliberate, providing the night life with a light. Once again the light of the moon lit up a section of the forest, a small pond shone in the strange blue haze. Billy remembered the pond. He remembered running because something had scared him, something had been watching him all the time he had been inside the forest. He remembered that too.

The Legend, he thought, trying his best to fight off an oncoming shudder, and remembering their fight at the same time.

I, Billy Cooper, did slay the Legend.

'Billy,' Amy said, seeing his little body trembling. 'What is it?'

'Nothing,' Billy said.

The Legend was dead, hopefully, so he didn't feel it necessary to mention anything to Amy. There was no use in

278

them both being scared right now, only Amy was, she had been for quite some time now.

'I think I fell round about here.' Billy shone the torch around fallen branches and roots that looked like huge biceps protruding out from the soil.

'OK,' Amy said, her tone of voice not able to hide how difficult she thought this was going to be.

'We have to find it,' Billy said, looking around. 'I can't leave without it …'

With what little light the torch had left they searched the bed of the forest, the light of the moon making blue patterns across their faces. It seemed hopeless but then Billy saw something gold twinkling in the light. Could it be? He turned around to Amy and was about to shout out in jubilation when he stopped. Amy had her hands down by her sides and was just staring at Billy, the moonlight catching the right side of her face.

'What's wrong?' Billy asked. 'Amy?'

'We're moving,' Amy said.

The torchlight then went out but Amy still saw the hurt on Billy's face just before it did.

'Oh.'

It was the only thing Billy could think of to say.

5

As Amy had guessed, Billy knew, deep down he had always known. But still, denial can sometimes be a wonderful thing, if not a damaging one at the same time. Billy had seen the 'For Sale' sign up in front of Amy's house. Once again though he had chosen to ignore it.

The Tunnel; that had been all he had thought about at that time and the 'For Sale' sign standing guard in front of Amy's house was something Billy didn't want to think about then. And who knew, maybe it would have gone away by the time they returned? Billy had thought about it on the way and on the way back too. But he knew it was not going to be gone when they returned, just like the dawn of a new day would surely always rise, the signpost would still be standing outside the Johnston family house. But still, Billy hoped, he really hoped. But he was now old enough to realise that sometimes hope is not always enough. Billy Cooper had always been a bit of a dreamer, he was now waking up.

Amy didn't plan to tell Billy then. She had wanted to do it back home, but the words just shot out of her mouth like automatic fire from a machine gun. Maybe she knew the longer she put off saying anything then the harder it would be on Billy, and her. And now the words were out she felt a weight leaving her, she thought she could float home, she felt that light.

The truth will set us free, Billy suddenly thought, not remembering where he had heard that phrase before, but probably from a film he had seen a hundred times.

There was a pause that seemed to last an eternity. Amy waited for a reaction from Billy; anything would do, and eventually she got one.

'Come here,' Billy said, starting to walk over to the pond.

Amy followed, really wishing she could read Billy's mind for real in that moment.

The pond rippled in the moonlight. Billy watched the water, taken over by a brilliant blue glow. He thought how beautiful it looked, tranquil and magical. The gold glow also grabbed his attention. It had to be the watch, just had to be. He couldn't be certain, but reckoned they were standing round about where he had fallen. He had never even felt the watch leave his wrist.

Amy looked on as Billy put down his bag and dropped to his knees and started moving his hands over the bed of the forest.

'Have you found it?' Amy asked after a short time.

Billy didn't answer, just carried on feeling through the dirt like a dog searching for a bone.

'So, about me moving,' Amy said casually.

'Wait,' Billy said, still feeling the bed of the forest.

'The watch,' Amy said.

Billy got back to his feet, turned and faced Amy. The watch was dangling between his right index finger and thumb.

Amy smiled, and watched as Billy put the watch back on.

'I guess there is nothing left to stay for now,' Billy said, admiring the watch on his wrist, and now feeling whole again. It was a little dirty, but Billy would soon put that to rights once back home, and what do you know, there was reason number two for going back home.

'Billy,' Amy said tentatively, 'about what I said ... I didn't mean to just come out and say it like that.'

'It's OK,' Billy said. 'I guess I have always known anyway.'

'I'm sorry.'

'Don't be,' Billy said. 'You have to be with your family, I know that. You don't ever have to say sorry to me, Amy, not after all that you've done for me.'

It was a brave sentiment from an even braver little boy.

Amy smiled, and realised Billy Cooper was not the same Billy Cooper who had run away from home four nights ago. Something about him looked different, and in that moment Amy realised he would be all right, that his family would be all right, and Amy was very rarely wrong when it came down to Billy Cooper.

'When do you leave?'

'Saturday.'

Jesus Christ, talk about the fastest train out of this shit hole, Billy thought.

And as Billy had said, there was nothing left keeping them here now. They left the forest and headed back up onto the track. Just as they reached the top of the embankment Billy heard another twig snapping, and was then finally glad that they were going home.

6

The watch was still ticking, and the luminous hands told Billy that it was now approaching 10pm.

Billy's feet ached, his back ached, his whole body ached. Tiredness had also crept over him, his eyelids suddenly felt like lead weights on his face. His shoes were almost sliding against the track now, like he was even too tired to pick his own feet up properly.

The trees and bushes thinned around them, even in the darkness Billy knew this. That told him that they were close to the end of the line. They walked on with nothing visible up ahead, apart from a blanket of darkness that seemed never ending. With each step Billy made, his body grew heavier, the bag he was carrying felt like it was filled with sand not clothing, he had even forgotten that Amy had been holding his hand since they had left the forest. But there was then a sound, they both heard it. Billy's eyes closed, he had to open them again quickly, otherwise the track would have been his bed for the night.

That sound again coming through the darkness.

Billy felt Amy's hand tighten in his own.

Whoosh ...

There it was again.

Whoosh ... *Whoosh.*

Billy now knew what it was. 'The end of the line.'

And it was.

7

Through the darkness something was starting to appear. The sounds they could hear were cars passing by on the A508 road leading to Northampton.

The street lights made the fencing visible, even the lights from the houses across the road could now be seen. Billy needed nothing else to tell him that their journey was coming to an end, and how thankful his body was. But as tired and achy as he felt, Billy did not go home that night after all. What had once been the beginning of their journey was now the end. Billy almost felt like he should say something deep, profound to Amy but she seemed content enough holding his hand, keeping pace with him.

When they reached the fence they both stopped and looked at one another. The truth was Billy had never expected to come back. And here they both were, and this particular adventure was now over and how relieved they both felt. Each one of them had their own story to tell, and their time to be remembered. Billy Cooper would now start writing again.

'We made it then!' Amy said, leaning against the fence.

'Yeah,' Billy said, resting his hands down onto one of the posts, 'I guess we did.'

It didn't feel like there was anything left to say, but Amy said it anyway. 'Are you ready to go home then, Billy?'

'Not yet,' Billy said, seeing little creases appearing in Amy's forehead as she frowned. 'Not until I walk you home first.'

Amy's frown disappeared and she smiled that same smile that Billy reckoned could light up the darkest place on Earth.

'A man with a gun, a monster, The Tunnel ... we had quite the adventure, Billy Cooper.'

'Yes we did,' Billy said with a smile. 'Yes we did.'

But had it all really happened, had they both really seen

the things they had seen? The images inside Billy's head told him that they did, and the pain he was feeling knowing Amy was going away was a welcome distraction, but either way he wasn't going to sleep that well tonight.

It didn't take them long to arrive back at Amy's house. The small garden at the front with low white fencing, long blocked paved driveway with the red estate parked on it, everything looked the same, and the 'For Sale' sign was still there.

The night sky was clearing and the moon lit up the house, but there were no lights on in any of the windows. Billy looked at his watch, it was now 10.30pm.

'Do you want me to come inside with you?' Billy asked.

'It's OK,' Amy said.

'You won't be in any trouble, will you?'

'Probably!' Amy said. 'But thanks anyway.'

Billy smiled, shuffled his feet a little and then said, 'So I'll pop around before you leave, you know, on Saturday ... if that's all right?'

Amy seemed to pause for a short while before saying, 'Of course it is, stupid.'

Billy smiled and nodded his head at the same time.

'I better go inside,' Amy said, turning and looking at the house.

'All right,' Billy said.

Amy smiled then started walking down the long driveway. Billy watched her, feeling like little pieces of his heart were being chipped away the further she walked away.

Amy stopped and turned. She just looked at Billy before saying, 'Are you going to be all right, Billy Cooper?'

'Yeah,' Billy said, but he knew he wasn't. Amy turned and started walking away again.

'Amy!'

She stopped, and turned around again, the whole thing now felt like some kind of dance routine.

'Thanks for coming with me,' Billy said. 'Thanks for believing in me. I know I couldn't have done it without you. Thanks for always being there for me.'

Amy smiled then quickly walked back over to Billy and kissed him on the cheek.

'We had quite the adventure, didn't we, Billy Cooper?' Amy said.

'Yes we did,' Billy said, smiling.

8

Billy stayed at the bottom of the driveway until Amy had gone inside the house.

'We could always try the long distance thing,' Billy said. 'What do you reckon?'

'*Maybe,*' Justin said. '*After all it did work for me.*'

'With who?' Billy asked.

'*Sue,*' Justin said. '*I had a long distance relationship with Sue.*'

'No you didn't,' Billy said. 'I remember this. She dumped you before she moved away. You sobbed like a baby for a week.'

'*Oh yeah,*' Justin said, laughing and putting his little brother in a head lock.

Billy laughed, and grabbed his brother around the waist. 'The long distance thing it is then.'

'*And why not, Billy Boy.*'

Billy looked up when he saw Amy's bedroom light coming on. She waved down at him before pulling the curtains. Billy smiled and waved back. He now had to start thinking about going home himself. With his bag over his right shoulder he crossed the road and started thinking where he could spend the night. There was only really one place he could think of, and there he could be with Justin for real.

'*Come on, Billy; let's get out of here*'

'Do you think that she will ever forget about me?' Billy said, turning and walking away.

'No,' Justin said. *'How could she? In my experience you never forget a pain in the ass.'*

Billy laughed and carried on walking with his brother, only seeing one shadow on the path underneath the moonlight.

21

Going Home Part II

1

Kate Cooper hadn't had much sleep last night. Alex was now sleeping soundly next to her, whilst Kate was listening to the morning chorus made by the birds.

It was already light outside so Kate got out of bed. It was hard for her to make sense of what she had seen the other day. She had always been a non-believer in the supernatural, a lady of reason, and had felt ridiculous whilst explaining it all to Alex. But she could not deny what she had witnessed with her own eyes. Something had told her to leave Billy alone, that he had to find out the truth for himself. Kate Cooper had taken something else away from that message too, and that was Billy would return home when he was good and ready to do so.

Kate had checked his bedroom yesterday morning, and she was going to do the same thing again now. She had even left the front door unlocked at night, since Sunday, in the hope that Billy would eventually find his way home and creep in. She wanted him to be in his bed, she prayed to God that he would be.

Kate walked over to the bedroom door and put on her white dressing gown. The carpet felt cold underneath her bare feet so she slipped on her slippers before leaving the bedroom. A quick look at Alex's alarm clock told her it was only 7am. This time last week the house would have been full of movement, Alex getting ready for work, Billy getting ready for school, but the silence was still the same. Kate hated herself for that.

Kate had lied for her husband. She had phoned his offices and told them that he collapsed on the Saturday and had been taken to hospital. Luckily her nosy fucking neighbour had been out the day it had all happened. Their business would be known by everyone now if the situation had been any different. Alex and Kate had had a long conversation last night about the way forward for their family. It was not going to be easy, but Kate had told Alex that they had to start somewhere. She had also told him that she reckoned Justin had left the message for her on the notepad. Alex had looked at her like she had been crazy for even considering such a ridiculous idea. But that had been before he broke down and started crying. He'd never got over losing his son, and was going to start opening his eyes to the one he had left. If Justin had left that message for Kate to find then that meant he was still a presence in their house, gone, but still part of their lives, and that filled Alex with hope, and right now that was all he had, hope that things could be fixed, hope that his son would give him a second chance, even if he didn't deserve one.

Kate looked in on Billy's room. The bed was still made, only a little crease in the quilt from where she had sat last night crying, hoping for her son's safe return. The curtains were still drawn and the room had an empty feeling to it that made Kate want to scream out. She heard Alex stir in the other room then everything went silent again. If Kate Cooper needed any proof that what she witnessed two days ago was not just her imagination then she was about to get it.

Billy's bedroom suddenly went cold again, just like the last

288

time. Kate had to pull her dressing gown out in front of her and tie it. Her breath was visible, looking like little puffs of smoke each time she exhaled. She folded her arms, rubbing her hands over them.

'Justin,' she said cautiously, 'is it you again, Justin?'

The window was not open but still the curtains blew inwards, Kate shuddered, her body started shaking, suddenly becoming impossible to control.

'Justin,' she said again.

Kate was about to ask what he wanted when the notepad on Billy's bed rose up in the air and then floated above the bed again. The page with the first message turned over. Kate looked on, her body feeling like ice. Another message, this had to be another message. Justin was communicating with her again; he had something to tell her. Kate wanted to go and wake Alex, she had been dubious about whether he had believed her when she had told him about her experience the other day, if he saw it with his own eyes then he would have to believe her, he would just have to, but Kate didn't want to move right now, she had a feeling that if she did then the message would not be written and she would then spend the rest of her days wondering what if. The last message contained information about Billy, so why would this time be any different? Justin was helping; he was helping Kate to find her son and to bring him back home. God how she hoped that was the case.

There was now a pen floating next to the notepad. It moved quickly in front of the paper and began writing. Kate could hear the scraping sound being made by the tip of the pen again. Was Justin actually writing this, was he actually in the room right now like before? Kate did nothing but watch. The message was now finished. Kate Cooper read it, her body erupting in goose pimples as she did.

2

Billy had a dream. It was a pleasant one for a change.

In it he had been sitting on his bed and writing a story. It was about a little boy who had gone to The Tunnel with his best friend called, Amy. Billy had written pages and pages of story filled with adventure and surprise in his notepad, all of which had felt so real, like he had actually lived through it. His little hand couldn't write fast enough, trying to keep pace with all the ideas flooding out from his head.

It must have been sometime ago, this dream, because Justin was in it, and alive. Billy hadn't realised at first but Justin was standing in the doorway and watching his little brother doing what he had always thought he was born to do. Billy turned yet another page of the notepad and continued writing at the same hectic pace. He didn't know the ending yet, but that didn't matter.

'It's not about the ending but the journey, right, Billy Boy?' he heard Justin say.

Then the pen stopped.

'Why is that?' Billy asked, looking up in wonder. 'If the journey has no regard for the ending then why even bother with it in the first place?'

Justin smiled and walked into Billy's room. Billy put down the pen and pad, he heard a bird singing outside, a car pulling up and beeping its horn, his own heart beating. Was it really real? Was he here right now sitting, writing in the past tense about something that had not even happened? If Justin was inside his room then it couldn't have been, could it?

'An ending is just that,' Justin said, sitting down on the end of the bed. 'But a journey is an on-going adventure, Billy. Life is a journey, the people you meet, the places you visit, the good and bad times that you experience.'

'So a journey doesn't have to end?'

'Maybe not,' Justin said. 'But always remember, a good journey always leads to an even better one at the end.'

'I don't understand,' Billy said, frowning and now sitting up.

'It's simple,' Justin said. 'When one part of your life ends, then the other part begins. There is never really an ending just little pauses along the way, allowing for change, allowing for growth. Sometimes the little pauses overlap, and sometimes you start anew. You are coming up to that part now, Billy.'

'A new start?'

'Yes,' Justin said, 'not an ending, Billy, just a short pause, bringing with it a new journey for you to take next.'

'Where will I go?' Billy asked.

'Wherever you want to, Billy … wherever you want. You are bound by nothing, little bro.'

Billy smiled and looked at Justin. Maybe it was time for a new beginning, a new journey, and the ending could be whatever he wanted it to be. After all, from now on he was going to be making the rules, hell, writing them.

The dream went a little hazy from there, speeding along like a film on fast forward, little images being recognisable but most of it all jumbled and hard to follow.

The sounds of the morning slowly brought Billy back. He opened his eyes and looked up at the dawn of a new day. The cool fresh air bit at his exposed arms like teeth, but he didn't care. He was with his hero this morning, had been for all of the night, and they had talked a lot, mostly about Amy, and that whole long distance thing.

You sobbed like a baby for a week …

Billy was lying on his back with his head resting on his bag. He ran his fingers through the damp grass next to Justin's grave. The headstone had weathered a little but the verse was still clear to read.

'JUSTIN COOPER – Called Away By An Angel,' the top verse read.

'Gone, but never forgotten, R.I.P.' Billy read.

Last night he had walked almost a mile from Amy's house to the cemetery, and was about ready to drop when he arrived. The night had been warm and Billy had slept like a hound dog next to his brother's grave. It had felt like the right thing to do last night, to be with his brother, his hero. When Justin died Billy had hated the idea of him being out here all alone. But he realised last night that Justin wasn't alone, and his journey may have ended, or paused, in this world, but surely continued on in the next. Like Justin had once said, it isn't about the ending. It is the journey along the way that matters.

Billy sat up and rubbed his weary looking face, his hair all ruffled and knotted. At first the morning light hurt his eyes but they were now adjusting. He yawned twice then put his red cardigan back on, which he had used as a blanket last night. The cardigan had been a bright red colour when Billy had set out. It was now more of a burgundy colour, looking stained from his journey.

Billy felt the need to stretch so got to his feet and started walking around and arching his back like a cat. He looked across the cemetery at the plot where he had first seen Amy. He wished Amy was here right now, he felt a little lost without her this morning. Spending the past few days with her, Billy had realised how much Amy meant to him, and now not to have her with him made him feel a little empty inside. She was also leaving, and Billy tried forgetting that, after all they still had a couple of days to spend some time together.

Another pause, Billy thought, a*nd another journey coming to an end. But what will be next?*

A new journey, not an ending, Billy now understood. Everything is connected, overlapping, the choices we take in life are no exception to this. Billy thought about Amy and smiled. For the first time in a long time he felt some hope, some direction, something to aim towards. He now believed what Justin had said about things improving, they had to, this part of his life had ended. With this fresh new morning came a fresh new start for Billy Cooper, he just wished Amy was here to share it with him.

When Billy looked away from where he had first seen Amy he noticed someone out of the corner of his eye. He turned quickly, half expecting to find Amy standing there and smiling. When he looked he did actually see Amy for a split second, but it wasn't Amy. Kate Cooper was standing there, trying to find the right words to say.

3

It all came down to this then: Kate Cooper had rehearsed what she was going to say to Billy a hundred times, but now nothing was coming out, it was like her lips had been stapled together. The first thing she noticed was how dirty Billy looked, small, his grubby face looking frightened and surprised all at the same time. She had to say something first, she just had to. Billy deserved that at the very least.

'I'm sorry, Billy,' Kate said, her voice was weak, her hands trembling down by her sides. Without realising she took a couple of steps forward.

Billy looked on, watching a lady that he loved but strangely didn't feel like he knew any more. He could feel his heart thudding inside his chest, and knew he should say something back but just couldn't. Maybe he had grown used to not saying an awful lot to his mother, in actual fact he couldn't remember the last time they had a proper conversation.

In that moment Billy wanted it to rain, for an earthquake to happen, even a bomb dropping out of the sky, anything would have been better than this awkward silence. It didn't seem to matter before, but now it did, so what did that mean? The cleansing had begun.

'Would you please come home with me, Billy?' Kate asked, reaching out with her right hand, her voice still straining a little. 'We can talk then. We need to talk, Billy.'

Home?

Home is where the heart is, Billy heard Justin saying inside his head. *Go, Billy Boy…*

And maybe that was the truth, but Billy felt too hurt, too angry, too disappointed to consider going back home with this woman. He had always known that this was going to be hard, but looking at his mum, the woman that had given birth to him twelve years ago, he hadn't realised that he would feel such rage inside, boiling up like a volcano that had once been dormant. Billy didn't want to feel like this, and hated himself for it, but couldn't think of one thing, anything that was remotely heart-warming about his mother. There was no memory of a hug, or her asking about how he was feeling. The woman had shown him zero compassion at Justin's funeral, she couldn't even bring herself to look at him, let alone touch and offer what little comfort she could have. Billy felt let down, let down by the one person that a little boy should never feel let down by. He wished it were different, he wished for a memory, a kind word, a smile, anything would have done. Billy remembered nothing.

'Billy…'

Kate stepped forward again, her palms now feeling sweaty despite the cool morning air.

'How did you find me?'

It was the only thing that Billy could think of to say. He guessed it had just been good luck, or maybe Amy. Yes Amy. Kate had probably gone around her house earlier on in the morning, hoping that Amy would be back and ready to tell her where Billy was. Amy would have guessed the cemetery; she always knew where Billy would be. And knowing how much Amy cared for him she would have told Kate with little resistance.

'I had a little help,' Kate said, her cheeks looking rosy red. She was wearing a long black coat, making her look rather like a pallbearer.

'Amy told you,' Billy quickly said.

'No,' Kate said, shaking her head. 'It wasn't Amy, Billy, it was your brother.'

'What?'

Billy was stunned, and could not hide the fact, his face looking like he had a million questions all over again.

'Justin told me where to find you, Billy,' Kate said, steadily walking forwards, her hands going up to cover her quivering mouth. She then had a horrible idea that Billy was suddenly going to bolt, like a frightened horse. But he didn't. If there was any reason for him to stay, any reason for him to listen, then this was it.

'He wants us to be a family again, Billy,' Kate said, crying. 'And so do I.'

Billy let his mum get closer.

Kate finally reached Billy then held him. Billy did not put any fight up. Kate just held her son next to Justin's grave, like she should have done a year ago.

4

The walk back to the car had felt like a walk on death row, but it wasn't Old Sparky waiting for Billy at the end of the path. It was his father, Alex, waiting in their family estate. They used to need the big car for family holidays, but it was now yet another painful memory of happier times. The boot packed tight full of luggage, Billy having to sit in between all the extra items Justin always took, but never used.

Kate kept an arm around Billy all the time whilst walking

back to the car, and occasionally looked down at him. She didn't do it for her own selfish needs or through fear of Billy deciding it was now high time to turn tail and run. No! She did it because it was the right thing to do. She wanted her son back, she wanted him home again. She wanted to be a mother again. Alex was waiting inside the car, mostly fidgeting his right leg and biting his finger-nails, something that he had not done since being a little boy. The truth was he had no idea what he was going to say to Billy. And watching as his son got closer and closer to the car he began to fidget even more. The man was acting like somebody had doused him with itching powder.

'It will be OK, Billy,' Kate had said in a reassuring voice as she opened the back door for him.

Step inside Billy, oh yeah, Old Sparky is waiting for ya boy...

Billy got into the car with the same unease as an animal stepping back into a cage.

Thud!

The door closed; there would be no running away now. His father turned around, he was about to speak when Kate entered the car. All Billy could see, all he could think about was the slap he received from his dad on the night he had set off for The Tunnel. That had been the final push that Billy had needed to go. In a strange sort of way he felt like he should thank his dad for that, it was that fucking ridiculous.

It will be OK, Justin's comforting words told Billy. *Just have faith.*

Billy's poker expression told Alex nothing, and that was what Billy had wanted. Alex was going to have to earn his son's respect, gain his love and trust again slowly.

There was so much water under the bridge, but Alex reckoned he could do it.

'I'm sorry, Billy,' Alex said. 'I'm sorry for everything.'

That was a nervous moment for Kate. When Alex spoke she turned in her seat, going from Billy then to Alex, Billy then to Alex, she looked like a woman watching a tennis match. Billy didn't answer, just stared blankly at his father. Alex stared back, praying for a response. Kate could bear it no longer. She had to intervene as this was starting to feel like a Mexican stand-off.

'Billy's, tired, Alex,' Kate said sincerely. 'Let's get him home. We can all talk later on.' She smiled a smile that Billy couldn't remember seeing in a long time. Maybe there was hope, maybe …

Alex nodded, and Billy leaned back in his seat and looked out of the window. The car started and Kate drove off. Billy could see his dad every so often looking at him through the mirror, almost turning to speak, then changing his mind. Billy was glad, he didn't want to talk right now. He was overcome with tiredness. He looked out of the window again, then back in the side mirror of the car. Alex was still watching him. The town flashed by in the blink of an eye, and when they finally arrived back home, Billy was fast asleep in the back seat. He dreamt about The Tunnel, but this time there was nothing to be afraid of. Billy Cooper was home again.

That's right, Billy Boy, you sleep now, you have had a busy few days.

5

Billy awoke. He was lying on his bed. His legs felt stiff and so did his neck. He didn't feel so tired any more though. He yawned then sat up, stretching out his limbs. The cemetery hadn't been that great for sleeping, Billy realised just how true that was now after waking up in his own bed. He was still in the same clothes, that wouldn't do. He looked at the clock on the wall. It was 5pm.

He now wanted a shower so left his room and went down the hall. He stopped outside the bathroom. He could hear voices, something that surprised him. He went into the kitchen and stopped outside the living room door, peering through the small gap. His parents were talking; they were both sitting on the settee and actually indulging in a conversation. For a horrible second Billy thought that he must still be asleep, that he would awake again to find that things were just as shitty as they used to be. But he wasn't sleeping.

Billy waited by the door for quite some time. He couldn't hear what was being said, but stayed there just the same. Maybe it was seeing his parents acting like husband and wife, not ignoring each other like they usually did, or maybe in that moment he saw hope, saw a family again.

The journey continues ... And never ends.

It's not about the ending; it's the journey that matters ...

Justin's words echoed like he was standing inside a large hallway whilst delivering them. *It will be all right ... I promise you.*

And Billy believed him. In that moment he really did. He smiled. But what he wanted now was far more important than anything else. And it was going to be the best shower he'd ever had in his life.

6

It was gone. The journal was missing.

Now he went for a shower, and before, BEFORE! It had been there. There was something else Billy was missing too. He left his room.

Hair still wet and hanging down over his face like spaghetti, he entered the kitchen. Billy was wearing grey baggy jogging pants and beige T-shirt.

His parents were sitting at the table. Kate had the journal. It was down on the table next to a brown folder that Billy immediately recognised.

'What's going on?' Billy asked suspiciously.

'Don't be mad,' Kate said softly. 'I couldn't help myself.'

Billy looked confused and made a step closer to the table. He looked at his father then at his mother, then down at the journal again.

'Your mum's been looking for this all year,' Alex said, tapping his right index finger down against the journal. 'Haven't you?'

Alex was now looking at Kate, and holding her left hand. Billy made a mental note, not being able to move his eyes away. He couldn't remember the last time he had seen his parents holding hands, probably another lifetime ago, far off in a land where little boys grew up to be gunslingers and still referred to a woman as ma'am.

'I knew he kept this journal,' Kate said, wiping her teary eyes. 'I searched high and low for it after the funeral. I just couldn't find it.'

'But you found it, Billy,' Alex said softly, and looking at his son like he once did.

'Justin wanted me to have it,' Billy said. 'He left it at the old tunnel just before he died.'

Alex and Kate nodded in unison, surprising Billy a little.

'I found your drawings,' Kate said, looking down at the brown folder. 'At least we now know what they mean. He came to you in a dream, didn't he?'

Billy didn't think that was strictly true. Justin had wanted him to go to The Tunnel, but the force hired to guide him there had been the Gate Keeper.

'Yes,' Billy said softly. 'He did, Mum.'

'Here you are, son,' Alex said, holding out the journal for Billy to take.

Son...

Billy reached out slowly with his right hand as if he were afraid the journal would be hot.

'I'm sorry, Billy,' Alex said, handing Billy the journal. 'I'm sorry for everything...'

They both looked at one another. Alex smiled a soft smile, one that told Billy he did still love him, but had just forgotten that somewhere along the way and that he had no excuses for the way he had acted. That smile told Billy more than words could ever have.

Looking at his father smiling, and listening to his mother's gentle sobs, Billy suddenly felt weak inside, like someone had taken away his essence. He wanted to cry too, but didn't.

'Thank you.'

Billy started walking back towards his room.

'Billy!' Kate cried.

He stopped and turned around.

Kate looked at him for a second or two, her eyes still running with tears. 'We love you, Billy.' There was a slight pause. 'We just wanted you to know that.'

'I know,' Billy said.

That night Billy said goodnight to both his parents for the first time in a long time. It was going to take some time to get things back on track, they all knew this, there would be no short cuts, but that was OK, time was on their side, and tomorrow would be a new day. Billy had wanted to phone Amy, to tell her that things weren't as bad as he'd originally thought, but didn't. She was most probably still getting the third degree from her parents for their little trip away. He would go and see her in the next couple of days, and say goodbye, close another chapter in his short life. He wondered who would be in the next one.

He also scanned through Justin's journal that night. There was one part that he found straight away, probably by accident, but Billy didn't think so.

It read:

1st July 2002.

I was so proud of Billy today. Mum and dad were too, I could see it in their eyes. I hope they look at me like that one day. Billy is not even twelve yet, but already he is becoming quite the storyteller. He let me read one today called 'Shadow Dancer'. Basically it's a short story about a little boy's fears of losing his parents. I loved it, and hope he carries on with his writing. I let mum and dad read it too. I know Billy only wanted me to read it (so if you are reading this, WHICH YOU HAD BETTER NOT BE, BILLY, sorry, Billy). I just wanted mum and dad to see you as I do, a talented kid who can do anything that he wants to. That's it really, apart from that I'm going to the tunnel over the next few days, have got to find out if there is any truth behind all those crazy stories I keep on hearing about before I leave for college next week. Have a present to give Billy before I leave, in actual fact I have two for him. Oh shit, I think I have just shot myself in the foot here. That's all then folks, a bit light today I know, but hey … The journey continues … And never ends.

Billy smiled, wiped his eyes then closed the journal. He slept well that night and dreamed his dreams.

Epilogue

It was raining hard when Billy arrived at Amy's house. It was
Friday, the day before she was leaving. The walk took Billy a
little longer than usual, perhaps because he knew it was
going to be the last time he was going to be doing it.

He waited in front of her house, wet and cold, feeling the
rain running down his back, his young face for the first time
in a long time showing signs of happiness and hope. But Billy
had a problem which he needed to discuss with Amy. And
since this was probably going to be his last chance to speak
face to face with her then he knew it was important that he
did.

Billy took note of the sign outside the house. It now had
'Sold' written on it. The sign now made it real for Billy, the
move was happening, he was going to have to say goodbye to
Amy today. He preferred saying goodbye to Amy today
instead of tomorrow, when she was leaving. Maybe this way
he had more time to change her mind, maybe?

Go to her, Billy Boy ...

Billy walked down the long driveway and before he could
even ring the door bell Amy appeared at the door. She was
wearing a white dress, her hair tied back into a pony-tail. She
also had a blue ribbon in her hair.

'Hi Billy,' Amy said.

Her voice was a little subdued, like she too was feeling the strains of the move, and she was. And all the hurt that Billy felt in that moment belonged to Amy too.

'Hi,' Billy said.

His jeans had damp patches on them and his jacket was soaked through. He looked like a drowned rat, just like he had done after his fight with the Legend.

'Come on in out of the rain,' Amy said taking Billy by the hand.

He went inside.

The house looked quite empty, Billy guessed most of their stuff had already been packed away and sent to the new house by now. It suddenly occurred to him as he followed Amy into the large front room that he hadn't even asked where it was Amy was moving to, but there was something else he had to ask first.

There was a brown settee against the far wall which they both sat down on. The rest of the room was empty, nothing but bare white walls and red carpet, windows without curtains and nets.

'How are things then?' Amy asked. sitting up straight with her hands clasped together on her lap. 'With your family, I mean.'

Obviously, Billy knew what she had been referring to.

'OK,' Billy said. 'I mean, you know … It will take time, but things are OK.'

'I'm pleased,' Amy said, smiling. 'I didn't want to leave if they weren't.'

Billy smiled and looked around the room then back at Amy, wishing he had now told her that things were really totally shitty with his family.

'*Yeah you know gal, things are just as shit-filled as they used to be, and in actual fact are worse … So I guess you will have to stay after all. What do you say?*'

303

Billy suddenly felt nervous, like this was the first time he had ever met Amy; his heart was racing and his palms all sweaty. He had planned what he was going to say to Amy last night and he had a dress rehearsal this morning in front of the bathroom mirror whilst squeezing a zit on his forehead.

'Don't go, Amy,' Billy said, taking her hand in his.

It hadn't quite sounded like that in the rehearsal, but that didn't seem to matter any more, Billy knew first hand that sometimes the words people say in their heads are never always quite as easy to say out loud.

Amy looked at Billy, her face full of admiration and love for him, for his bravery, for his integrity, and most importantly for his willingness to wear his young heart on his sleeve.

'I have to go,' Amy said softly, gripping his hand. 'I'm sorry, Billy, but we have to leave tomorrow.'

Her voice trembled, Amy didn't want to leave; it was just the way it had to be. It was her time to move on, just like it was Billy's too. The pages of the story were turning again, and unfortunately for both of them they were not going to be together in the next chapter.

'It's OK,' Billy said, swallowing hard, feeling that lump there again. 'I know … I've always known … I guess.'

And he had, Billy Cooper had, he had always known who Amy really was. His young heart had just chosen not to see what had always been there standing right in front of him.

Amy frowned. 'Billy, please don't. It will only make it harder on the both of us.'

'I don't care,' Billy said shaking his head. 'It is not important to me, and never has been.'

Amy let go of Billy's hand then stood up. 'If you have always known,' she said, turning back towards Billy, 'then you know why I have to leave.'

'It doesn't change anything,' Billy said standing, his hair dripping, making little wet patches on the carpet below.

'Yes it does,' Amy said.

'Why?'

'Because I should never have broken the law, Billy,' Amy said. 'We have rules you know.'

'But you did it for me,' Billy said softly. 'You did it for me, Amy.'

'I know,' Amy said tenderly. 'But you have to let me go now, Billy. You have to let me leave. Please see me for who I really am and let me leave.'

'I do,' Billy said. 'I always have, Amy.'

'No,' Amy said. 'I don't think you have, Billy. But now you must.'

Before Billy could speak the room started changing around him. Instead of looking modern yet empty, it was now old and forgotten. The red carpet was replaced by old dusty wooden flooring – the windows were now boarded up, only allowing a little light to penetrate into the vast aged room. The walls were no longer bright white, but had dulled into a murky yellowy colour. The fireplace was dusty and black, probably hadn't been used in fifty years. That was where Amy now stood.

'What happened?' Billy asked.

'You must see what is really in front of you, Billy,' Amy said. 'Not what you want to see.'

Billy frowned, and then started looking around the room in bewilderment.

'Look, Billy,' Amy said pointing at the mantelpiece.

Billy stood and walked over to it, and then looked and saw what Amy was pointing at, her name written in the dust as clear as the day she had done it.

'I died a long time ago, Billy,' Amy said softly. 'You have to see me with your eyes. Not with your heart now.'

'I don't care,' Billy said defiantly, tears beginning to trickle down his face. 'Who cares if you are a ghost? I see you, I believe in you. Isn't that all that matters?'

305

Amy wasn't just a ghost, she was Billy's guardian angel, always had been. Billy had seen the writing. Kate had shown him the messages left on the notepad last night which she assumed had been left by Justin. Billy knew differently though. He recognised the writing style immediately. It was Amy's. When they had been filling the time capsule back inside The Tunnel, Billy saw one of the things Amy had written. He knew, but didn't say anything. It all now made sense, and hurt like hell at the same time. The house, the talks with Amy's parents, Billy had played the whole thing, he had seen what he had wanted to see, not what had really been there because he had longed for the family he had been without for so long.

'You no longer need me,' Amy said.

'Yes I do,' Billy said quickly. 'You're my best friend.'

'Please, Billy,' Amy said. 'Don't make this any harder than it has to be.'

There were other people in the room now, Billy felt them, he turned around and standing there next to the door were Amy's parents. Billy knew them, except for one thing.

'Don't be afraid,' Amy's father said, raising his right hand. He was wearing a black suit with a white shirt underneath.

Billy now saw properly. 'The Gate Keeper,' he muttered. He looked at Amy in a mist of confusion.

'I was the messenger,' the Gate Keeper explained. 'My charge is now done. But before we can pass to the next world I must show you what my daughter couldn't.'

Billy closed his eyes and watched.

He could taste the water again, wanted to spit it back out. They were now back at the lake. Billy could feel the sun on his face each time his head came out of the water, bobbing like a float. Panic was starting to set in, his body began to tighten; he wasn't swimming in water but glue. He went under again, this time he didn't have the strength to pull himself back to the surface. The lake was consuming him, swallowing him whole. Billy closed his eyes and accepted his watery grave.

Billy looked on, his eyes were still closed but he could now see. The images fast forwarded then stopped. He could see light, the sun reflecting down on the surface of the water, making it look like a huge mirror. He was getting closer and closer, his hand being held all the time. He surfaced. It was like being born again. Amy held his hand the entire time, she would not let him fall, it was not his time, she could not let this happen, she was his guardian angel, she brought him back, cleansed him free from the asthma. Billy slowly opened his eyes, he saw an angel, the sun shining down creating the illusion of a white figure standing over him, an angel, Amy. He was now seeing her for who she really was. He coughed then sat up, the sound of sirens now all around him, help was coming. Amy was then gone.

But before she went, she caught a glimpse of things to come. She read Billy, she could always read Billy. There was trouble ahead, family breakdown, loneliness, and Billy was going to shoulder all the blame himself. His parents were not going to help matters, they would both shut themselves off from Billy, enter a world of their own full of hurt and misery. Black, that place was, dark and damp, Amy could see it all, this would eventually lead to Billy's demise, she couldn't let that happen. So Amy made a decision, she broke the laws of her world and physically crossed over into Billy's. She would be the friend he would surely need in such a dark time of his life, she would be his light, his comrade, his best friend. The time was coming. The cemetery, they would meet in the cemetery. The house, the tombstone, Amy knew them as hers. Billy needed her, and she would not let him fall, never. She would guide him home.

'You sent me the dream,' Billy said, opening his eyes. He felt refreshed, like he'd just had the best sleep of his life. 'About Justin dying, it was you.'

'My daughter did,' the Gate Keeper said. 'She sent your father a message also, but it was too late. She whispered to your mother in the house, two words, Billy Cooper. She was not supposed to interfere in that way, Billy. She was your guardian angel, not Justin's. It was his time, and time eventually takes us all.'

'You understand, Billy?' Amy asked, looking a little scared of how he was going to react to all of this.

And she was afraid that Billy would not understand that if she saved him then how come she didn't save Justin too? But Billy did understand. Amy had broken all the laws of her world to spend the last year with him. She couldn't have saved Justin if she had wanted to, there were greater laws governing even her. An accident is just that, but the difference being Billy was meant to live on, his guardian angel had done her work, would continue to do her work. She would never really leave his side.

'That's why you stayed with me,' Billy said. 'You blamed yourself for not being able to save Justin.'

'I stayed because I wanted to,' Amy explained. 'You needed me, Billy, and that was all that mattered.' She noticed Billy frowning again. 'Please don't hate me, Billy,' she said.

The Gate Keeper looked on, standing next to a woman that Billy only knew as Amy's mother, from a time when he had felt like he hadn't one of his own.

'Hate you?' Billy asked, both sounding and looking surprised. 'How could I ever hate you? You gave up so much for me. You saved me. You're my best friend, Amy, my only friend and I –'

'*Tell her, Billy … Just tell her that you love her.*'

But Billy didn't have to, Amy knew, yes, she knew all right.

Amy was now crying, so Billy quickly stepped forward, reached out and embraced her. They held one another for a long time, in an empty old house that Amy had once lived in long ago, two best friends from two different worlds that had shared so much together over the past year. Billy didn't want to let go of her, because he knew Amy's work was now done, and when he did she would be gone.

'Billy Cooper!' Amy said. 'What would the files say on this one?'

Billy smiled, and carried on holding his best friend in the whole world who just so happened to be the ghost of a little girl whose grave lay on the same plot as Justin's. The pages then turned again, and the chapter ended, but the journey would continue, a chorus sang, Billy heard it. Then the calling, they were returning, and the higher powers were calling all ...

Calling All Angels –

*

The pages stopped ... The next chapter had now begun.

When Billy opened his eyes he was standing back outside the house. It was no longer raining, the sun was shining and he could feel it on his face. It was Amy.

The crooked sign standing outside the house now read 'For Sale' again, which it had done for a long time now. The house had been there for a long time. Nobody seemed to want to live in it, but that was fine by Billy, that way the house would always belong to Amy, just like The Tunnel would always belong to the both of them. He could now see what was really in front of him, like a thick mist had cleared, and he was no longer afraid of what he might find.

—

Time passed by and Billy was back standing in a familiar place. His parents were both at his side. It was cool today, the last day of summer 2003. Billy looked around, he had somewhere to go.

'I won't be long,' he told his parents.

They smiled, watching him walking away; they knew where he was going. They then looked back down at their other son. Alex had his arm around Kate, the freshly laid flowers danced in the wind.

Billy knelt down and placed the flowers next to her little grave. He rubbed his fingers across her tombstone and remembered. He knew she would always be with him, sometimes he heard her voice saying out his name in the wind, he saw her in his dreams. Amy would never be that far away. Best friends never really are.

He stayed sitting next to her grave for quite some time, telling her about his day like the way he used to. And that night after he had gone back home, Billy Cooper was going to carry on with his new story. It was called 'The Tunnel' and was about two best friends who went off on an adventure of a lifetime, one of self-discovery and wonder. Billy didn't care much about the ending, because he knew it was the journey that was what mostly mattered. Everything else would take care of itself. It always did. And this one was most definitely for Amy Johnston, his best friend in the whole world.

<u>The End, of this journey anyway.</u>

Afterword

There is an old disused railway line in Market Harborough. And it does come complete with tunnels. Hopefully not haunted though. I remember as a kid, riding through one of those tunnels on my bike with a friend of mine called, Simon. It was pretty scary. The ground was rough, and there was always that fear of some smart ass hiding somewhere getting ready to jump out on you. Plus the fact that if you got a puncture then you were in for a long walk back.

There were stories about those tunnels, honest, probably not quite as frightening as the ones Billy Cooper had been told, but they were still just as real back then, and scary to hear as a kid. There are in fact four tunnels, I only ever went down one of the straight ones, which was long enough but at least I could see the light at the end of it. I never had the balls to go down the bendy one.

Readers familiar with the old railway track will know that I have taken certain liberties within this novel, which I hope you will not hold against me too much. And incidentally I did hear stories growing up, that a man did die after being hit by a train, and supposedly haunted one of the tunnels. Yes, my friend and I both agreed we would be better off giving that tunnel a miss. But looking back on it all now, it really had been magic. So until next time, keep those pages turning.

N P 2006

311